The Asset

Samara Black

ISBN 979-8-9898465-0-4 (eBook)

ISBN 979-8-9898465-1-1 (paperback)

Library of Congress Control Number: 2024902041

Printed in the United States of America

Book Cover by Cheshire Gato Media

Front cover:

Photo by: Samara Black

Cover model: Jessi Rae

Background image: RDNE Stock Project (via Pexels)

Back cover photo credit: Darius Krause (via Pexels)

First edition 2024

To Heather

Because if we'd never had the crazy idea to play around on your typewriter that weekend, Larissa probably wouldn't exist.

Contents

Author's Note

The following story includes the following content that may be inappropriate for readers under the age of 18:

- Cursing, profanity, dirty words

- Violence, sometimes graphic in nature

- Nudity and consensual sexual activity

This story also contains the following content that might be sensitive or triggering for some people:

- Sexual assault (mentioned, not described)

- Human trafficking (mentioned, not described)

- Child witnessing violence against another person (described)

- Graphic violence against women (described)

Chapter One

Night Shift

Prague, Czech Republic
July

God bless the IT Department of the CIA.

Jamie Sayers was hired right out of college. Within a few months she'd developed several apps to help simplify the often tedious bureaucracy for field officers. During a team lunch, I realized her sense of humor was nearly as twisted as mine and we'd joked about the app that was now helping me solve the curious question before me. Well, it technically sat in the front seat two rows away. From my seat in the cargo van, I swiped my finger back and forth between the two screens, unable to decide.

At the sound of Vasil Lesky's voice, the lead officer for our mission, my jaw tensed and my finger stopped moving. Based on the faces of those around him, everyone else had long stopped listening to his incessant droning as well. After he summarized everyone's job for the third time, my mind was made up and I swiped to the next screen. Pressing my lips together to hide the smile at the image, I was more than happy with the size of bullet I'd chosen for the middle of his forehead.

A 38. Definitely.

"I cannot stress this enough," he said for what seemed like the fiftieth time. "It is imperative that Becek comes to no harm during this operation."

Closing my eyes, I tried to block him out. Two minutes. That was all I got before his grating voice broke through and with it the name "Becek" repeated at least three more damn times.

I bolted upright, causing several agents to jump. "Can you please turn the radio on?"

Six pairs of eyes looked as if I'd asked to light them on fire. Hell, I would've done so if it meant the pompous pain in the ass in the driver's seat would shut the hell up long enough so I could clear my head. After several tense moments and a few awkward stares, I leveled my gaze at Lesky.

His eyes narrowed. "Officer Fallon, I'm sorry if we're cutting into your leisure time, but we need to focus on this mission."

"With all due respect, I'm here to keep the professor, as well as your team members, safe. I don't know if you've noticed, but it's pitch-black outside with a light breeze. When I get up there, those conditions must be considered. If I'm off by so much as a millisecond, it could be the difference between this mission being a success or having to explain to the State Department why we're bringing their missing scholar home in a box."

I leaned forward, silencing his muttered irritation. "I'm guessing Mr. Lynch didn't tell you I have certain requirements for all my jobs. One thing I need is fifteen minutes of quiet time to mentally prepare. Being a sniper might seem easy. Just point the gun and shoot, right? Yeah, I get that a lot. However, I assure you that's not the case. I could bore you with all the details, but I'd rather focus on the mission you've spent all this time talking about."

"He mentioned something about certain requirements, yes." He jerked his chin toward the door, and the team exited the van. As I grabbed the handle, he brought his enraged face within inches of mine. "You'd better be worth all these little... eccentricities of yours, or I'll see to it you never work another mission again."

He stomped away, and I nodded at the other two snipers, who returned the gesture and left. We'd spent hours poring through the pictures and walking through the operation, holding one last meeting an hour before leaving the hotel. Our tasks were engrained in our heads with no detail left uncovered.

I blew out a relaxing breath. Sweet, sweet silence at last. I closed my eyes and imagined the view from the roof, my worksite for the night. Prague wasn't known for many flat rooftops, but we'd lucked out and the target was next to a newer building in the financial district that met all our needs. That didn't mean it would be easy, however. Ten guards were stationed on several floors, and that was plenty to keep us busy.

My next thoughts were of Professor Anton Becek, the elderly man with tired eyes, a warm smile, and an astonishing level of knowledge about weapons of mass destruction. His file detailed the sad story of a nuclear physicist who sought asylum in the U.S. after the Czech government tried to kidnap his grandson. When that didn't work, they grabbed Anton from his hotel and brought him back to Prague. His work with the government made him an asset, one the Czechs couldn't afford to slip through their fingers.

The look on his grandson's face as he moved from the pediatric cancer unit in Baltimore to a safe house was a rare bright spot in their story. His large brown eyes filled with hope at my vow to bring his grandfather home. I rarely made such a promise, but the family had seen more than its fair share of heartache. Reuniting that little boy with Anton was imperative. The family needed at least one small sliver of joy as he battled a disease that threatened to suck every drop of it from his family.

I sat up and the clock on the dashboard showed six minutes until show time. My hands wove sections of my black shoulder length hair into a quick braid. Lesky was jabbering at the team yet again when I approached the command center. Ignoring him, I grabbed a headset and busied myself with adjusting the cables and earpiece. By the time our eyes met, it surprised me his teeth hadn't ground to dust.

With a saccharine smile, I pressed my palms together in front of me and bowed. "Shall we begin?"

The smell of pastries lingered as I passed the bakery that made, hands down, the best apricot mini danishes in the second district. I slipped through a side door in the alley. The only sounds were my footsteps as I entered the stairwell and climbed eight stories to the roof. Alas, one major downside of covert missions was elevators were always forbidden. Well, that and the danger of being discovered and killed.

The wind was stronger when I stepped onto the roof, making me thankful for the braid against the back of my head. My drill instructor's constant barking at me to "keep my damn hair out of the way" was an edict I'd never forget. I made it to the southeast corner and praised the genius who selected this location. The balustrade provided excellent cover from being detected and several vantage points.

I gazed at the skyline, marveling at its beauty before settling behind the railing. Switching my earpiece, I rolled my eyes as Lesky's grating bark filled the line with another repeat of his earlier instructions. Once he quieted, I made my presence known.

"F3 in position. Please limit chatter from this point forward."

F3. That was my name over comms for the mission. In meetings and at the pub, the team knew me as Officer Davina Fallon. That wasn't my real name, either. I was on a team full of people I'd never worked with, except for one, and we both respected each other's anonymity. Fellow CIA officers or not, my trust was a premium few could afford.

Silence descended upon the area as everyone moved to their places. I opened the case strapped to my back and assembled the British sniper rifle given to me for the mission. My gun would've been preferred, but a last-minute logistics snafu bumped me from the German-bound military transport plane in favor of an extra pallet of equipment. I wound up on a commercial flight instead, which meant options for weaponry was whatever could be scrounged together. This model was smaller and had less range than mine, but it would get the job done.

After checking each magazine and arranging them in a semicircle to my left, I practiced unloading and reloading to get a feel for the mechanics. Satisfied, I crouched down and scanned the roof of the targeted building through my scope, locating the four guards assigned to the floor that our recon watched daily for almost a week. After several minutes of watching their movements, it was time.

"Roof guards are in position," I whispered. "Standby."

I licked the back of my hand and placed my finger on the trigger. Gross? Sure, but better than relying on an unfamiliar scope to gauge wind speed and adjust my position and timing for all four shots. I centered the target and held my breath. The steps I'd recited from dusk until dawn in training beating through my head. Hold, squeeze, breathe. It was all over in three seconds. Four suppressed shots fired, four bodies down.

"Targets neutralized."

Neutralized. Eliminated. All the euphemisms amused me. They were dead. Use all the pretty, fifty cent college words you wanted, but the fact remained someone was dead.

"Copy, F3," the command center responded. "Any line of sight on the guards inside?"

"Scanning now."

My eye returned to the scope and found four guards on the fifth floor where Anton was located based on our intel. Two more guards on the second floor slouched against a window ledge, chatting and laughing. I watched them for several minutes, long enough for them to speak into their walkies and hustle back to work. Eventually, they settled into a rhythm.

"Six guards, four on the fifth floor and two on the second. They've timed their movements to avoid being near the windows at the same time. Are M7 and K4 in position?"

I'd met M7 and K4 the day I arrived, and we'd bonded over tea and pastries in the very shop I'd strolled past earlier. M had only been with the Agency for a year. K and I worked together once before. Since I had the dubious distinction of the most kills between the three of us, they considered me the lead. This gave me the "honor" of killing the four guards on the roof.

"K4 in position."

"M7 is moving to an alternate location. Civilian too close to original position," Lesky replied.

I paused. A civilian walking through this part of the district at three in the morning was unusual. Nothing could be left to chance, even if it was just a drunk. "Do we have a visual of the civ leaving the perimeter?"

"Affirmative. M7 and I observed a male, Caucasian, approximately six foot one, wearing black tennis shoes, blue jeans, dark gray hooded sweatshirt, and a black skull cap. L2 confirmed he left the perimeter headed northwest toward the metro station. Over," an unfamiliar voice responded.

My body tensed. "Identify?"

"X5, over."

X5 was the chubby blond guy who made it a habit to stare at every female team member's ass when he wasn't telling anyone who'd listen how he'd run the mission. He was skeevy, but he was a skeevy team member and therefore safe.

"M7, please respond when you're in position."

"Affirmative. M7 in position," her lightly accented voice answered.

"Copy. Welcome to the party. Keep a visual on five. K4, take two. Maintain position and identify timing to eliminate targets. I'll watch the perimeter."

"Copy," they answered in unison.

The earpiece fell silent, and I trained my scope on the building, watching for the car scheduled to arrive and move Anton to another location. A location farther away from his family and closer to his death.

"Targets on two eliminated," K4 whispered.

"Copy."

"Black sedan heading into the area, approaching from the north," Lesky announced.

"Copy. Status, M7?"

"Stand—," she began. My stomach dropped until her voice returned. "Targets on five eliminated."

"Copy. Ground team in position?"

"Affirmative."

The sedan stopped in front of the building and the driver remained behind the wheel, smoking a cigarette that dangled from his mouth. I ordered my team to standby and moved into a better position. The usual tension was in the air, but something else unsettled me. I tried to shake it off, telling myself it was just because of the civilian M7 spotted. I looked through the scope and got back to work, watching two guards escort a shorter person with a fabric bag over their head.

Seconds later the driver and guard on the right were dead. My gaze on the last target was fixed and I was preparing to fire when a small spark flashed, and something flew past my leg. Following the movement, I found a bullet embedded in the metal wall of my rifle case.

"Shots fired," I calmly reported and rolled under the solid part of the railing.

"Shots fired! Shots fired!" a voice screeched.

"Lesky, calm the fuck down and get a status on the last target."

"Second guard eliminated," K4 answered. "However, the payload was hit."

Fuck. Fuckity fuck. "Any other shots fired?"

"Negative. Scanning area now," K4 replied.

"Status of the target?" Lesky barked.

"Appears to be a minor injury to the forearm. I'm not sure he was a—"

"Black out comms now," I ordered. "Debrief back at the command center once I get my ass off this roof."

"Area secure. No additional shots fired. No suspicious persons in the area."

Getting shot at never bothered me, but the uncertainty afterward was an anxiety filled hell. I shivered as the wind battered my skin. My senses were hyperaware, causing a jolt to any sense of calm with the smallest of sounds, or even an unfamiliar scent in the air. When I heard the first morning train whistle in the distance, I steeled my nerves and decided to take a chance. Rolling onto my stomach, I studied the bullet before packing up the rifle. After several more minutes of convincing myself it was safe, I crawled around the perimeter to the exit.

Shoving the case against Lesky's chest should have eased my frustration, but his blank face only pissed me off more. "There's a bullet inside to analyze. Wanna tell me what the fuck happened?"

"We're trying to figure that out. Becek's arm was grazed. He's being taken to the hospital now."

I glared daggers at him and pressed my comms button. "K4, meet me in the med transport in three minutes." He looked like he wanted to argue, but I tossed the earpiece into the van and left without another word.

The two EMTs working on their patient looked uncomfortable at my approach, but relaxed after Anton's gravelly voice assured them I could be trusted. We sat quietly as the beeps of the heart monitor filled the small space. He scratched at the stubble on his chin and winced when the IV slid into his arm. The tech watched the line and nodded to us once she was done.

"Dušek was moved and had a round of chemo last week," I murmured. "He's safe and can't wait to see you."

He nodded and closed his eyes as a petite blond sat down next to me. At her creased brows, I cast my eyes to the right, aware we'd caught the interest of the two men up front. She nodded and instead we watched Anton's chest slowly rise and fall. After arriving at the hospital, we stayed behind while they wheeled him inside. Once everyone was gone, we checked our surroundings and closed the doors.

She eyed me, crossing her arms over her chest. "What the hell is going on, D?"

I laid my head against the wall. "You tell me, Elle."

"He wasn't the target. Whoever it was had a clear shot the minute you dropped the first guard."

"They wanted me pinned down. But why? What did it accomplish?"

She shrugged and thought for a moment. "Why did you black out comms?"

"That wasn't X5. He was way too quiet and agreeable."

"Lesky's going to have a shit fit once he finds out. What are you going to do?"

I shrugged. "Lesky can figure it out. My guess is it's some little snot trying their hand at freelance and thought infiltrating a CIA job would get them some notoriety. They'll be dead soon enough."

We stayed inside and chatted until the doors flew open. The EMTs were startled and annoyed to see us still sitting there, so we made a hasty exit. As we crossed the ambulance bay, Elle dropped the names of several government officials to ensure their silence.

She hugged me once we got to the corner of the street. "Be careful, yeah?"

"Always. When you get to the command center, make sure they find X5. I'm willing to bet you'll find his body in the alley behind that horrid café across from the pub."

"Lesky's bound to be close to hysterics by now."

"He needs to switch to decaf and chill the hell out," I groaned, rolling my eyes.

She smiled before taking off at a sprint. I remained, tilting my face up to the fresh air. The city was beautiful. I wanted to stay longer, but there were important phone calls to make and an escape plan to execute. After one last breath of fresh air, I headed toward the building behind me.

The wonderful thing about the basement of almost any hospital was that nobody cared who else walked past them at an ungodly hour. Exhausted night staff were too busy seeking a rest from their hellish schedule. Janitors just wanted to get their job done without being bothered by some uptight jackass telling them what to do or where to go. The people working in the morgue only cared about the dead. Basements also had plenty of equipment rooms that were the perfect place to stash duffel bags.

Unless, however, that same room was the location for a secret rendezvous for Dr. Vasko and sweet nurse... Frana. It was only after ten torturous minutes of listening to their pants and moans that he finally groaned out her name. Not long after their voices traveled away from the room, I grabbed my bag from its hiding spot and jogged down the nearest hallway. Once hidden in a different supply room, I dialed my cell phone and hid behind what looked like an iron lung. My call was late, and no doubt he'd be pissed.

"About damn time!" an angry voice burst through the line. "I was expecting your call ten minutes ago."

"Yeah, sorry about that. I had a horny couple playing doctor in the room where I hid my bag."

"How did it go?"

I blew out a breath and prepared for the explosion. "Someone decided to join the party. Payload was injured but will be okay."

My boss, Felton Lynch, was one of four Senior Operations Officers in my division of the CIA. He'd also raised me after my parents died when I was six. He had my complete trust, something I shared with less than ten people on the planet. It was his tendency to act like an overprotective father when things went sideways that made me dread his reaction.

"Son of a bitch," he thundered, a loud sound banging close to the phone that sounded as if he'd just punched something. "How bad?"

"The shooter got inside the perimeter and accessed our comms. Shot at me, but the rifle case took all the damage."

"Are you okay?"

"You should know by now it'll take more than a rogue shooter to do me in," I scoffed. "Give me some credit here."

"I do. I wouldn't be doing my job if I didn't worry."

"Is that concern I hear? Don't tell me the old man is starting to give a shit."

"Smart ass," he grunted. "Get your ass home, Officer Donovan. I want to see you before you disappear again."

"Yes, Boss. See you soon."

After hanging up, I tossed my clothes into a medical waste container destined for the incinerator and changed into a simple black hoodie and jeans. Loud voices in the hall warned me of several bodies arriving at the morgue, the result of some mysterious shooting in the financial district. By the time I slipped out, I was bone tired and actually looking forward to sitting in the crappy seat for the short flight to Amsterdam before the long flight home. It would take fifteen hours to get there, but Felton's pancakes were an enticing reward. The rogue shooter was barely a thought in my mind once I took my seat on the plane.

I fastened my seatbelt and pulled out my phone to complete my last unofficial task. Following each assignment, I disappeared to an undisclosed location in case someone tried to track me. Felton found my method reckless, but I enjoyed choosing a random spot in the world each time. Opening my geography app, I pressed the dice icon and glanced at the results.

Well, at least I wouldn't be cold.

Chapter Two

Activation

Brian

Six Weeks Later

"This is Special Agent Brian Kenmore. I need to speak with Barton Kane ASAP," I barked into the phone. "Yes, I'll hold."

I stood outside the airport, trying to force the stifling air into my lungs. In the few minutes since I stepped outside, the sweat poured down my back as if I'd run a marathon. As the hold music warbled in my ear, I watched the sliding doors and wished the cell signal inside the terminal wasn't so shitty. When the scorching heat penetrated my shoes, I cursed and moved to a tiny patch of shade near the building. Why in the hell would someone come to a place like this?

Kane's secretary came back on the line and told me he was in an important meeting and couldn't be disturbed. I bit back the string of profanity I wanted to yell and left a message for him to call me. After shoving my phone in my pocket, I jumped into the first taxi that stopped and tried not to moan too loudly when I discovered it was air conditioned. The driver laughed at me before handing me a couple of tissues.

Even sweaty and miserable I was still one lucky bastard, I reminded myself. Less than a year with the Bureau and they had sent me out on my first solo job. Agent Alex Wahlstrom was assigned to an undercover operation in, strangely enough, some back-water one horse town in Arizona about an hour east of Tucson and hadn't been heard from in almost a week. Foul play wasn't suspected, but they needed to be found.

I'd taken my buddies to lunch to celebrate and brag, rolling my eyes when Roger said the name sounded fake and joked that I was being sent to round up some deep cover spy. We'd all heard the rumors of the ultimate secret agent during our field training so many times this person was a legend. Helena, the realist, pointed out the unlikelihood of a rookie being trusted to find someone with such an elite resume. We left her to pay the check while I headed home to pack.

Unfortunately, in my excitement I neglected to meet with the crotchety bitch in the logistics department to get all the details for the assignment. As if she was ever much help. I wasn't sure how someone who had never been in the field was fit to give me advice about undercover work. I usually tuned her out while she muttered nasty comments under her breath, shoved paperwork into my hand, and threw me out of her office. Since I didn't even know if I was looking for a man or a woman, the joke was on me.

I hadn't heard from Kane by the time I'd showered and changed, so I decided to grab some food and get acquainted with the town. After that I'd try to figure out what to do next. Everyone at H.Q. would be impressed when I found this person with no information, I told myself.

The sun was brutal as I shuffled into the rundown bar across the street. The cool air was a welcome blast on my skin after almost burning my hand when I pushed open the worn, green metal door. A few patrons nodded as I strolled to a worn barstool. My eyes were still adjusting to the dimmed light when a perky voice chirped in my ear.

"Hey there! What can I get ya?"

I turned and tried my best not to gape at the giant tits crammed into the tiny red tank top mere inches from my face. My gaze moved up to a beautiful set of ocean blue eyes that now watched me with curiosity. I moved back in the seat and tried to look like I wasn't leering at her.

"I'll take whatever light beer you have on tap."

With a megawatt smile she turned, her long, curly dark blond hair swaying, to grab a glass from under the counter. My eyes scanned her body as she filled the glass at the taps, and it didn't disappoint. Her ass was damn near mouthwatering the way it filled the short black skirt she wore. The thought of her toned legs wrapped around my waist, hell, around my shoulders, made my cock twitch.

She set the glass down. "Three dollars."

I handed her a five and told her to keep the change. She served other customers as I sipped my beer and surveyed the bar. It looked like your typical dive, loved by the locals and avoided by the few tourists in the area. That made it the best place to keep my ears open for anything that could put me on the trail of my missing agent.

The bartender's gaze met mine when she returned. "So, what brings you to Rio Rico?"

"I'm doing some consulting work for the water treatment plant."

"Sounds exciting."

"Not really. I make a living dealing with dirty water."

She giggled. "Never thought of it that way. I'm sure there are worse jobs though."

"That's true. And it's not like I can complain. Been here not even fifteen minutes and I've already made a friend."

With a quick wink, she shifted to the other side of the bar. Her easygoing personality and killer body made her a sweet temptation. After watching that delicious ass of hers bounce around the bar, I decided maybe the night wasn't a total bust. I could find the MIA agent in the morning.

"So, can I get you anything else?"

Feeling bold, I flashed a smile. "I don't know. How about a menu and your phone number?"

The husky laugh she let out as she passed me a small, laminated sheet of paper made me think of other ways to make her breathless. "A menu is easy enough. However, I don't think you've quite earned a phone number yet."

"And here I thought I was getting somewhere."

"Ha! Nothing comes easy. Not even me."

"Well, who doesn't love a challenge? But even I'll admit I can't convince you on an empty stomach. I'll take a cheeseburger."

A few minutes later, she set my plate down, grabbing an onion ring as she walked away. "I believe that's mine," I called after her with a wide grin.

"Guess I owe you," she snickered over her shoulder.

Our flirting continued as the bar filled with patrons. I made small talk with an older guy who shuffled in and dropped himself onto the stool next to me. He worked as a cook at a nearby resort and was in no rush to go home to his senile mother. I nodded my head and threw out the occasional comment but didn't pay close attention to him as he rambled on. Instead, I locked eyes with the cute bartender almost every chance I got.

It was almost nine, and as much as I wanted to stay and try to seal the deal with her, I needed to head back to the hotel and figure out my next steps. "Wish I could stay and chat longer, but it's getting late, and I have to be at the plant early."

Her mouth formed the cutest little pout as she handed me my receipt. "Aww, that's too bad. I'll be off soon. Maybe I'll see you again before you head back home?"

It was my turn to wink. "You can count on it, darlin'."

I jammed my card into my wallet and watched her approach the other bartender, who nodded at whatever she said in his ear. She shot a heated look my way before heading toward the restrooms without another glance. I folded the receipt and was sliding it into my wallet when I saw blue ink at the bottom of the paper. It turned out to be a note directing me to follow. My cock sprang to life as I thought of all the dirty things I wanted to do to her luscious body. So what if it was in the back of some dive bar in the middle of nowhere? It wasn't like I had anyone at home to answer to, and it sure beat the hell out of jerking off to shitty porn back in my room.

The light in the hallway was dim when I pushed through the door. "Hello?"

The stillness of the warm air caused the hair on the back of my neck to stand up. Once I realized my mistake I turned to leave, but my back slammed into a wall. The sharp inhale as I tried to catch my breath became a yelp at the sting in my neck. I looked down to see my potential one-night stand holding me against the wall with one hand while the other held the syringe that pierced the skin.

"Start talking," she snarled. "Now."

· · · ● · ● · ● · · ·

Larissa

It was hard not to laugh. Brian was a wall of muscle well over six feet tall who could have easily broken me in half. His hands, which were large enough to crush my head, shook as they came up in surrender. I moved the needle enough to make his eyes bulge. He pressed his body against the wall and inhaled slowly.

My thumb hovered over the plunger. "Three seconds."

"I… I'm, uh… Special Agent Brian Kenmore, FBI. I'm trying to find a colleague assigned to a special project in the area. They were supposed to contact the local field office several days ago, but never checked in, so they sent me to see if I could find them."

"Try again, Brian. I know that's not true, but I'll give you points for coming up with an almost believable story. Let's start with who sent you."

"B—barton. Barton Kane."

I released him from the wall and held out my hand. "Phone. Now." My fingers swiped through the screen as soon as it fell into my hand. "Verification code?"

"Um, pink firecracker, red rose, and… um… Fuck!"

"Last word is incorrect. Ten seconds."

He closed his eyes and his Adam's apple bobbed. "Pink firecracker, red rose, and… gray flowerpot."

I patted his shoulder. "Relax. You get to live for now. By the way, you have the wrong number to reach Barton. I'm sure that means you did something to piss someone off."

He rolled his eyes skyward and muttered under his breath. I suppressed a snort as I watched him wipe the sweat from his closely shaved copper hair. It was almost insulting they sent someone this green to find me.

"Verification code?" a brisk voice asked over the line.

"Pink firecracker, red rose and gray flowerpot. What in the fuck, Barton?"

While Felton was my handler for the CIA, Barton Kane was his FBI counterpart. Since the law forbade working for both agencies at the same time, I bounced between the two. After completing an assignment and a required break, my position was terminated and the other hired me. My job history looked cringeworthy on paper and to the outside world, but the truth was far different.

"Hello to you too, Lissa."

"What the hell are you doing sending some rookie out here? I'm insulted."

"Yeah, it was a last minute thing, and the guy seemed eager. Look, I know you're not done with your break, but I need you to come in."

"Why? You know the rules. Breaks can't be canceled without executive authorization."

"And I have it. Felton and I met with the higher ups, so here we are. I need you back at headquarters in two days."

I tensed, causing a small gasp from Brian. "What's going on? There's no way Felton would agree to this without a damn good reason."

"You know I can't go into details over the phone. Just trust me. I'll tell you everything when you get here. When you hear the situation, I think you'll even be happy I'm calling you in."

"We'll see about that. What's the deal with the moron here who I'm pretty sure just pissed himself? Were you trying to get him killed? Did he spill coffee on your computer or something?"

He sighed. "Mel suggested him and now I know why. The chatter in the office is he's been pissing her off the last few weeks."

I watched Brian tremble and tried not to laugh. Melanie was a veteran logistics tech assigned to my unit. Her knowledge and clout commanded a certain amount of respect. If you didn't want to wind up at a shitty hotel or paired with an agent you couldn't stand, she was the key.

"Yeah, I could see Melanie doing something like that," I replied, meeting Brian's gaze. At the mention of her name, his eyes widened. Bingo.

"So, Agent Donovan, do you think you can tear yourself away and come in as requested?"

I sighed dramatically. "I guess. But I'm not traveling with Brian here. Lord knows he'd tip off every spy between here and Dallas."

"Fair enough. I'll see you in two days."

My finger lingered over the button to end the call, but decided Melanie wasn't the only one who got to have some fun. As his eyes widened, I brought the phone back to my ear. "I didn't catch that last part, Barton. Is he allowed to return to headquarters, or do I need to execute a Code Sunset?"

"Lissa. Enough! Before he actually pisses himself."

"Agreed. I'm not sure Max still works at the morgue, but there's always the desert. I'll make sure to dump the body in that one spot before I leave. Thanks!"

I stared at him and lowered the phone. His breaths quickened, almost hyperventilating. I scrolled through his pictures until I found the one that had piqued my curiosity earlier. When he saw it, his shoulders sagged.

"Who's the blond? You two look pretty cozy right here, but you spent the night eye fucking me."

"That's the love of my life, ma'am. She'd be my wife if I hadn't screwed up and let her slip through my fingers."

"So, your coping mechanism is to be a walking cliché and hook up with random chicks while you're on assignment?"

"I'm not proud of it, but yes. It—"

I held up my hand. "I'm not your mom or your priest. We're all messes in one way or another. However, I wouldn't recommend using the field to find your dates. Rookie mistake, really. Pun intended. Your dick will not solve your cases, Agent. Only your brain can do that. I recommend you use it."

He nodded but remained silent. His gaze never wavered from the picture, nor did the sorrow in his voice. There was still a lesson to be learned even though I sympathized with his situation. I returned the phone to his pocket and stared at him.

"I know I screwed up. I'm sorry. It won't happen again," he pleaded in a rush.

Without another word, I emptied the contents of the needle into his neck. My hand clamped over his mouth as he tried to scream. Once he calmed down, I gave him a stern look.

"Agent Kenmore, I'm going to give you some advice right now. I highly suggest you take it to heart. First, do some basic research on your assignment's location. The water treatment plant in Rio Rico is a secure facility that doesn't hire consultants from NGO's. If you understand, just say 'understood'."

"Understood."

"Second, don't piss off Melanie. Or any of the other logistics people. They're part of your team. When you return home, buy that woman an obscene amount of chocolate and beg for her forgiveness. Heads up, she prefers British chocolate over domestic. And for the love of god, *do not* give her any white chocolate or anything with peanuts. Understood?"

He gave a weak nod. "Understood."

"Lastly, you're a rookie. You may think you're hot shit because you're working for the feds, but you still have a lot to learn. This assignment was a test, and you failed miserably. This time you're just dealing with short term embarrassment and a good story to laugh about should you last long enough to be a veteran. Your next screw up could get you or someone else killed. Then if you ever find your way back to that woman you love so much, she'll have to mourn your loss."

He blew a ragged breath. "Understood. Again, I'm sorry."

"Don't apologize, Brian. Learn. And be better than the rest of us. Make that your mission instead of getting your dick wet."

"Yes, ma'am," he answered. "May I ask what you injected me with?"

"I won't tell you the specifics. But you should hustle back to your hotel room and get comfortable. You're in for a long night."

Chapter Three

Mothership

Visiting FBI headquarters in Washington, D.C. was a nerve-wracking experience. A person's every move was scrutinized upon entrance to the building, from not holding the elevator door for a nerdy looking guy to loaning a quarter to a woman in the bathroom for the tampon machine. Karma worked differently when the walls saw and heard everything. Offend the wrong person and you could find your network access "accidentally" revoked or sent to work a case in some hell hole.

My path to the Bureau was purely accidental. Felton recruited me to the CIA, and after training I was just another officer who traveled to exotic and foreign destinations, became immersed in new and fascinating cultures, spied on the locals, and sometimes killed them. It was during an assignment in Germany less than a year later that I first straddled the line between the two agencies.

I was investigating a prominent businessman in Hamburg when his five-year-old daughter was kidnapped. I traced the group responsible back to a compound in North Dakota, which ended my involvement once she entered U.S. airspace. After multiple calls from the lead FBI field agent asking for information on the father, Felton called the agent's boss and snidely asked if he needed to loan me to the Bureau to solve their case. The next day I met Barton Kane in a hotel outside Fargo. Within minutes, I was relieved of my duties with the CIA and

Barton swore me in as a temporary agent. Sixteen hours later, I carried the little girl in my arms from the compound. Not long after, Felton and Barton came to an agreement, and I was off to the FBI training facility in Quantico.

I smoothed the phantom wrinkles from my black pantsuit and waited for the elevator in the lobby. My hair was still blond, but now free of the extensions so it hung in loose waves above my shoulders. I pulled loose strands behind my ear as people walked past, feeling exposed despite their smiles and friendly nods. Upon my arrival to the fourth floor my back straightened, and I pushed everything aside. Work mode was on at full power.

Special Agent Barton Kane, my boss in all things related to domestic intelligence, stood in the lobby typing on his phone as I approached. Based on his disheveled chestnut brown and silver hair, my best guess was he'd been in his office since before the sun came up. That usually meant he'd been arguing with Felton and was in a crappy mood.

He nodded at my hair, eyebrows raised. "Blond?"

"Worked for Agent Kenmore," I quipped, following him down the corridor. "How's he doing, by the way?"

"He was released from the hospital this morning and scheduled to fly back to D.C. this afternoon."

My grimace was immediate. The laxative I shot into his neck, regrettably, worked a bit too well. A night of explosive diarrhea left him severely dehydrated, which caused him to pass out and hit his head on the bathtub. When the hotel staff came to check on the noise complaint, an ambulance was called, and he was diagnosed with a concussion.

"I probably used too much and shouldn't have done it in the first place, but he had to learn before he got someone killed."

"Sounds like he learned several valuable lessons."

I stopped in the doorway to his office. "Why am I here, Barton?"

He dug through a drawer behind him and dropped a thick manila file onto his desk. "Always straight to the point."

"Well?"

"What if I told you we have a line on Gio Sardi?"

My eyes rolled. "I'd say I've heard that before and it's never panned out."

I was fifteen when I learned a man by the name of Giovino Sardi, the underboss of the Sardi family, ordered the hit on my parents. Located in Bari, a coastal town in southeastern Italy, the organization was small but influential, thanks to their alliance with the Genovese family. Over the years they'd gained a foothold in the power structure south of Naples, holding most of the southern coast. They had made several attempts to expand their operations to the U.S., but the Genovese limited their reach to a few small cities on the east coast.

Gio was a power-hungry sadist who was believed to be the true head of the family. He moved in shadow, much like me, and ruled with an iron fist. His power was absolute, as was the level of loyalty he demanded of his underlings and family. If he had any weakness, I had yet to find it.

"I get that you're skeptical. But I know you, and I know you're going to hunt down every lead available to find him."

Dammit, he was right. I closed the door and sat down in front of his desk. "What have you got?"

He thumbed through the file. "We're still trying to establish how they know each other, but Sardi has ties to a history professor who's spending a semester teaching at a college in Portland."

"Maine?"

"Oregon. It looks like they had regular contact for the last few years, but it slowed down a year ago."

"Why wasn't it a case back then?"

"There was a CIA team working on it in Italy for eighteen months. A few weeks ago, we busted up a drug ring in Syracuse run by a couple low-level Sardi associates."

"Which now makes it a Bureau matter," I finished.

"Precisely. DEA called us in once they found the mob link, so here we are."

"Felton wasn't part of the job in Italy?"

"No. Contrary to what he thinks, other people are perfectly capable of gathering intel in Italy without his involvement."

I said nothing. There was always a general mistrust between the two agencies, but Barton barely tolerated Felton. He did his best not to involve me in their issues, but it made for a chilly reception whenever Felton Lynch came up in conversations.

"So, what's the plan?"

He handed me a small envelope. "You'd be going undercover as one of his graduate teaching assistants."

"Spying on a teacher and babysitting college kids sounds like a ton of fun."

"Oh, come on. It'll be like your fourteen again. Wasn't that when you were a grad student?"

"Fifteen, actually. But I was never a teaching assistant. Like Felton would ever allow me around that many college guys."

Before my parents died, the school tested me, and determined I was an exceptional learner. I graduated high school at age twelve and spent the next six years earning multiple degrees, including a doctorate in math. Some people used yoga or meditation as a coping mechanism; I'd used academia.

"My mistake," he chuckled. "Are you in?"

"Of course. Maybe I'll make it my last hurrah."

"Stop joking about that. You've said that before every assignment for the past year."

"Who said it was a joke?"

His face turned serious. "Why? Why now?"

"I agreed to this weird arrangement hoping to get close enough to that damn family to bring them down once and for all. Five years later, I'm not any closer. I'm starting to think it would be easier if I just went off the grid and handled it myself."

"Not if I have anything to say about it. What you're describing is suicide."

"Last time I checked, there's not much anyone can do once I submit the papers."

"What would Felton say about this?"

I leaned forward and narrowed my eyes. "If that's a threat, go right ahead."

He held up his hands. "All right. You know I was bluffing. But that doesn't erase the fact that what you're talking about is insane. You need resources if you're going to take him on. Also, it's only been five years. Don't you think you're being impatient?"

"It probably looks that way to most people, but every October reminds me I haven't made good on my promise to avenge them. It's been twenty years since they died. To me it feels like I've failed them."

"Promise me you'll think about this long and hard before you decide. I'm not saying that as your boss and someone whose job would be a lot more difficult without you. I say that as a parent who doesn't want to see someone else's child get themselves killed if I could prevent it."

"Fine. I promise not to make any snap decisions."

Satisfied, he handed me the file and turned to his computer screen. I was reading through the information about the school when the phone on his desk rang. He glanced at the display and smirked.

"She found you," he announced, grabbing the receiver. "Yes, Melanie? How may I help you today?"

As the voice on the other end spoke, I tossed the file in my bag. "Tell her it's your fault I didn't stop by to see her first."

"I'll send her right over," he snickered before hanging up. "You're in trouble. You better get over to her office. And don't be there all day. You have a trip to Portland to prep for."

"Yes, sir."

· · · · ● · ● · · ·

Since Melanie's office was on the other side of the floor, I'd intended to stop by and catch up first before meeting with the boss. The element of surprise was now gone, which meant she greeted me with a flurry of foam darts as soon as she saw me. When I dashed through the office door, her short, and stocky body vibrated with laughter.

"You know, the last time I checked it's against the law to fire at a federal officer," I told her, dropping the darts on her desk.

Her brown eyes crinkled, and a grin spread across her face. "My cuffs or yours?"

"I'd pay money to hear you say that to Barton."

She laughed and rounded the desk to her chair as I closed the door. Most logistics techs didn't get an office. Melanie Barnes was nothing like most techs, however. When a fellow agent who was one of her close friends was gunned down in a series of shootings in D.C., she worked tirelessly to help any way she could. From ordering coffee by the gallon for all-night task force sessions to personally doing laundry for several agents, she'd been there. Unable to give her a bonus, or even a raise, they freed her from the cubicle farm she hated. A large picture of her and her friend taken during a trip to Vegas sat in a frame on a filing cabinet behind her.

"So how was Arizona?" How she kept her voice so even was amazing.

"Quiet until some damn rookie walked into a bar. By the way, that little prank reeked of you."

"As I understand it, something else reeked after you were done with him."

"A tiny part of me regrets he wound up with a concussion, but I don't think he'll do whatever he did to piss you off again."

"I felt a little bad about that too," she conceded. "But I doubt he'll ever refer to me as his 'travel girl' again."

"I'd guarantee it."

She typed on her keyboard. "All right, Portland. We have an apartment secured on campus. The local field office will leave a car in the airport parking garage for you. You have orientation first thing Friday morning."

"How many others are in the program?"

She glanced at the screen. "Four aside from you. Identities appear to be clean. No red flags when we screened them, but you know the drill. Report anything that's suspicious as soon as you can."

"Always. Who's my local field contact?"

"Jack Marlowe. I've worked with him a couple times. No nonsense but doesn't have a stick up his ass."

"Thank god. Felton had me working with a pompous douchebag on my last job. Identity details?"

"Printing now," she replied. "Your name is Jessica Ross. Shane will meet with you tomorrow morning to start work on your appearance."

"Sounds like a plan. What's the intel on the target?"

"Professor Caleb Winters, visiting adjunct history professor at Portland College. Besides teaching the standard history courses, he's also teaching a combined grad and undergrad class on the history of the mafia."

She spent the next few minutes combing through his education and background. We joked about the death wish he must have to want to teach a class like that. As she continued to read his stats, I skipped through the file to the pictures. When I held up his picture, her eyebrows raised.

"Not bad looking," she replied.

Nodding in agreement, the picture dropped back into the folder in my lap. I studied it, taking in the deep brown hair and eyes. Yep, he was definitely a looker. The only problem? Based on the small smirk that curled his lips, he knew it.

"You can smell the bad boy vibes coming off him. He's going to be drowning in coeds."

"Nothing you can't handle."

"It's not," I agreed. "But nothing I hate more is wading through layers of bullshit, and that would be a tough one. It's going to be hard to find out if he's still cozied up to Gio Sardi if he's got a flock of potential conquests around him all the time."

"As a reminder, it's still illegal to shoot people just because they annoy you."

I rolled my eyes. "You're no fun. What's his last known location?"

"Arrived in Portland three days ago. Let's see here," she paused. "Well, that's interesting. He has a short-term lease on a condo, but intel hasn't seen him there."

"Maybe he's already found someone to give him an extra special tour of the campus. I'll give Portland a call before I head out and see what else they might know. Since Barton alleges this is supposed to be a simple case, it would really suck if it started with my target going MIA before I even get there."

She looked unconvinced. "Sometimes the simplest of assignments are the furthest thing."

We chatted for a time before I remembered I still needed a place to crash for the night. She reminded me of my appointment the next day as I put all the papers back in the folder. I was gathering everything together when my phone buzzed. She stopped talking as I read the message.

In town. Meet?

"I think I know the reason for that smile," she sighed.

"Don't know what you're talking about," I hedged, typing out a quick reply.

Her smile faded. "I thought that was over. At least that's what you made it sound like the last time we talked about him."

"We haven't seen each other in months, so there really isn't anything to end anymore. We send a text when one of us is in town. If we meet up, great. If not, no worries."

"Yes, but you said it was over for a reason."

Time for a subject change. "Hey, do you know if Georgia is in town? Or is she in San Diego?"

"We had coffee this morning. She'd be a much better choice as far as where to spend the evening."

"I'll stop by her office and see what she's up to. I've been meaning to talk to her about some things. Might be time to make some changes."

"Hon, you're fast approaching that line where you've done it all and seen it all. More than me," she drawled. "Change might be the best thing for you."

"It's not a popular opinion, but it's time to start thinking about it. I won't make any decisions until after this case, though."

We stood, and she gave me a bone-crushing hug. "Which means you really need to be careful, Lissa. This case seems too easy, which makes it the perfect kind to swallow you whole. I mean it."

"You know I'm always careful, Mel. But for you I'll swear to it."

As she sat down behind her desk, I glanced at my phone and saw a text from Georgia basically ordering me to be at her house no later than six. Barton must have told her I was in town. I slung my bag over my shoulder and turned back with a mock salute.

"All right, I'm out. Do tell our favorite Agent Kenmore hello from me when he returns to the office. And tell him I still owe him that onion ring."

Her boisterous laugh echoed down the hall behind me.

Chapter Four

Dine and Dash

A WARM HAND CARESSED my hip. I rolled over and my eyes followed a tan, muscular arm until I was looking at the handsome face of Officer Jackson Michaels. He smiled and brought his lips to mine for a lazy kiss. My fingers wove into his mussed dark blond hair and the kiss deepened. The hand tightened its grip, reminding me how he clutched me to him when I rode him like our lives depended on it.

Jackson and I worked a job for the CIA in St. Petersburg infiltrating a human trafficking ring. Our work resulted in the rescue of several teenaged girls, and afterward we celebrated. A lot. I still looked back on that night filled with way too much vodka and zero inhibitions fondly. As we nursed our respective hangovers on the flight home, we agreed to be friends. The kind who often met up when they were both in town for hot, dirty sex. We sealed the deal with an extremely depraved romp in a corner of the cargo plane, a memory that still made parts of my body quiver two years later.

Our hook-ups were the few free periods of time our jobs allowed. Hours spent together without interference from bureaucrats and politicians. Brief respites to escape the watchful eyes of handlers and exist as human beings, enjoying our freedom. No rules, expectations, and most importantly, commitments of any kind.

He pulled the white sheet away and rolled me onto my back so quickly I squealed. Chuckling, he nuzzled between my breasts and moved lower. He placed several open-mouthed kisses from my belly button to my left hip. I shifted and parted my legs, but instead of taking the hint, his lips moved to my right hip.

He braced his body over mine and gave me a deep kiss. "I believe it's time to make you come again."

"Who am I to say no?"

He winked one of his dark green eyes and brought my right breast to his eager mouth. I squirmed as his tongue swirled around my nipple. The stubble on his cheek tickled when he gently bit down and sucked.

"Jackson—"

He leaned on his elbow as his mouth moved to the other breast, giving me enough room to slide my hand between us. The low growl that came from his throat when my hand closed around his cock only urged me on as I stroked him in a steady rhythm. His lips devoured mine in a wild, desperate kiss as I felt a tiny dribble of pre-cum on my hand. In a flash, he flipped me onto my stomach. His hands grasped my hips as he pulled me onto my knees and trailed kisses against my spine.

"Fuck, I need to be inside you now," he groaned, grabbing at the box on the bedside table.

As soon as the condom was on, he filled me with one deep thrust. He drew back, almost pulling out, only to slam back inside. I gripped the sheets and yelped when he slapped my ass. His hips pistoned faster, and soon my legs quivered as my orgasm teased me. My body exploded a few thrusts later. He held my hips in place and fucked me like a demon until I slumped forward.

His cock was still deep inside me as he pulled my body upright. He wrapped his arm around me, pressing my back to his firm chest. I turned and gave him a kiss, which turned into soft moans when he moved. He nuzzled my neck and shoulders, and I bucked against him until he tightened his embrace.

"Hold on to me." His voice was a ragged whisper.

I grasped his arm with both hands as he rolled his hips. His hand slid around my side, and I cried out when his finger grazed my aching clit. He tortured me with a slow pace that he refused to increase no matter how much I begged. After what felt like eternity, his finger moved faster. He scraped his teeth against my neck, and it was all I could do to not combust from the sensations pulsing through my body. When my orgasm ripped through me moments later, I feared I'd actually explode. He cursed when he came not long after. Breathless, I leaned against him as he kissed me and lowered us onto the bed.

His head rested on my chest as we caught our breath. I tangled my fingers in his hair and felt him smile against my still heated skin. His hands moved under my shoulders and held me for a moment before raising his head. I watched him mull something in his mind before he spoke.

"Stay with me tonight?" His eyes were hopeful.

A chill invaded my mind and with it a growing unease. Sleepovers were risky, especially in the epicenter of the intelligence community. It was because of that we never spent more than a few hours together. That, along with this new desire to hang out, made me nervous and thankful Georgia texted me before I left the office.

"I wish I could, but I have dinner plans."

His shoulders slumped, but he nodded. "At least stay for lunch? I could order some takeout."

"Sounds good to me. We've certainly worked up our appetites."

Fifteen minutes later we laid in bed with an assortment of food boxes between us. He'd put on a pair of gray sweatpants to answer the door and I'd thrown on his black t-shirt, much to his chagrin. We ate in comfortable silence, long enough for my anxiety about his earlier question to fade. As we cleaned up, I took in the new tattoos littering his arms and chest. Knowing their significance, I wondered how much deeper into hell he'd gotten in the last few months.

"How are things in Russia these days?"

He shot me a weary look. "Peaceful for now, but it's a powder keg. The Svetskaya's second got married about three months ago, basically with a gun to his head."

"Anton finally settled down?"

"Hardly. He might be married, but he's not settling down. That's the problem."

I nodded my understanding. Anton Volko was second in command to the largest bratva in Moscow. He was well known for both his cruelty and mental instability. Everyone believed the only reason he kept his position was because it was easier to watch and control him if he stayed within the power structure. I'd had the misfortune of crossing paths with the madman once, and the scar from the bullet that grazed my thigh served as a bitter reminder of my only failed mission.

"And this is why I don't miss Russia," I sighed. "That's a cluster-fuck just waiting to happen."

His brow furrowed. "You haven't been back? Not since we were there?"

I marshaled my best poker face and shook my head. In truth, I'd been back. Twice. However, Jackson thought I was a fellow officer in the same European division. Keeping that knowledge to myself not only ensured my safety, but his as well. The fact we hadn't worked together since that mission also made me wonder if Felton already knew about our encounters.

"Nope. They've had me banging around the central states for the past eighteen months. Haven't been east of Budapest in over a year."

"Well, you're not missing out. Where were you before Arizona?"

"Berlin. Another day, another arms dealer. About the only exciting part was someone got inside the perimeter and shot at me."

His eyebrows shot up. "Any leads?"

"Not a one aside from the poor bastard with a broken neck in an alley."

"Just another day at the office, right?" he laughed, moving closer.

His arms enveloped my body as he dragged me into another slow kiss. The few articles of clothing between us disappeared and soon our bodies were joined once more. When my body detonated in climax, he clutched me to him and shouted through his release. Afterward, his arms held me in place.

"Can I ask you something?" he murmured after a pause.

"Of course."

He rolled to his side and propped his head up on his hand. "Have you ever thought about maybe something more between us?"

My skin prickled, and I felt cold, exposed. I pulled the sheet tighter against me and tried to slow the jumble of words and emotions percolating in my mind. Jackson's fingers moved down my back, but he thankfully stayed silent.

Of course, I'd thought of more. I was only six when my parents died, and they had forever etched the love and affection they showed each other into my memory. One day I overheard my mom on the phone describing my dad as a prince she loved with every part of her soul. In no time my doll was swooning over her own dashing prince and his accent. Their wedding had been epic, and my dream was to find a love like that someday.

Twenty years later, it was a goal I decided was unobtainable. It was hard to dream of a hero when my line of work brought me close to some of the worst people in the world. One of the worst was Konstantin Lydyev, the leader of the trafficking ring Jackson and I helped bring down. He was a sexual sadist who used a ceremonial knife to cut a small line into the upper arm of his "girls" each time he raped them. The things we saw in his compound were a whole new level of evil. It was only thanks to Jackson that I made it through with my life, cover and sanity intact.

And there was the paradox. Jackson well understood the perils of the job. He would've welcomed the challenges of juggling both a career and a relationship. An assignment on the other side of the world with no end date and limited contact? No problem. That should have made the answer easy, but I knew it would be grossly unfair to him.

Could I trust him with my life? I already had. My heart, however, was another matter. While I liked him, it was nowhere near the love he deserved from someone he wanted more from. He deserved the spiritual love my mom spoke of, the kind that created butterflies in one's stomach and all sorts of flowery shit. Sadly, the butterflies in my stomach as I considered his proposal were the wrong kind.

"Lissa?"

I rolled to my side to face him. "Honestly? No, I haven't. That's not to say I don't enjoy when we're together, but I just can't see more between us."

"Do you think that might ever change?" Hurt shone in his eyes and tinged his voice. "I'm willing to wait."

"And that wouldn't be fair. I don't want you or the person you're meant to be with to miss out because you're waiting for me. I can't and won't do that to you."

He nodded and then laid his head on my chest. We stayed in our silent embrace. After a while, he took a deep breath and sat up. His eyes were gentle as he caressed my cheek. "Thank you," he murmured. "I appreciate your honesty."

I started to reply, but my phone buzzed from somewhere on the floor and brought an abrupt end to the conversation. He cussed under his breath and strode to the pile of clothes.

"Real world, line one," he grumbled as he slipped the black phone into my hand.

I groaned and tossed it on the bed as soon as Felton's name lit up the display. No way in hell was I answering. He'd figure out where I was and who I was with in less than sixty seconds, and I was in no mood to deal with an interrogation. The buzzing stopped, only to start again.

The phone kept ringing, making it hard to put the damn thing in airplane mode. Jackson put on his sweatpants and brought my clothes back to the bedroom. He busied himself in the kitchen while I got dressed and returned with two cups of coffee. I thanked him and took a long drink.

"So, where are you off to next?" His tone was casual.

"That's probably what Felton wants to tell me when I decide to take his call. What about you? Back to Moscow?"

"Probably. Things are getting hot over there with Anton, but it's a risk worth taking."

I took one last gulp. "Be careful wherever you wind up, will ya? You're not allowed to get your head blown off, whether it's by a crazed Russian or anyone else."

"Same goes for you, Officer."

"I'm always careful. When have I ever not been?"

"Do I need to remind you whose idea it was to mouth off to that cop in St. Petersburg?" he challenged with a laugh.

"No, no you don't," I conceded with a dramatic sigh.

He kept his hands in his pockets as we walked to the door, a far cry from a few hours earlier when he removed my clothes in a frenzy the minute I arrived. Though neither of us said the words, we knew our affair was over. We lingered at the door before I pulled him into one last hug.

"Take care of yourself. You'll make some woman incredibly happy someday," I whispered.

"I wish that woman was you."

My smile was sad. "Part of me does, too. But I know it's not."

He nodded and opened the door. After one last kiss on the cheek, I stepped into the hallway. The door closed. I took one look at the young couple heading toward the elevator and headed in the opposite direction toward the silence of the stairwell. In that moment, ten flights of stairs were preferable to watching the two of them hang off each other in a small space.

Thoughts of Brian wandered through my head as I made my descent. He never told me what happened with the woman in the picture, but the obvious pain he felt at her memory was enough to make me wary. That was a level of emotion I had neither the ability nor desire to feel. Did that mean I was destined to a life of nothing more than the occasional secret fling? Only time would tell.

I zipped up my jacket and secured my helmet before straddling my motorcycle. The engine roared to life, and I zipped away, my heart feeling lighter the further away I drove.

Chapter Five

Assets & Liabilities

THE AROMA OF HOMEMADE marinara sauce hung in the air while I finished wiping down the counters of the now spotless kitchen. After scolding me for having to hear I was in town from Barton, Georgia told me where to find the hidden spare key and that she'd be home before seven.

Georgia Kaplan had been with the Bureau for almost twenty years. She was one of the few I trusted with my real name, as well as most of the details of my past. Her reputation was one of a protective hardass in the field and a loyal friend and mentor to her colleagues. I was someone lucky enough to see both parts, and it was because of that she was one of my closest friends.

We hadn't spoken in a while, and I was looking forward to catching up and talking to her about my possible retirement. Barton might claim he was framing his concerns objectively, but he was still my boss. Georgia had no agenda. Now that Jackson was no longer a distraction, the issues that had been pushed aside now roamed free in my head. Aside from my possible career change, there was one other lingering concern.

The rogue shooter in Prague hadn't been captured or even identified. I wasn't comfortable going into the field while this person was still on the loose, but I also wouldn't turn down an opportunity to get my vengeance. It could be argued, and it had been often, that I was obsessed with bringing down the people responsible for my parents' death. To those critics I offered no apology.

I never got to ask my mom about my period or get advice about boys. Rather than my dad teaching me to drive, I learned from a fellow doctoral student. My graduations were bittersweet affairs that I got through with a stiff upper lip and cried myself to sleep at the end of the night. I strived to make the best of the major milestones in my life, but their absence always left a hole.

And it was all thanks to Gio Sardi. The same shithead mobster I vowed to kill and was no closer to finding five years after Felton promised me that joining the CIA would do just that. As my thoughts grew bitter, I shook myself mentally. I really needed to get my head clear and talk to Georgia about my career path.

The life of a secret agent probably sounded cool to the average civilian. Go undercover, travel to exotic places, and sometimes kill people. Dream job, right? What could go wrong?

In a word, everything.

Working in intelligence was a job that required a level head and a clear understanding of the consequences of every action. It sounded like hyperbole, but errors in my line of work were sometimes fatal. Testifying before Congress was no walk in the park but the guilt that someone else suffered or perished because of your fuck up was worse.

Death was part of the job, but as a sniper I was more often the dealer than the savior. It sounded callous, but it all depended on the will of the person or committee who ordered me to pull the trigger. Not that everyone I saved was a good person or vice versa. Unfortunately, that was how the world worked.

The phone rang, bringing me out of my reverie. I grabbed the receiver from the kitchen wall. "Kaplan residence."

"Hey, I should be there in about an hour," Georgia's voice beamed through the line. "Should I grab anything on the way for dinner?"

"Maybe some garlic bread?"

"I'll see what they have at the store. How are you doing?"

"Just a lot on my mind."

"Well, let's see what you, me, and a bottle of wine can figure out after dinner. See you soon."

I stared at the clock above the stove and contemplated my reasons for retirement. I'd been with the CIA for almost five years but worked for both agencies as "The Asset", straddling the line between the FBI and the CIA, for a little over four. It didn't seem like a long time, and it wasn't based on most people's career paths. Most people, however, didn't have a continuous supply of deception, death and destruction as parts of their job.

It was a strange career path, but one I was destined for according to Felton. The night my parents were murdered, I ran to his house after escaping my own. While I immersed myself in schoolwork to deal with the loss, he dealt with all the legalities of my custody and dealing with their estate. Since nobody knew if I was still a target, he made it his mission to ensure I was able to defend myself. I spent the first few years in his care enrolled in martial arts training and countless self-defense classes.

Living with a CIA officer who knew people in law enforcement, I saw plenty of guns. It wasn't until I was eleven, however, that he took me to a shooting range for the first time. His expectations were low when he placed the pistol in my hand. I didn't even know how to load the damn thing. He showed me how, and then motioned toward the target. Nobody expected that I'd empty the entire clip with deadly accuracy.

After that, my after-school activities changed from gymnastics and scouting to more advanced self-defense classes, weapons training and survival tactics. I was too young to join any ROTC program, but Felton saw to it that several of my instructors were former military members familiar with the curriculum. By the age of sixteen, both the Army and Marines were clamoring for me to join once I was old enough.

When I turned eighteen, I enlisted in the Marines and left for South Carolina barely three months after receiving my doctorate. Felton boasted to anyone who would listen that I chose the Corps because they were the best of the best, but the truth was I sought the training as an escape. No longer able to lose myself in schoolwork, I buried myself in surviving basic training.

After graduation, I was fast tracked into Scout Sniper School based on my sharpshooting scores. Any pride I felt was squashed on the first day when my drill instructor told me that my spot in the class was thanks to Felton. I was nothing more than just another bureaucrat's pampered brat, he'd bellowed, and my days of buying favors and easy rewards were over. His words stung but had their intended effect. With a shrug, I told him I wasn't in the business of easy and when I graduated in the top five, he'd owe me an apology. I never said I wasn't sometimes an arrogant pain in the ass.

For the next thirteen weeks, I lived for the single goal of being the best sniper that grouchy old bastard ever saw. Every shouted order was followed without question or complaint, and I completed every assignment at the highest level of precision. After a damn near perfect score on my final exam, an endurance test performed in the dead of night, I graduated at the top of my class.

He pulled me aside after the ceremony and not only apologized, but he also shared a picture of himself at his own graduation. I blew all his records out of the water, he'd told me, and he was happy to be proved wrong. He wished me luck, ordered me to stay safe during my deployment, and told me not to lose my humanity. At the time I didn't give that last bit of advice much thought. I'd spent three months training to view a target as nothing more than something to be eliminated. Awash with the emotional high of victory, I headed to Iraq.

Within a week, everyday life turned into a desperate quest to find even the tiniest shred of humanity. No stories, lectures or courses prepared me for the hell of a war zone. The friendships forged within my platoon were a godsend, helping all of us to cope with what we saw and experienced daily. However, my moral compass never stopped screaming about the brutality we committed in the name of our country.

It was a cynical worldview, but I knew I was just a pawn in the bigger picture, a means to an end. People with more stars on their uniforms and zeros in their paychecks sat in a room and decided where to send their pawns to perform the jobs we were trained to do by the military industrial complex. It was cold comfort on those nights spent watching for insurgents hell bent on killing us, but it provided the needed perspective when the chaos of life made it damn near impossible to focus on anything else. Until it all changed.

An IED explosion left me with a severe concussion and an unexpected visitor. Felton strolled into my hospital room in Germany in his stiff black suit and informed me I was coming home. Within two years I had training certificates from both the CIA and FBI. I'd barely gotten home from my Bureau graduation ceremony when leaders of both agencies met in a SCIF, also known as a Sensitive Compartmented Information Facility, to sign a top-secret agreement. From that day forward, I was The Asset.

According to Felton, the idea of an agent tied to both organizations wasn't new. A former Army sniper was recruited a few years earlier. Caught up in a bureaucratic pissing contest, he stayed an official CIA officer who completed a handful of missions for the Bureau while on unpaid leaves of absence. The rest of the man's story was nothing more than rumor since everyone refused to speak of him.

The tale as it was told was the same tired cliché as seen in the movies. He got sucked into the life and sex, drugs and debt followed. When the bottom dropped out, he was almost outed as an agent and an innocent woman was killed. After multiple stints in rehab, he was fired or forced into retirement depending on the version of the story. The details always varied depending on the storyteller, but he served as a failed experiment and everyone went back to the drawing board.

The current Asset program had an exhaustive list of rules and protocols. No tattoos, piercings, or identifying marks. After every mission, foreign or domestic, a minimum of two weeks was required as a "cooldown" period. My location was always known by at least one member of both agencies, including during my forced vacations. And if all of that wasn't enough to make it the funnest job ever, I got to randomly pee in a cup and submit to regular psych evaluations every few months.

While it wasn't forbidden, both agencies heavily discouraged friendships and relationships with people outside the intelligence community. That meant very few friends and you could forget about having any kind of normal love life. My dating history was short and miserable thanks to Felton and his background checks. I'd somehow managed to keep Jackson and a couple other flings under the radar, but there were too many risks and too few rewards. All parts of a life I wasn't sure I wanted to live anymore.

The ringing of the kitchen phone again interrupted my train of thought. Thinking it was Georgia, I smiled and grabbed the receiver. "Larissa Donovan!" a loud voice snarled before I spoke a single word.

"Felton Lynch," I shot back, lowering my voice to mimic his angry tone.

"Barton Kane just called and had some interesting information for me. About your retirement."

"Well, that's news to me since I'm not retiring."

"How was your afternoon with Officer Michaels? Anything I should know about there?"

I clenched my jaws and bit back my first response. "Actually, he told me about some of his adventures in Russia. Not so sure you really want to hear how the rest of our time together was spent."

He expelled a long sigh. "Why is this the first time I'm hearing about this, Lissa? What's really going on?"

"I'm about to head to Portland on a job. I only mentioned it in passing to Barton and he had a complete shit fit."

"Promise me you won't make any rash decisions."

"Promise me you'll leave Jackson alone," I countered.

"Fine. I just need to know we'll talk once you know what you want to do. Retirement is a huge step, and there are things to consider that I'm sure you haven't thought of."

"Like I said, it was an offhanded comment. I joke about shooting you at least once a week and I haven't. Not yet anyway. *If and when* I decide I want to retire, we'll talk."

"All right. I probably could've handled this better." Wait. What? "His call just caught me off guard."

The front door opened, and I saw Georgia enter with a grocery bag in her hand. Thank god. "Okay, Felton, I gotta go. Dinner is ready."

"Tell Georgia I said hi," he replied, pausing. "Safe travels."

"Always."

I stared at the phone in my hand after the line clicked, thrown off by his behavior, or more accurately, that he acted like a human being for more than a few seconds. Felton wasn't the warm and fuzzy type and he sure as shit never admitted to ever making an error. Georgia erased my concern in the next second, when she wrapped her arms around me.

"So nice to see you again," she greeted.

"It's been too long! How's the family?"

"Regina has her own practice in San Francisco and is doing well." Her daughter was a child psychologist.

"And Jay?"

"He's doing what he calls 'freelance work' while his friend finishes school. When she graduates next year, they're starting a consulting company together. I'm sure it will do well, but I wish he'd find something reliable in the meantime."

"We kids are terrible at doing what you guys want us to do," I joked. "I was officially on Felton's shit list until just before you got here."

She pursed her lips as she opened a bottle of wine and poured us each a glass. Since she didn't work with him, it limited her exposure to the occasional nod in passing or the stories she'd heard from me. After taking a sip, she smiled. "Something tells me I want to hear the story of what you did to annoy the great Felton Lynch."

After dinner we moved to her living room and her ridiculously comfortable couch. For the next hour, she sat in silence and let me vent about Felton, question my decision to dump Jackson, and my reasons for considering retirement. She expressed no judgement. Instead, she proposed certain scenarios and asked how I felt about them. After a day of emotional twists and turns, it felt good. By the time we finished the bottle I wasn't much closer to a decision, but the conversation had given me some much-needed clarity.

Afterward, she excused herself to call her husband who was at their home in San Diego. I headed upstairs to the guest room, pausing to look at the pictures on the wall. I smiled and studied the Kaplan family's history, their large, joyful smiles stared back at me in images that captured so many moments in time over the years.

As I studied the pictures, I wondered if I could ever have a family of my own someday. I knew it was impossible in my current life. Hell, I didn't even have a permanent home. Would my life ever be safe enough to include innocent people? A dull sadness followed almost as the question passed through my mind. Had I been hell bent on revenge for so long that I missed my chance for a family and a life in the ordinary world? I sighed and headed to the guest room to finish packing for my next, and possibly final, mission.

Chapter Six

Hello

MY FLIGHT TO PORTLAND was long and uneventful. The pale September sun greeted the plane as it touched down on the runway. Since I didn't have any other luggage aside from my backpack, it didn't take long to reach the parking garage and search for the car issued to me. Following the directions sent to my phone, I found a dark blue sedan that reminded me of the model I raced in college before Felton caught me. After checking the car and finding no threats, I tossed my backpack into the passenger seat. Soon the GPS was on, and I was speeding down the highway toward the Portland College campus.

I parked the car and walked a couple blocks until I saw the tan brick exterior of the Broadway building on the corner. The first floor was full of retail shops while the upper floors were student apartments. I crossed the crowded lobby and made my way to my room on the ninth floor. As requested, I was at the end of the hallway and near the staircase. The high numbered floor wasn't ideal, but at least I was near an escape route.

My new "home" was a one-bedroom apartment that had a plain light wood student desk with a black metal office chair, a dark gray couch with a light wood coffee table. The tiny bedroom held a queen-sized bed with no headboard and a plain night table with a single drawer that fell off the track if it opened too far. The small but livable closet hid a box full of clothes that I'd need to wash and hang up, which wasn't the end of the world. Another box sat in the kitchen. Inside I found bedding, towels and just about every other essential I'd need aside from groceries. Once again, the logistics team came through.

The team even selected my favorite colors. Warm earth tones, mostly red and brown for the kitchen and deep, bold jewel tones for the bed and bath. After spending most of my lifetime hidden in the shadows with no permanent home, I craved colorful surroundings whenever possible. Would deep purple sheets solve all my problems? No, but they made waking up in a strange location suck less.

"See, Brian? All you have to do is be nice to your logistics peeps," I mused, hanging a bright blue shower curtain over the bathtub. A small snort of laughter escaped my lips as I thought of how his next interaction with Melanie would go when he came back to work. Hopefully, he heeded my advice and bought her a ton of chocolate or his path to forgiveness would be long.

I tucked a piece of my now long black hair over my ear and finished organizing my towels. My appearance was usually the last thing I cared about on a job, but I found myself in love with the lush, curly extensions. My hair was so dark it looked blue black, which made my skin look paler. The cobalt contact lenses were darker than my natural ice blue but complemented the hair nicely.

A loud knock at the door sounded as I left the bathroom. After making sure nothing suspicious was laying out, I checked the peephole. A tall young woman with long pink and purple hair stood, nervously glancing down the hall. She turned to my open door and smiled.

"Hi there! I was wondering if you had a couple double 'A' batteries. I forgot to pack some for my mouse and keyboard."

"Let me check. Come on in," I opened the door wider and held out my hand. "Jessica Ross."

"Nicole Turner. Nice to meet you."

It took a couple minutes to rummage through my box of office supplies before I found a small package at the bottom and held them up. "Jackpot."

"Oh my gosh, you're a lifesaver! I owe you."

"No worries. I know how that goes. I forget the power supply for my laptop all the time."

She laughed, her dark green eyes twinkling. "So where are you from?"

"Seattle. You?"

"San Francisco."

"I've heard it's beautiful."

"It is, though I have to say I loved Seattle the one time I was there. So, are you undergrad or graduate?" She sure got to the point in no time.

"Graduate. History," I answered.

"Me too! I thought I was the only once around here since everyone I've met so far has been business or pre-law." She leaned against the counter. "Did you sign up to TA with anyone? I wasn't going to because I was a little nervous about balancing it with the workload, but after I heard Caleb Winters was teaching here this semester, I knew I had to get in."

"That would be awesome if you matched with him. Then I'd know someone."

She grinned. "I did!"

As we chatted, I learned she arrived a few days earlier and spent the time exploring the campus and city. After learning I hadn't been to the bookstore, she escorted me to the building a few blocks away. I thanked her as she carried one of my overstuffed bags back to our building. During our walk from the elevator to my room, we made plans to sit together during our orientation the following morning.

"Hey, I almost forgot," she said as she dropped the bag on the couch. "An acquaintance of mine invited me to a party. He has a place close to the campus. Wanna come?"

Seeing an opportunity to blend in with the students, as well as blow off some steam after traveling all day, I accepted. We agreed to meet up later and head over to the party for one last night of fun before school swallowed our schedules up and, in my case, spying on the professor.

After checking my hair and makeup one last time, I headed to the bedroom and grabbed my black flats from the closet. Wearing a pair of now laundered dark blue skinny jeans and a simple black crop top, I stood at the full-length mirror and gazed at my reflection. Maybe after I retired I could get my belly button pierced. My eyes moved to my plain arms as I grabbed a light purple cardigan. Or maybe a small tattoo? I shook my head, mentally scolding myself. I needed to get through the job and decide if I was even going to retire first.

My eyebrows shot up when I found Nicole in the lobby. "I appear to be underdressed."

She waved her hand dismissively and smoothed out the tight black dress that clung to her. "Don't. You look great. I'm just seeing if I can catch an eye or two tonight. Nothing wrong with that, right?"

"Not at all."

I offered to drive, which not only gave me a chance to learn my surroundings but also ensured I had a way to get back to my room. Fifteen minutes later we parked and walked to a large, old house on the corner. Both streets were lined with cars and the front steps and porch were crowded with people.

"Garrett owns the house but said it's too big for him," she explained as we walked through the front door. "So he converted the downstairs to an apartment and rents out most of the rooms upstairs."

I nodded and scanned the scene in front of us. People greeted their friends, smiling and hugging each other and looking like they were out to have fun. Nicole waved and chatted with several people before pointing toward the kitchen. She went to snag a couple beers and told me to find a spot for us to hang out. The loud music directed me to my destination.

The living room furniture had been pushed to the walls and partygoers danced on the floor. A few people waved at me as I entered the room, and I returned their greetings with a warm smile. Nicole appeared with two bottles and pulled me up onto the large coffee table. Soon we were both lost in the music, dancing and laughing.

By the time the fifth song started, I knew I was being watched. I'd felt plenty of eyes on me from the time we arrived, but those were brief. This was different. My senses sharpened, and I scanned the room. Was my watcher out for a date, or did I have a bigger issue on my hands?

My question was answered when I locked onto a pair of deep brown eyes in the hallway that led to the kitchen. I returned the man's stare, and he grinned. Nicole and I resumed dancing, but I stole the occasional glance in his direction as the song continued and noticed he was working his way closer.

The song ended, and I asked if we could get a drink. We hopped down and left the room, breezing past my watcher. As I felt his stare, my own eyes scanned the house for potential escape routes.

I grabbed a bottle of water and handed her another beer. We hung out in the kitchen for a little while. Nicole was quite the social butterfly who knew almost every person who passed by our corner. We were chatting with a drunk woman we discovered lived down the hall in our dorm when I excused myself to use the restroom.

Crawling under the plastic chain blocking people from going upstairs, I found the hallway at the top empty. Several of the doors were closed but the rooms weren't empty based on the noises I heard as I walked past. I'd just left the bathroom and was almost to the stairs when the sound of footsteps made me freeze.

"Hello."

I turned and swallowed a gasp. He stood several inches taller than my own five foot seven. My best estimate was six foot two, possibly a couple inches more. His black t-shirt clung to his chest, outlining the muscles beneath. I caught a whiff of his cologne, a mixture of warmth and spice, and images of making out in front of a campfire on the beach conjured in my mind.

Coming out of the bathroom at a house party was not how I envisioned meeting Professor Caleb Winters for the first time. The pictures in the file hardly did him justice; he was the perfect mixture of sex and sin. While my libido surged, warning bells also rang through my head. Did he know who I was? Until I knew for sure if my cover had been blown, I was just a girl at a party.

I met his gaze, trying and failing to ignore his chiseled jawline and the stubble that covered it. "Do you make it a habit of following women to the restroom?"

He chuckled softly before dragging a hand through his mahogany brown hair. "No, I promise I'm not some sort of creeper. I just wanted to say hello."

"Ah. Well, hello." Before he could say another word, I was gone.

A loud, cleansing exhale escaped my lips once I returned downstairs. Hot bad boys had always been my weakness, and even though his file was more than enough warning, he was still a temptation. Add to it the question of whether or not my identity was still intact, and it was for the best that I kept a distance.

Nicole pulled me back onto the table as soon as she saw me. Deciding my encounter with our professor was something we'd laugh about later, I let the music take over. Several minutes later, I felt his stare once again. Determined to enjoy the night, I ignored him.

As the evening wore on Nicole started flirting with a guy named Rob. Soon they were grinding on each other on the floor as I continued to dance above them. When he left the room, she pulled me aside to tell me she was going back to his place for the night. After telling her to be careful, I headed out.

"Leaving already?" a familiar voice inquired as I stepped off the porch.

I turned and faked a yawn. "What do you mean 'already'? It's almost one in the morning."

He moved closer. "Ah, but the night is young!"

"For some, but it's a school night for me."

His smile widened. "You shouldn't have told me that. That creates all kinds of naughty images of you in my mind."

I was thankful in that moment for the darkness that hid both the tension on my face and the small blush of my cheeks I couldn't stop. His persistence would've been charming if not for the fact he was under investigation. Was there a reason he was following me? A subtle scan of the area revealed we were alone; no accomplices but still no assurance I was safe.

His grin widened as he moved closer, officially invading my personal space. My stomach jolted and the hair on my arms stood up, but I refused to show weakness. I stepped off the sidewalk, not caring that he loomed over me. He stepped down as well, but stayed in place when I moved backward once again. The scent of his cologne came over me as he leaned closer. I glanced up and caught him staring at my lips.

Deep breaths. Focus, Lissa.

I arched a brow. "That's the best line you could come up with?"

"It's the best I could come up with on the fly. You can't say it didn't work at least a little bit since you're still standing here."

"If that's the best you've got, I think it's safe to say I'm not the only one who needs to get some sleep."

He closed his eyes for a moment. "Now I have even better images in my head. Care to join me?"

"And all those images should be enough to get you through the night," I teased before heading toward my car.

"Not even a name?" he called after me.

I turned around. "Not a chance. But when I tell this story to my friends, you'll be forever known as Bathroom Guy."

"See? I'm memorable enough to tell your friends about."

"Good night!" I yelled over my shoulder.

He didn't follow, and I drove away. It was only then that I expelled the breath I'd been holding and my pulse calmed. My mind continued to whirl as I replayed each of our interactions and tried to decipher if he'd realized my identity or if the evening was a collection of the world's strangest coincidences. The GPS on my phone directed me down a hill and back toward the brightly lit downtown area. As I drove past several bars and a large bookstore, I said a silent prayer he hadn't followed me.

My stomach plummeted when a red Audi turned behind me. It was just another coincidence, I told myself, even though my gut told me otherwise. A quick glance in my rearview mirror showed that, sure enough, Caleb was the driver. I pulled up the local number to call for backup on my phone and placed it in the cup holder. As he followed me through a yellow light, I gripped the steering wheel and cursed. It would be so much easier if I could just shoot his damn tires out.

He pulled into the lane next to mine at the next light and rolled down his window. I shot him a bored glance and lowered mine only halfway. "Can I help you?"

"Well, it appears fate is smiling on me and we're both heading in the same direction."

"Trying another pickup line, huh?"

"Is it working?"

The light turned green, and I waved before speeding through the intersection. He paced me for a few blocks until I turned and sped down a side street. I paused several seconds to see if he'd found me again, but it was just me and a few people on the sidewalk. I pulled into a parking garage and killed the lights. The phone number I dialed was ringing before I'd brought it to my ear. He wouldn't be thrilled at a call at such an ungodly hour, but he'd get over it.

"What's wrong?" Barton mumbled.

"I'm sorry to call so early, but we may have a situation. I have a plate on Winters, and we need to run it to get some idea of how he's spent the last three days in Portland."

"What happened?" His voice was more alert.

"I went to a student event. He was there, and we had two interactions. It could be a coincidence—"

"But better safe than sorry," he finished. "Send me the info. I'll get someone in the office to tear it apart ASAP. I should have something for you before you go to class. You are not, I repeat, not to go to that class until you hear from me. Understood?"

"Loud and clear."

I hung up and texted him the license plate of the Audi before heading to my apartment. The trip was thankfully quiet and uninterrupted. By the time I shuffled to my room, my legs weighed a ton. I changed into a pair of yoga pants and a t-shirt before collapsing into the middle of my bed. Finally relaxed, I allowed myself to think of the guy who flirted with me that night. The fact he might be a dangerous criminal who might know who I was would be resolved in a few hours. Until then, he was just a cute guy I met at a party.

Calling him cute was a gross disservice, however. He was one delectable piece of man candy. But just like any other piece of candy, too much was never good. I resolved myself to spend just one night entertaining my impure thoughts and then back to business in the morning. After tonight, however, one thing was certain. To hell with a tattoo or a belly button piercing. Once I retired, I wanted a boyfriend who didn't need a security clearance.

The alarm went off way too early a few hours later. I dressed quickly, selecting a pair of faded jeans and a simple white t-shirt under a black hoodie. I was tying my shoes when my phone rang. Barton.

"Winters spent the last three days staying at a hotel on the water-front," he reported. "For whatever reason, he opted not to stay in the condo the initial intel placed him in. There's no unusual activity on his credit card and no suspicious activity on the traffic cameras near the apartment."

"So, what's the verdict?"

"Proceed, but with caution. At this time, we have no reason to believe you've been compromised. You have your first class with him today, so let's talk again afterward and go from there."

Relieved, I hung up and grabbed my bag since I was now running late and my body was desperate for coffee. My plan to stop at the cafe around the corner was shot to hell when I saw a red Audi parked in the adjacent lot and decided not to push my luck. I found another cafe closer to the building where my class was located and soon I had a large, hot cup of energy in my eager hands. Nicole texted that she had saved me a seat as I rounded the corner of the building ready to face the day.

"So now you're the one following me."

I looked skyward and counted to ten before turning around. The jeans and t-shirt from the night before were gone and instead he wore a black business suit with a crisp white dress shirt underneath and a dark blue paisley tie. And damned if he didn't look even hotter than he had less than twelve hours earlier. Our eyes met and he smirked.

"Or proof that you're stalking me," I retorted.

"That was some impressive driving. Looks like you know your way around a gear shifter."

I rolled my eyes. "As much as I'd like to sit here and have another conversation dripping with cheesy pickup lines and sexual innuendos, I need to get to class, Bathroom Guy. Maybe we can do this another time."

Without another word, I dashed inside the building. My phone buzzed with another text from Nicole asking where I was since orientation was about to start. Picking up the pace, I shuffled down the hall, ignoring his casual, untroubled gait behind me. I walked into the classroom with under a minute to spare. After a quick walk down the stairs at the side of the room, I joined her in the front row.

"Just in time," she whispered. "Anything fun happen at the party after I left?"

I opened my mouth to answer when Caleb's deep voice broke through the hushed voices around the room. With a silent agreement to catch up later, we turned to the front. I grabbed a pen and opened my notepad to look like an adult with her shit together.

"Good morning. Welcome to my graduate teaching assistant program for the next semester."

He opened his briefcase and grabbed some papers while I took a large gulp of coffee. When I peered over my cup, a small smile tugged at lips I'd fantasized about kissing. Amongst other things. The skin hidden under my hoodie heated and my stomach fluttered.

Fuck. My. Life. This guy was going to be trouble.

Chapter Seven

Detention

HE LEANED AGAINST THE table behind him and smiled. "I asked the History Department to give me the best applicants they could find for this program. Based on everything I've read from your applications I'm extremely impressed with all of you. I look forward to working together."

He paced the room as he shared his background. I zoned out and sipped my coffee for several minutes until a hard nudge on my arm brought me back to the present. Nicole glared at me over the top of her own cup, causing me to mouth an apology. She arched an eyebrow, and I whispered that I'd fill her in later.

Caleb outlined our duties as his teaching assistants. We would grade papers for his undergraduate classes, design tests and exams, and other assorted tasks. Everyone perked up when he said each of us would present a lecture in one class, with the possibility of leading his flagship course, The History of the Mafia.

It was this class that earned Professor Winters so much attention in the education community, as well as an invitation to lecture at the college for the semester. Popular culture couldn't get enough of the mob, so a course about the topic taught by a young and handsome professor was sure to draw a lot of attention to any school who invited him.

It was also bound to attract the attention of the very groups whose history he was exposing. Most mafia groups were bound by a code of silence. The Italians called it *omertà*, and the term translated across most languages. In the literal sense, it meant silence and a refusal to give evidence to the authorities. However, I doubted any group would be thrilled about some professor discussing their histories for college credit.

After he finished speaking, we went around the room and introduced ourselves, including our hometown, undergraduate college attended and if we already had a specialty area of research. The first to speak was the short and stocky man with thick glasses named Karl Fischer. He ran his hand through his close-cut light brown hair as he told us about his parents who moved the family from Germany so he could attend NYU for his undergrad degree. His light green eyes darted around the room as he finished by saying he had no specialty yet. His body relaxed the second he returned to his seat.

The tall, reedy woman several rows in front of Karl stood up next and introduced herself as Rachele Tulo. She was originally from Milan, where she received her degree from a local college. Because organized crime had been a persistent threat in her hometown, she had an interest in the history of the mob. Karl seemed quite captivated, staring at her the entire time she spoke. As she took her seat, she tossed her long blond hair over her shoulder and shot him an uneasy look.

Nicole was next, telling everyone about her hometown of San Francisco and earning her undergrad with an emphasis in European history from Cal Berkeley. The sudden breathiness of her voice as she addressed Caleb was worthy of an eye roll, but my face remained blank. I wondered if she was a natural flirt, or if our professor was another eye she was trying to catch.

She eyed me expectantly, so I stood up and looked around the room. "My name is Jessica Ross. I grew up in Seattle and went to the University of Oregon, where I double majored in history and sociology. My specialty is modern American cultural history," I said, reciting my fake CV almost verbatim before sitting down.

Caleb's eyebrows shot up. "History and sociology? That should make for some interesting lectures."

The last member of the group, Trevor Grigsby, stood. He looked a few years older, which was confirmed when he told everyone he grew up in Bristol, England, and had taken a few years off from his studies to travel Europe and help take care of his ailing grandmother. He then received his undergraduate degree from Oxford. As he sat down, I felt his gray eyes on me.

Caleb stood and announced class was ending early so everyone could pick up their keys to the shared office and set up their desks. Nicole and I exchanged glances, silently agreeing to sit close to each other. I tossed my notebook into my backpack and was heading toward the door when his voice interrupted our plans.

"Ms. Ross, may I speak to you for a moment?"

Nicole's brow furrowed. "What did you do?"

"No idea," I muttered. "Try to grab me a good desk, please."

Once the room was empty, he checked both doors. Satisfied they were closed he turned back to me. We stared at each other for a second before he pointed to the desk I'd occupied during class. "Please sit."

"I prefer to stand, *Professor*. Since I'm guessing the reason for this meeting is about last night, I'll cut the crap and ask if you make it a habit of attending college parties and flirting with students?"

"I didn't realize it was a college party."

My eyes narrowed. "Really?"

He nodded ruefully. "Okay, I get how it looks bad. A buddy of mine rents out the basement in that house. He asked me to come hang out and mentioned the party. We decided to check it out, and it wasn't long before we realized we were the oldest people there. College parties aren't our scene, so we stayed downstairs after that. I'd gone up to grab a couple beers when I saw you."

"And it never occurred to you that I was a student? I remember mentioning I had class the next morning. Not only did you keep flirting, but you also followed me! That didn't seem inappropriate at all?"

He lowered his head. "You're right."

His comfort level plummeting, I pressed on. Relenting too soon could cause suspicion. No, I had to play the outrage a little bit longer. "Is this a regular thing you do? Is that why you're so popular with the students? Because I'm sure most colleges have something in their code of conduct about it."

"Look, I'm sorry. I should've left, but then I saw you, and just had to talk to you. I know it was wrong, but—"

"You *followed* me! I've got half a mind to go to the department and ask to be placed with a different professor. How do I work with you and act like you didn't do and say all those things?"

He studied me. "You're right. I was way out of line and I'm sorry. You're well within your rights to ask to work with someone else, but I think you bring a lot to the program. Is there a way we can move past this? Let me prove to you that I'm not who you think I am right now?"

Crossing my arms, I focused on a cracked floor tile near his polished loafers. The silence was uncomfortable, but my eyes stayed focused on the floor. He was seconds away from folding.

"Please," he begged, breaking the silence. "I promise it won't happen again."

Time to reel him in. Slowly, I lifted my eyes to his. "I'll stay for now. Don't give me a reason to regret it. Am I clear?"

"Crystal."

"Now, if you'll excuse me, I need to go get my keys and try to not get the crappiest desk in the office."

His shoulders relaxed. "I'll come with you," he offered, only to retreat a step when I raised my eyebrows. "If that's okay. I mean, I'm guessing you don't know where the office is."

The air was tense as we walked down the corridor. I'd lost count of the number of awkward glances and smiles we'd exchanged, and by the time the elevator doors closed I wished I'd taken the stairs. Of course, the elevator looked like a relic from the 1950s and was painfully slow. This gave me plenty of time to stare at the ancient linoleum while ignoring his gaze. When the doors finally opened, the sharp intake of breath over my shoulder told me I wasn't the only one thankful to be free of the confined space.

He turned to me as we rounded another corner. "So, history and sociology? How exactly does one wind up with a degree in both?"

The memories conjured from that time of my life brought an instant smile to my lips. It was while working on my master's in math that both topics caught my interest. My grad school advisor was a free spirit who challenged her students to look beyond our textbooks. Some of my most engaging and entertaining discussions took place during our advisory meetings over cups of tea. She was the first person who treated me like someone who didn't require special handling.

"I started as a history major. The cultural side really interested me, so I made that my sub-specialty. Add to that a couple sociology courses I took to meet the general ed requirements, and the next thing I knew I was a double major. Sociology ties into history more than people realize. And to be honest, a course on the history of the mob is interesting to me for both subjects."

"How so?"

We arrived at the History Department office before I answered. After saying goodbye, he continued down the hall and turned to the left. I went inside, grabbed my keys, and then followed the same route. The last door on the right opened to a small reception area with another door at the back of the room. Voices and laughter grew louder as I approached. Once inside the larger common room I found Nicole, who was laughing with Trevor. She excused herself and ran over to me.

"I did the best I could." She pointed to the far corner of the room. "It can always be worse."

She nodded, and we sat in the old metal chairs in front of each desk. "What did he want to talk to you about?"

Over her shoulder, the door on the wall across from our desks opened. Caleb sat down and opened his laptop. He stared at the screen for a minute before looking up and smiling. I cursed the flutter in my chest. He wasn't Bathroom Guy at the party anymore.

I shrugged. "Just about the sociology part of my studies and how it might enhance some of his classes."

We chatted until Rachele handed us a sheet to sign up for office hours. We signed up for the same time slots and agreed to meet at the coffee place by our dorm. We'd meet every Monday and decide as a group who would handle the weekly assignments and meetings. We both listened as she rambled on, clearly relishing that she was the one to share this information. I stifled my laugh when Nicole rolled her eyes.

Sensing we weren't listening to her, she busied herself with reading through the stack of papers on her desk. Seeing we all had the same packet, I thumbed through the pages that outlined Caleb's classes and expectations. Nicole and I discussed what we'd read, and after a little while decided to grab lunch. As we reached the door, I turned around and saw him hang up his phone and stand.

Nicole was practically bouncing on her feet as she waved to him on our way out. "See ya, Professor!"

He smiled at her before giving me a small nod and pinning me with his gaze. "Bye, Nicole. Until next time, Ms. Ross."

Chapter Eight

Spy in Aisle Three

HAVING NO OTHER CLASSES after lunch, I went back to my dorm. Three missed calls, seven text messages, and one annoyed voicemail from Barton made him the immediate priority as soon as my door closed. I'd just tossed my backpack on the couch when my phone buzzed yet again.

"Jesus, it's about damn time you answered," he grumbled. "Where the hell have you been?"

"We had to pick up our keys and then the usual dog and pony show where everyone sizes each other up. After that I went to lunch with one of the TAs who happens to be my neighbor. I literally just walked through my door."

"Well? Did anything else happen?"

"He asked me to stay after class and apologized for his behavior at the party last night."

"Interesting," he said. "And now you've met him both formally and informally, what are your first impressions of the esteemed professor?"

I flopped down next to my backpack. "He's charming, that's for sure. No doubt he uses it to his advantage whenever he can. Between that and the mafia class, I can see why he's so popular. That said, I'm struggling to understand how a history professor has any connections to the mob. But maybe that's the idea."

"I thought Felton was crazy when he brought it to me, too. CIA has pictures of them meeting on several occasions, so at some point they needed something from each other."

"But nothing in the past year?"

"Nothing, which I also find odd. They met every few months before, and then they just stopped."

"That definitely sounds strange," I agreed. "What else did Felton have to say about it?"

"He heard they didn't part on the best of terms. And to add to the mystery, the rumor is that the Genovese family is tracking Caleb. He's not hiding, so make of that what you will."

Something didn't add up. "What's Gio up to these days?"

"He was living it up in Bari with his brother until six months ago when he started making regular trips to Rome. He's up to something, but we have no idea what it could be."

"Am I wrong to think we're missing something? How does a college professor go from teaching classes to an unexplained relationship with a crime family to now being watched by one of the largest mafia organizations in the world? Did Felton give any insights into why?"

"I tried to ask him for more info and got his standard bullshit about it being classified. Not sure what the point is of him asking us to help him out if he's not going to share the info." The bitterness in his tone was unmistakable.

"I'm not going to defend him, but I'll say that he takes that whole 'need to know thing' seriously. And it's not like he'd tell me any more than he'd tell you."

"I'll do some digging and see what I can find out myself. I had copies of the pictures sent to you, so you should go check your mail soon."

"That was going to be one of my first errands since I don't have any other classes today," I said.

"Good idea. Don't forget to touch base with Marlowe if you haven't already."

"Already done."

"Sounds good. I'll call you if I hear anything else. In the meantime, stay safe."

"Always," I replied.

The sunny weather and heavy traffic made my decision to walk an easy one. Ten minutes later I strolled through the door of a mailing and shipping store near the waterfront. The woman behind the counter cast a sharp glare my way as the door closed behind me. I showed her my key, earning a curt nod before she turned back to her desk.

I grabbed two envelopes from my mailbox and shoved them into my purse. The alarm inside the small metal door emitted a loud beep. I placed my thumb on the panel to my right and entered my code. When the light turned green, the woman relaxed. Her hand that had been beneath the counter, no doubt clutching a gun, was now back on the desk. She nodded at my plain manilla envelope and got back to work.

The store was not a conventional business, but rather a communications hub set up by the Portland field office designed for agents in deep cover. It wasn't a frequent practice, but when it wasn't possible to keep in contact through electronic means, snail mail proved to be an important alternative. Messages in certain color-coded envelopes that held highly sensitive information weren't allowed to leave the building while plain messages were approved once the agent's identity was confirmed. Since my dorm room didn't have secure phone or internet lines, it was decided the hub was the best choice. Getting out of my apartment on a sunny Friday afternoon was a bonus.

My next destination was a small bookstore tucked away behind several bars and restaurants called Paige's Pages. The stories I'd heard about the store and the family who ran it were a comfort over the

years, and I promised to visit if I ever found myself in town.
An electronic door sensor rang, announcing my arrival. As I ap-proached the front counter a man yelled from the back room that he would be with me in a moment. Recognizing the voice, I smiled.

"I sure hope so. Haven't got all day!" I called back.

Something fell to the ground with a thud. "No way!"

A very tall and muscular Black man with dark hair in a military buzz sprinted to the front and around the counter to envelop me in a bear hug. My feet left the ground, causing me to laugh until his arms tightened around my ribs.

"Jake, I can't breathe," I wheezed, slapping his shoulder.

He grimaced and then released me. "Sorry about that. It's been a while." His eyes widened as he scanned my appearance." I can't believe I get to see you in the field! What do I call you?"

Jake McGuire and I had been friends since sniper school when we were paired into our spotter and shooter teams. After gradua-tion, that partnership continued in the same platoon in Iraq and we were assigned together on patrols. It was during those times spent hiding in abandoned buildings and dodging bullets that I knew he was someone I could trust with my life.

Our convoy was traveling through what was left of a demolished town when we started taking fire. The truck in front of ours swerved for reasons unknown and hit an IED. Our truck was knocked over, throwing our bodies several feet. Barely conscious, I choked on smoke and sand for what felt like hours. When I was mentally clear enough to know what was going on, my ears rang too loud to process my screams. The shrapnel ripped through the right side of my body and upper arm like my skin was made of paper. Jake tossed me over his shoulder and ran for cover, and the first sound I heard was the bullet that tore through his arm before he tossed me behind a brick wall. He collapsed a few feet away, only to crawl and cover me with his body in case we were discovered.

I woke up three days later in Germany with a severe concussion. Jake was in the bed next to mine with his arm held together with a shit ton of pins and gauze. A few days later, I was set to be discharged and returned to my company when Felton walked into my hospital room and informed me that he was bringing me home to Virginia.

Jake received a medical discharge when the nerve damage was found to be too severe. He returned home to Portland and when his mother tired of his moping, she put him to work organizing shelves. When she passed away, he took over the store to keep her dream alive. We stayed connected over e-mail, and his stories about strange customers and even stranger books that crossed his path always made me laugh.

I offered him my hand. "Jessica Ross. Pleasure to meet you."

"That has a nice ring to it. And the hair and the contacts make you look exotic."

"Yeah, that's me," I laughed. "Just your average, run of the mill exotic grad student."

"Well, I always promised you that if you were in Portland to stop by and we'd have a beer. So, let's go."

"You sure? If you're working we can go another time."

"Nah, it's almost closing time, anyway. Besides, I'm the boss and I want to take my buddy out for a beer."

"Well, all right then," I said as he grabbed his coat and locked up.

He took me to the bar next door with promises of cold drinks and amazing food. In no time we were sharing a giant plate of onion rings and laughing as he told me about the elderly woman who visited the store every few weeks in search of books on sex toys from other parts of the world and throughout history.

"Can she not look that stuff up on the internet?"

He shrugged. "I suppose she could. But, hey, it means money for me. And stories I get to tell other people."

"That's true. And not like I have any good stories I can share. So, how's Sami these days? You two better still be together."

His face lit up. "Yeah, we're good. More than good."

"Oh? Do tell!"

"We're going to Oktoberfest with her parents in Washington next month," he confessed, pausing. "Where I'm going to ask her to marry me. It's time I made an honest woman out of her."

Sami was Jake's high school sweetheart. They broke up when he first shipped out because she didn't want to be in a long-distance relationship. They'd remained friends and when she learned of his injuries, she flew to New York to meet his flight home. Within a few weeks they were back together and still going strong five years later.

I pulled him into a hug. "That's awesome! I know she'll say yes, but you still have to tell me once she does."

"Ha! You'd kick my ass if I didn't."

We talked a little while longer and when I mentioned I needed groceries, we headed to a small market a few blocks away. When we arrived, he steered the cart while I tossed items inside.

He laughed at the boxes of macaroni and cheese in my hand. "This is just like every supply run we ever went on. You're the grabby one and I'm left to carry everything."

"And if you hadn't grabbed the wrong batteries for my scope, you wouldn't have been relegated to cart duty," I laughed in a low voice.

We got to the beer aisle, and I'd just asked for his recommendations when the squeak of shoes coming to a stop drew my attention to the left. I looked up and found myself face to face with Caleb, whose eyes darted to Jake before meeting mine again.

"Hi, Professor Winters."

"Ms. Ross, what a surprise."

Jake dropped a six pack into the cart before stepping forward and extending his hand. "Jake McGuire. I'm guessing you're one of Jessie's professors?"

Jake, who was a couple inches taller, stepped closer and crushed Caleb's hand as they shook. I counted the wine bottles behind them before giving in to the urge to punch him in the shoulder. In that moment it didn't matter that I was an international spy, or that I had more combat kills than him. Whether we were in a bar in Baghdad or a grocery store in Portland, he just had to slip into overprotective brother mode.

The fake smile damn near hid the grimace. "Caleb Winters. Pleasure to meet you."

Jake's phone rang. He grabbed it from his pocket and looked at the display. "I need to take this."

He rounded the corner, and I turned back to Caleb. "So, did you get your office all set up? It still looked pretty messy when we left."

"After a while, yes. I'd hoped to con a couple of you guys to help, but everyone took off."

"Nicole promised the best sushi I'd ever had, so I had to go see if she was right."

"And was it?"

I shrugged. "Eh, top five."

He nodded in Jake's direction. "So, how long is your boyfriend in town?"

"Oh, Jake lives here in Portland. His family owns a bookstore near the waterfront. Paige's Pages? You should check it out. It has a nice history section."

"I just might have to do that. Any chance you could hook me up with a special discount?"

"Don't tell me you need a discount. Something tells me you're doing better than I am," I joked, pointing to the frozen and boxed dinners in my cart.

Jake jogged toward us before he could reply. "Hon, I'm sorry but I've gotta go. I promise I'll make it up to you."

I groaned inwardly. Way to lay it on thick. "Okay, no worries."

He pulled me into a tight embrace, his lips hovering just above my ear. "Is this guy clear? Or do I need to stay? I can call Sami and let her know you're in a situation if you need me here."

"He's clear," I murmured against his chest. "I'll text you when I get home. Tell her I said hi."

His phone rang again, and I stepped back. "You better get going if she's calling again."

He shook his head. "It's not mine."

We turned and found Caleb scowling and pressing buttons on his phone. The anger on his face dissolved the moment he looked up. Jake's arms tightened around me. "Everything okay, Professor?"

"Yeah, just a friend of mine. I can call back later," he answered as the phone rang again. He rolled his eyes. "Or I can just take it now and stop annoying everyone. Nice meeting you, Jake."

He nodded. "Likewise."

Caleb stabbed the screen of his phone with a finger and pressed it to his ear. "What?" he bit out.

Jake steered me around the cart. "I'm not sure you should be alone with him. Are you sure you're okay? You armed?"

"I have a knife hidden on me and one in my bag. I'll be fine. From the sounds of it, Sami needs you. I'll text you once I leave here and when I get home."

"Five-minute increments the second you walk out of this building. I'm serious," he commanded before stepping back and kissing my forehead. "Call me later, yeah?" he added in a loud voice before he turned and left.

When I walked back to my cart, Caleb had set his basket on the ground and was shooting Jake a nasty glare. His jaw clenched at the caller's shouts but remained silent. When he kicked the basket a couple inches away from him, I pushed my cart to the next aisle and busied myself with selecting a tub of ice cream.

"Look, I fucking told you I'd do it. I just need more time," he growled in a loud whisper.

Milk. I needed milk, which was in the cooler and about ten feet away from whatever verbal altercation he was having. My cart glided to my destination until his arm punched a package of paper towels, causing me to jump.

"No, *you* listen to me, you impatient fuck!" he seethed.

I grabbed a carton and moved to the safety of the bread aisle. The sunny weather had turned into a downpour when I strolled outside, so I texted Jake and then called a taxi. In the meantime, I occupied myself by eating a couple grapes and playing games on my phone.

"You might be here a while if you're waiting for the rain to pass," a voice said behind me.

"Ah, but the night is young," I joked, turning to face him.

Caleb smiled and looked skyward. "That may be, but this rain isn't going anywhere. Do you need a ride?"

"That's really nice of you, but my cab should be here any minute."

A loud swarm of voices cut through the sounds of traffic and rain just before I was shoved forward by a group of people. I would've crashed into the flower cart next to the entrance if his arm hadn't grasped me by the waist and pulled me against his body. At once the smell of his cologne flooded my nostrils and my skin heated. I brought my arm to his side to steady my feet. His hold on me tightened, and he leaned closer.

"Are you okay?" his voice rasped low in my ear.

I nodded, unable to speak, and he loosened his grip. It took a few seconds for me to realize my arm was still around him. Feeling my cheeks burn, I stepped back. Once my heart rate returned to normal, I smiled and tried not to fidget.

He moved closer. "So, um—"

A bright yellow taxi turned the corner. The driver yelled my name, and I glanced at Caleb one last time before yanking the door open and flinging myself and my bags inside. When the door closed behind me, he gave a small wave, which I returned as we pulled into traffic. A buzz from my phone broke the spell. I'd forgotten to text Jake, who threatened to storm the market and fill the professor with more holes than swiss cheese. Rolling my eyes, I explained I was on my way home and to stand down.

Deep brown eyes plagued my subconscious as I dragged the soggy bags inside my apartment. Putting on dry clothes, I shoved all my groceries into the fridge with the mental promise to put them away later. Not in the mood to cook any of my frozen dinners, I grabbed my pint of ice cream, a spoon and my mail before settling onto the couch with a blanket.

The first envelope held a stack of photos with a note attached saying they'd been taken two weeks earlier in Rome. My jaw clenched at the image of Gio Sardi as he stood next to a cargo van and watched several men loading it up with large crates from a ship. Another man, whose face I couldn't see, stood next to him and pointed toward a large truck parked nearby. The smug smile and expensive sunglasses on his face filled me with disgust. He looked like an ordinary businessman, but I knew what a sadistic, cold-blooded killer he was. I set the pictures down and grabbed the second envelope.

The next set of pictures piqued my interest. The note on the front said they were taken fifteen months earlier in New York. Gio stood in front of what looked like an abandoned building. With Caleb. Each image showed them arguing, and at one point Caleb poked Gio in the chest. The last four pictures showed him tossing a wad of paper at Gio before storming away, but not before flipping off the older man first.

"Well, well, Professor Winters," I muttered as I brought a spoonful of ice cream to my mouth. "You're just full of surprises, aren't you?"

Chapter Nine

This Little Piggy

"WHY IS PARTICIPATION ONE quarter of our grade?" The redhead who looked like she'd just rolled out of bed asked in a huff.

I straightened my posture behind the lectern. "Two reasons. First, how do you expect to learn anything if you don't come to class? Second, why would you pay money for a class you don't take part in?"

"Hmph." She shared an annoyed look with the woman next to her.

Caleb scrawled in his notepad before clearing his throat. "This has always been a policy in my classes. If you have any concerns, Ms. Bennett, please schedule an appointment with me and we can speak further."

Part of our TA duties included attending and teaching classes. Trevor was supposed to take this one but asked to switch with me because of a last-minute appointment. After forty-five minutes of asinine questions from freshman about everything from the price of the textbook to how grades were calculated, I wanted to pull my hair out. Luckily, the class was scheduled to end early so the students could go to the computer lab and set up their online accounts. If they needed any help, I'd written Trevor's cell phone number on the whiteboard behind me for all their support needs.

"Did anybody have any other questions?" My voice broke through the low din in the room. Caleb tapped his wrist, signaling for me to wrap it up. "All right, then we'll stop here so everyone can get over to the lab."

He stood up as the students gathered their bags. "Good first week, everyone. I promise we'll start actually learning history at our next class." He nodded at the board. "If you have any questions or problems, please call the number up front or stop by during office hours and someone can help you."

A few students approached me with questions. Caleb had a department meeting to attend, so he motioned to the door before leaving. A little while later I arrived to an empty office and a ringing phone. Tossing everything in my hands onto the couch, I raced to the table, only for the caller to hang up. Blowing out an annoyed voice, I moved everything to my desk and started going through e-mails.

The phone rang again, only for me to hear another click when I answered. After the fourth time, I cursed and pressed the button to direct all calls to voicemail. Nicole came in later with sandwiches, and seeing my name on one of the bags brightened my mood. After a morning of whiny students and prank calls, I was ready for a break.

She tossed me a bag of chips. "How did class go this morning?"

"The next time Trevor needs someone to cover for him, he can find another sucker. It was nothing but endless whining and griping about anything they could find to pick apart."

She eyed the red light on the phone. "Is that why this is forwarding to voicemail?"

"No, some jackass keeps calling and hanging up." I flashed a guilty smile. "And I may have given out Trevor's cell number to the class for tech support."

"Well played." Pressing a couple buttons on the phone, she tossed her wrapper in the trash. "I'll handle any calls. You look like you could use a break."

"You're awesome. Thank you."

"How was your weekend?"

I sat next to her on the couch and dug into my turkey sandwich. "Uneventful. Met up with a friend of mine who lives in town and we hung out for a while. Spent most of Sunday doing laundry and watching football. What about you?"

She smiled. "I met up with a friend, too."

"Was this the guy you were telling me about?"

Nicole had a boyfriend named Matt back in San Francisco. However, they had an open relationship which allowed her to play the field. She'd explained it all to me on the way to the party, and it was during this same conversation that she told me about her friend with benefits in Portland.

"Yep. And let's just say I was definitely not happy to see Monday morning roll around."

"Ugh. Not jealous at all! Nor am I going to ask if he has any friends because I may need to find one of those for myself."

"Find one of what?" a voice interrupted. We both looked up to see Caleb enter the office. When Nicole's cell phone rang and she left the room to answer, he turned to me.

"Oh, just an app on my phone for keeping things organized." My eyes darted to my screen to hide the subtle blush on my cheeks. Jesus, I was trained to control these reactions. What the hell?

"Ah. Well, great class today. I'm sure it wasn't the class you were expecting. That was probably why Mr. Grigsby switched with you."

"Which is why I returned the favor."

Nicole burst into the room. "A bunch of the students are having trouble trying to get logged in and Trevor isn't answering his phone."

"Of course he isn't," I muttered, rolling my eyes.

"Which is why I'm heading over there to help them. I think you've dealt with them enough today."

"Have I mentioned that you're my favorite friend?"

"Trevor owes me now, too. All it's going to cost you is doing the mail this afternoon."

I gave her a thumbs up. "Deal."

Caleb opened his mouth to speak again but was interrupted by the phone. I held up a finger and grabbed the receiver. *Click.* Silence. Sighing, I hung up.

His brow furrowed. "Problem?"

"We've had a bunch of hang up calls today. Kind of annoying."

"That's odd."

"Hopefully they'll figure out another way to entertain themselves soon."

I returned to my desk and the long list of e-mails needing my attention. No matter how hard I tried to focus on work, his presence bugged me. "Professor, was there something you needed help with?"

His posture straightened. "Now that I think about it, there is something I wanted to talk to you about."

"Okay?"

He leaned against the desk behind him. "I wanted to apologize for my behavior the other night at the store. I shouldn't have pried so much about you and your boyfriend."

I nodded but said nothing. The day after the infamous shopping trip, I'd had to endure an hour-long interrogation from Jake. Afterward, I had thought little of Caleb's less than friendly attitude. Listening to him lose his shit with the mystery caller had been far more interesting than the pissing match between those two.

"I also wanted to apologize if I made you uncomfortable at all during my phone call," he added, as if reading my thoughts. "You left pretty quickly, and I can't say I blame you."

"Oh! Nothing you need to apologize for. Once I saw you were upset, I figured it was personal, so I let you have some privacy."

"Well, I was still rude and unprofessional."

I gave a one-shouldered shrug. "Well, it's not like you knew you were going to run into one of your students and her plus one raiding the beer aisle at the grocery store, so don't worry about it."

"Plus one? That's an interesting way to refer to a boyfriend, isn't it?" He paused, chuckling at my silence. "Sorry, I did it again. I'm just going to go in my office before I stick my foot in my mouth any more than I already have."

I gestured to the pile of letters and a package on the table. "I need to get mail done, anyway."

"Well, I won't keep you. Other than to say that if there's food in that box over there, I call dibs on any chocolate."

"We'll see about that. Besides, you'll be in your office so it's not like you'll see anyway," I joked.

"Lying and stealing from the professor who determines your final grade, Ms. Ross?"

"All bets are off when chocolate is involved. And now you're keeping me from getting work done. Scram."

He laughed and disappeared into his office. After sorting through the letters, I noted the Italian postmark on the box before slicing through the tape. It was probably more historical documents from Rome, which meant no chocolate, I thought wistfully. My mind was elsewhere as I pulled away the blank sheet of paper on top. The rustling of plastic made me look down in time to see a bag open and revealed a severed pig head. The vegetables surrounding it were plastic, but the smell confirmed it was very real. Genuinely startled, I screamed and shoved away from the parcel.

"What's wrong?" A pair of firm hands shook my shoulders. "Jessica!"

I snapped out of my daze and found his face inches from mine. With a shaking hand, I pointed to the table. "There's a pig's head inside."

He approached the box with caution, swearing when he pulled the flaps away. The office phone rang, and I jumped. He stalked to the desk and ripped the receiver away from the base.

"Caleb Winters," he barked. "Look, I don't know who you are, or what kind of sick game you're playing but I'd advise you to knock it the fuck off."

I backed away when he slammed the phone down. The shock of everything had worn off, but now an endless barrage of questions and possibilities about what just happened percolated in my mind. His eyes widened, and he stepped closer.

"Jess? Are you okay?" His tone was low and soothing as he gently touched my shoulder.

"Just give me a minute. That was… unexpected. And gross."

"I'm going to call the police, okay? Let's sit down while we wait for them." He put his arm around me and led us to the ugly red vinyl couch.

His hand touched the bare skin on my arm, and goosebumps erupted. I leaned into him and inhaled his scent for several seconds before realization set in. Sitting upright, I scooted sideways to put some distance between us.

"Who was on the phone?" My voice came out shakier than I'd planned.

"Don't worry about it," he muttered as he dialed his cell phone. I peeked at his face and saw the tension in his jaw. Our eyes met, and his were blazing. As he spoke into the phone, he rubbed my shoulders and moved his arm to my lower back.

When two Campus Security guards appeared at the door less than five minutes later, his hand disappeared. Not long after, two police officers in suits arrived, introducing themselves as Detectives Sam Nelson and Mark Ross. Nelson took my statement while Ross spoke with Caleb in his office. I recounted what happened and was just about to mention the phone calls when Detective Ross came out and asked about them.

"Did the caller say anything?" he asked as Nelson took my fingerprints on an index card.

"No, they hung up each time. Did you ask Professor Winters about the calls? The phone rang right after I opened the package. He spoke to someone when he answered."

"He told me the caller stayed on the line but said nothing."

I wiped the ink from my fingers and found Caleb watching me from the doorway to his office. He gave me a small, sad smile. My stomach churned, and I turned away, desperate to be free of his scrutiny. I needed to think... away from him and the literal stench of the day.

"Thank you for your time, Ms. Ross, Mr. Winters," Nelson said. "You two are free to leave. Campus Security will lock up the office once we're done here."

Caleb spoke to the detectives as I packed up my things, but his voice was nothing more than a deep and vague rumble. I stared at the fake wood grain pattern on my desk as my brain continued its assault of rapid-fire questions. When he touched my arm, I jumped and turned around.

"Sorry," he murmured, moving his hand away. "Are you okay?"

"Um, yeah."

The detectives escorted us out of the office and one of the campus security guards followed us until we exited the building. The cool air was a welcome change when I stepped outside. I took a few deep breaths and tried to calm my frazzled nerves.

"Jess?"

His touch was soft on my shoulder as he turned me toward him and stepped closer. I licked my suddenly dry lips and retreated several inches. My body's physical reaction to his closeness was confusing and alarming.

"Professor, I'm fine."

"I think after that we can dispense with the formalities. Call me Caleb."

"All right. I'm fine, Caleb."

He grinned. "That's better. Would you like to grab something to eat? It's the least I could do."

It was a tempting offer, one that could've gotten me some good intel. However, between the endless questions in my head and the way my body insisted on being stupid around him, I knew it wasn't a good idea.

"As nice as that sounds, I'm going to head home. It's, uh, it's been a day."

"Yes, it has. Rain check?"

"Um, sure." I rubbed my forehead and glanced down the street.

"Are you sure you're okay?" he persisted. "You seem really shaken."

"I'll be fine. It just threw me off guard. One minute we were joking about chocolate, and then suddenly it turned into a police situation."

"That's one way to put it. If you're sure you're okay, go home and relax. Don't be afraid to call me if you need anything."

"Thanks," I responded with a slow wave. "Good night."

His eyes followed my every move as I turned toward my apartment. My pace picked up the moment I turned the corner and was no longer in his field of vision. Calls had to be made, first to the field office about the small matter of the police having my fingerprints, and then to Barton. For a moment, I thought about calling Mel, but I wasn't in the mood for that much gloating. The simple case of babysitting a professor just hit an interesting and possibly complicated speed bump.

Chapter Ten

Whisky Tales

I DIALED MY PHONE as soon as my door was locked. Agent Marlowe answered and after I told him what happened at the school, he assured me there was no cause for concern. Relieved that I wouldn't be discovered, we agreed to debrief after he spoke to the cops and hung up. The next conversation would be longer and more involved, so I put on pajamas, warmed up some leftovers, and grabbed a beer. The caller picked up on the second ring.

"Is Caleb Winters in witness protection?" I asked without preamble.

Barton paused. "Why?"

"Just answer the question. Is he or not?"

"No, he's not. What the hell is going on?"

I told him everything that happened since the last time we spoke, including Caleb's phone call in the grocery store. He put me on hold while he checked with the U.S. Marshal's office and confirmed that he wasn't involved in the witness protection program.

"Have you found out anything from Felton?" I grumbled. "Something's going on and we need to know what."

"I haven't heard a damn thing from him and it's pissing me off."

"What about Ginnie?"

Ginnie Matthews was a colleague of Felton's and had worked with him as far back as I could remember. Over the years she'd been an amazing resource and helped me when he wasn't available. Barton had commented more than once that he wished she was my handler.

"Called her yesterday. All she said was he was traveling, and that she'd let him know I needed to talk to him ASAP. He usually responds once I get her involved, so I imagine I'll hear from him soon."

"Let's hope so."

"So, how did Winters react?"

"A lot happened all at once. I found the head almost the same time that the phone started ringing. He completely lost his shit on the caller but was completely calm when he gave his statement to the cops."

"What's your gut telling you?"

"Maybe a warning? A bunch of mobsters in Italy killed a guy and disposed of the body by dumping him in a pig pen. What I want to know is who is this caller who seems to piss him off so much?"

"And is that person related to the special delivery?"

"That's why I called you since you're supposed to have all the answers," I joked.

"And I would if some asshole from the CIA would share them with me."

"Fair point."

"Well, just keep on it until you hear otherwise. It's a definite concern, but I'm not sure how much of one yet. I'll be in touch."

After tossing my phone on the cushion next to me, I decided on an evening of mindless TV. I grabbed some ice cream, and then stared at my front door from the couch while paying little attention to the crappy movie I'd selected. As I was debating whether to spend the energy needed to grab a second beer, my phone rang. My eyebrows shot up at the screen.

"Jess? Hi, it's Caleb. Winters."

"Oh, hi. I didn't expect to hear from you so soon. Did you already hear something from the police?"

"No, I wanted to apologize again for what happened, and to tell you to take a couple days off. I'm sure all this still has you pretty rattled."

I headed to the fridge to grab the second bottle. "Are you sure?"

"I insist. You're not to come back to the office until Monday."

"All right," I relented, leaning against the counter and taking a drink to calm the fluttering in my chest. "I'll see you Monday."

I glared at my phone before leaving it on the counter and taking another drink. What was with my body's reaction to this man? Never one to swoon, I cringed at the memory of practically sitting in his lap on the damn couch. Hell, my pulse raced when I heard his voice. Time away from him was just what I needed.

Abandoning my TV plan, I turned off all the lights and headed to my bedroom. I tried to decide how to spend the next four days as I brushed my teeth. An idea came to me and soon I was making another phone call.

A gruff voice answered. "Donovan, to what do I owe the honor?

"Evening, Drill Sergeant. How's retirement treating you?"

"Jesus, kid. Cut the bullshit. What's up?"

"I need to get away for a few days and was wondering if you'd be around."

"I'll be here. Wouldn't mind if you brought my old buddy Jameson along with you."

"You got it," I laughed. "I should be there by dinner time tomorrow."

"Sounds good. I'll thaw an extra steak and pull out the good glasses. Drive safe," he drawled before hanging up.

I sent a text message to Barton and Marlowe informing them of my trip. Barton called barely a minute later and wanted to know all the details. After telling me to be careful and reminding me to get the good bottle of Jameson, I joked that he needed to remember those words when he approved my expense report.

The sky was the pale blue of early evening upon arrival at the training facility in Oak Harbor, Washington. After parking near the hangar I walked inside, easily finding the grouchy old bastard as he put away supplies. I crept toward him with a smile, waiting for him to say something.

"You should know by now you can't sneak up on me," he growled.

I stood at attention and saluted. "Drill Sergeant."

"Oh, for fuck's sake! Give me a damn hug."

My arms flew around him. "Good to see you, Connor."

Sergeant Connor Minton, USMC retired, was my instructor from Scout Sniper School who told me about Felton's involvement in getting me into the program. He and Jake were the only two people who didn't work in the intel community who knew my true identity and occupation.

He stepped back and gave me the once over, narrowing his brown eyes. "Well?"

I held up the paper bag in my hand. "Gold Reserve. You almost done here?"

"I'm done whenever I feel like being done. Let's go."

When Connor retired two years earlier, he returned to his native Washington State. After two months he got so bored he said it felt like he was just waiting around to die, so he did volunteer work with other veterans at the Air Force training facility. Every year he and Jake met up for a hunting trip in Montana. They'd invited me on several occasions, but work had always kept me away.

He grew up a Naval brat around the shipyard in Bremerton a couple hours to the south but rebelled and chose the Marines, much to his father's annoyance. After graduating with perfect scores on all his exams, his father muttered a few terse words of praise and then left. It was then, he said, that he learned one of the most important life lessons to know.

After my return from Iraq, he told me that when he met me in training, he saw the same need for acceptance and approval that he'd had. That was why he told me the truth. I already had Felton's approval he'd said, so much so that he tried to make things easy for me. Taking the job with the FBI, something that relied on my own skills, was a smart move. According to him, however, I was still a work in progress... just like everyone else.

"So, tell me what's going on in the world," he instructed as he unlocked the door to his small apartment. "You on a job?"

"I am, and it's a weird one. And possibly my last."

His eyes widened. "Whoa. Slow down. What do you mean by your last?"

"I'm thinking of retiring from both agencies."

"Why? What the hell else would you do? You're only trained for one thing: killing. You gonna become a merc or something?"

"No, but I'm wondering if maybe I should set out on my own to find my parents' killer."

He placed two glasses on the counter with a bang and pinned me with a hard glare. "You realize that would be a goddamned suicide mission, right? You'd be going up against the mob. It's a small family organization, I'll give you that. But it's still the fucking mob, Larissa."

"I'm sick of waiting around for this asshole. Felton said I'd be able to look for him in between assignments, but that's never happened."

He sighed and rubbed the top of his bald head. "And there's your problem. You listened to that shithead."

I looked skyward and prayed for strength as he turned away. Compared to Connor, Barton and Felton were best friends. Like Barton, I got the impression there was more to the animosity than either would ever tell me. Long ago I had resigned myself to the fact that Felton wasn't a nice person.

"Yes, I know. Felton is always the problem."

He grunted in response and busied himself with seasoning the two steaks on the counter. After finding vegetables in his fridge and chopping them for a salad, I continued to prepare dinner in silence until he returned from his patio grill carrying the steaks. By then I'd set the small table in his dining room.

"So, here's what we're going to do," he paused as he poured himself a glass of Jameson and sat down. "We're going to eat our dinner and you're going to tell me what has you in such a state that you bought an expensive bottle of whisky and drove over four hours to come see me. And then we'll get this figured out."

"The case sounded simple enough when I got it. Spy on a college professor with ties to the Sardis. But a lot of things aren't adding up. For example, how do these two even know each other? We have pictures of them together about a year ago, so it's not like I'm chasing a rumor."

He stared at his glass for a moment. "He knows exactly who sent that little gift in the mail."

"Well, you don't have to be a rocket scientist to figure out Gio had something to do with it. It looked like they wanted to tear each other's heads off in the photos I saw."

"That seems too easy to me. What's Felton have to say about all this?"

"He's traveling so Barton hasn't been able to talk to him."

He narrowed his eyes. "But I'm sure there's a way you can get a message to him."

"There is. I just try to avoid using it if I know he's in the field. Plus, I don't want to make it seem like I'm trying to sidestep Barton."

"Something tells me he won't mind. We both know he'd enjoy stepping in to help."

"He would," I conceded. "I just didn't want it to come to that. You know how well that would go over."

"I would think Felton would see pissing Barton off as a bonus."

The ancient metal dining chair squeaked when I rolled my eyes at the ceiling. "He's not your favorite person, but he was there when nobody else was. When he found me that night, he could've turned me over to the state, but he didn't. He raised me, kept me safe and taught me how to defend myself."

"And I'll never take that away from him. But I think sometimes you trust him blindly and this could be one of those times. Something isn't adding up, and the person who could easily clear this up is nowhere to be found."

"Connor, how many times did you tell me that if you know someone has a known bias to treat anything they say as a load of crap? Bit hypocritical right now, wouldn't you say?"

His smile looked proud. "And the fact that you're calling me out on that tells me that you have been listening to me. Yes, I've never liked Felton and I'll tell you why. He came to see me a few weeks before your graduation. I think he was trying to use whatever clout he thought he had to get you a better score. Dumb bastard didn't know you were already on track to graduate with the best scores of any class in decades. We played cards and not only did that shithead cheat, but he also drank all my good whisky. Never liked him before that night, and after that he confirmed my first instincts were correct and to never trust him."

"This coming from the guy who told me he refused to give me a perfect score on my final exam on principle," I grumbled.

He grinned and downed the rest of his drink. "And the fact you're more pissed about that than what I just told you about Felton is why I still have hope for you."

Chapter Eleven

Did You Try Flowers?

I STAYED AT CONNOR'S for two days, sleeping on his couch, tagging along when he volunteered, and reminiscing about our days in the Corps. Our trip to the shooting range proved I was still a better shot than the grouch, something I reminded him about often. He rolled his eyes, but I caught a smirk now and then. As I packed up to leave Saturday morning, he cooked breakfast. Neither one of us mentioned the case, Felton, or my thoughts of retirement since my first night.

"Before you decide, I want you to do something." His voice sounded like gravel as he sipped from his giant mug.

"What's that?"

"Close your eyes and try to envision your life one year and five years later. Where are you? What are you doing? Who's in your life? What do you hope to have accomplished? And then think about where Giovino Sardi fits into all that."

I set my cup down louder than intended. "What are you saying? That I shouldn't go after him? That I shouldn't avenge their deaths?"

"Not at all. What I'm saying is you need to think about the life you want, what you want your future to look like. Is he still alive? If not, what are you doing with your life now that you aren't chasing him?"

He watched as I let his words sink in. When I looked up moments later, he gave the slightest of nods, as if he already knew my response and was waiting for me to say the words.

"I've never thought about it."

"That's what I'm getting at, Lissa. You're a killing machine. You had the skills long before you ever came to me. I just helped make you better. But at some point, this battle is going to end. What will you do if the target you've spent most of your life hunting is gone? Can you move past it all and live a life that isn't soaked in blood?"

"You don't think I can?"

"It's not about what I think. Not what Jake McGuire, Barton Kane, or even Felton Lynch thinks. What do you think? Can you do more with your life than just avenge the deaths of two people whom I'm pretty damn sure wanted more for you than this? That's what you need to do before you decide to retire."

"I will."

He walked me to the car and gave me a rough one-armed hug. "Stay safe, kid."

"Yes, sir."

With one last salute, which earned a spirited middle finger from the old fart, I was on the road. Between the cloudless blue sky and my need to walk around, I decided to stop for the night in Seattle. The deluge of tourists allowed plenty of cover to breathe in the salt air as I strolled along the waterfront. Nobody gave a second thought to a girl in a dark blue hoodie who tossed food to the seagulls and watched boats sail across the Sound. Retiring to my room for the night, I watched the sunset from the balcony before heading inside for a long, hot bath.

The buzzing of my phone drew me out of the bathroom, where I found messages from Barton and several others. What should have been a quick response about my location turned into a long exchange about the case and then another rant about Felton. By the time I told him we'd talk more later, I was too damn tired to respond to the multiple messages from Nicole and flopped on the bed. When my phone chimed again, I groaned loudly and grabbed the offensive device. The message almost made me drop the damn thing on my face.

Hope you're enjoying your time off. Let's get that beer next week.

Caleb, the man who occupied my thoughts the most and whom I should trust the least. He was the target of my investigation, I'd scolded myself, a man tied to my parents' killer. I had no business turning into a hormonal teenager around him, and my finger sure as fuck shouldn't have been hovering over the keypad to type out a reply.

ME: Having a great time. Skipping school is fun.

CALEB: Is it skipping school if your professor gives his blessing?

ME: It is when you have other classes led by professors who aren't so
     charitable. My pile of homework will be horrid next week, so if
     I'm too busy to get that beer it's your fault.

CALEB: If that happens, I promise to make it up to you.

ME: Nah, I'm good.

CALEB: Please. I insist.

ME: *insert grateful but noncommittal response here*

CALEB: *my firm rebuttal and insistent offer goes here*

My entire face flushed. I'd felt an attraction to other targets be-fore, but this was different. Most of my reaction to the mail incident had been for show, but my reaction to his touch was not. I'd enjoyed it, craved it, and felt a small pang of sadness once it was gone.

That was when I knew I needed space, more than the few blocks between my apartment and the office. No, I needed hundreds of miles to sort out the hormonal shit storm in my head and quiet the craving. To my frustration, the memory of the warmth I felt from his touch lingered at night, even while trying to fall asleep on Connor's lumpy couch.

Disgusted with myself, I shoved my phone under a pillow and grabbed the remote. Several hours spent watching trashy reality TV and eating pizza in my bathrobe helped, but soon my channel surfing traveled to the steamier side of the dial and I grabbed the plain shopping bag that sat next to my purse.

Ah, hell. Even spies had needs, I reasoned as the plastic toy in my hand came to life. It wasn't often that I sought battery operated companionship during a job, but lately my resolve faltered more than once. If Cosmo, my new sparkly purple friend, helped then it was money well spent.

Images of Caleb's deep brown eyes and the sound of his voice carried me away. The fantasy of his warm skin against mine was nowhere near as thrilling as the real thing, but at least it didn't break any laws. Several orgasms later my body was sated, and I fell asleep without another impure thought.

Another text was on my phone the next morning, but I forced myself to ignore it. Instead, I dragged my ass outside for a jog. The autumn sunrise made for a stunning backdrop as I explored the waterfront. I passed several bakeries and cafes until I could no longer resist the delicious smells and bought a bag of mini donuts. Wiping powdered sugar off my fingers, I sat on a bench near the aquarium and watched the large green and white ferry boats cross the glassine surface of the Sound. I tossed chunks of the last donut to the seagulls and watched them battle for several minutes before touching the rainbow ice cream cone icon on my phone. The secure messaging screen appeared, and I typed out my message.

I'm interested in purchasing some Italian pastries for a special event. What's your standard shipping time?

My phone chimed with another message as I returned to my room but it was almost checkout time so I ignored it. It was late afternoon when I made it back to Portland and cursed the state of my filthy apartment. I tossed my phone on my bed and didn't pick it up again until I crawled under the covers. After promising Nicole I'd explain everything after class, I confirmed to Caleb I'd be in the office in the morning.

Four days offline meant a mountain of work. I spent the morning catching up and combing through the upcoming lesson plans to make sure the team was prepared. After I translated my third document in Italian, a pot of coffee was needed. Nicole was due to arrive, and with her an interrogation that would start as soon as she walked in the door.

"Girl, you scared the shit out of me! I tried to get a hold of you and never heard back. I was going out of my mind," she practically yelled when she burst through the door. She unloaded her bag and then pulled me from my chair into a rib-crushing hug. "Where were you? I stopped by, and you weren't even home!"

"Sorry about that. I wound up turning off my phone and then going to Seattle for a couple days."

"Well, it looks like the trip did you some good."

I smiled. "Thanks. It helped clear my head."

We headed to a study session with several underclassmen. Afterward, Nicole went to class while I returned to the office. When I entered, Karl was leaning against Caleb's door while they talked about an upcoming mafia class. I waved to them both and sank into my chair, glaring at the stack of papers on my desk. Not wanting to waste any time, I took a huge gulp of iced coffee and dug in. A short time later I felt a presence to my right and looked up.

Karl gave me an awkward smile. "How are you? We all heard what happened."

"I'm a lot better, thanks. Sorry for leaving everyone in the lurch. Is there anything you need me to help with?"

"No, I'm all right." He glanced at the clock. "I should go. Professor Winters asked me to look for a couple articles for next week's class."

"Okay, well, it was good seeing you. Let's catch up later."

With his usual silent nod, he left. Karl was quiet and awkward around most people until the subjects of European history and New York sports entered the conversation. The football season hadn't been kind to his teams, which led to several entertaining and spirited talks around the office.

Caleb came from his office with a warm smile. "Welcome back."

"Thanks. And thank you for giving me a couple days off. As it turned out, a road trip was just what I needed."

He dropped into the chair next to mine. "It was the least I could do, and it's great to hear that it helped. While you were gone, we made a couple changes. The biggest one is that all incoming mail is being scanned before it comes to the office. Suffice to say that after what happened, you don't need to sort it."

"I'm fine. It's not like it's going to happen again from the sounds of it."

"Well, you now have a great excuse to get out of it."

"All right," I relented, holding up my hands. "So, is there anything else I should know about?"

He leaned forward. "I owe you an explanation."

"No, you really don't have to do that, Professor." Lies. All lies. I couldn't wait to hear it.

"Well, for starters, please call me Caleb. And, yes, I do. It's a situation that shouldn't have escalated, but it did, and you got sucked into it. You deserve to know why."

"Okay?"

He took a deep breath. "The box came from an ex-girlfriend of mine. She's been warned to stop contacting me, but still acts out from time to time. I didn't know you'd be on the receiving end of her craziness, and for that I'm sorry."

My eyebrows shot up. "Something must have gone wrong between the two of you for her to be sending something like that."

"That's an understatement."

"Did you try flowers?" When his eyes widened, I smiled and shook my head. "I'm kidding. Based on what I saw, she'd probably turn them into some weird and gruesome potpourri."

"I don't know whether I should be worried or not by that comment. The last thing I want to do is give you any ideas if you ever break up with your boyfriend."

"I wouldn't stoop that low. Besides, I don't see that happening anytime soon."

"Right," he muttered. "But I wanted to explain. And apologize. I'm sorry my personal life affected you."

"Life happens," I replied with a shrug. "We can avoid it all we want, but it does. About all we can do is try to learn from it and move on."

"That's a pretty healthy way to look at it."

"You can live a good life, but there will always be things and people you can't control. Sometimes you just have to sit back and let things happen."

He raised an eyebrow. "Like fate?"

"Fate takes credit for way too many things."

"You don't believe in fate?"

I shrugged. "I believe fate only gets you so far. It can lead you to something or someone, but it's what you choose to do with that opportunity that decides the outcome. For example, fate brought you and this woman together. You both took the chance on a relationship. It didn't work out and here we are. Is that fate?"

"Definitely not."

"Exactly. But if you two had lived happily ever after, everyone would say it was. It's not that I don't believe in it. I just think it's too easy to call something fate when it works out, but not when it's a crappy outcome."

"Excellent point."

"Just the humble musings of someone who's been there more times than I'll ever admit."

I shrugged and started going through the papers. A comfortable silence settled between us for a time. Of course, that all went to shit when I caught him watching me. I snapped the file folder in my hand closed. "You know, there are plenty of better things to stare at in this room than me."

"Sorry. Couldn't help it."

"Please try harder."

He moved closer. "I know we agreed to never talk about it, but since you brought it up, I'm going to say what's on my mind. I think about that night a lot. Do you?"

I scoffed and ignored my body's traitorous reactions. "No. Once I realized we'd be working together, how I felt was no longer relevant."

"Are you saying that if I wasn't your teacher, I would've had a shot?"

"I still have a boyfriend, so your chances would've still been nonexistent."

"People break up all the time."

"You're one of those people who thinks persistence pays off, aren't you?"

"I think it would be worth it in this case."

My feet hit the floor with a loud thud before I rolled my chair backwards. I pressed both hands on my thighs to hide my sweaty palms. After all the filthy images in my head from the other night, I took a cleansing breath. This was the wrong time for this conversation.

"I think all of this is a sign that it's not meant to be," I finally managed to get out.

His voice was rough. "Let me ask you something. Let's say two people meet at the worst possible time, but you know they'd be awesome together. What would be your take on that?"

I tried to pretend his words had no effect, but doubted he believed my blank face. After years of successfully sidestepping temptation, it was practically dropped into my lap in an undeniably sexy package and said all the right things. I dug my fingernails into my arm. The sharp sting gave me the few seconds needed to steel my resolve. When I snapped my gaze up to his, his flinch was small, but unmistakable.

"I think that unless you're talking about your ex, you need to change the subject to something related to history or my job as your teaching assistant, Professor."

"Jess, I—"

"No, we agreed to keep things professional. I'm Ms. Ross and you're Professor Winters."

His chair moved back several inches. "I'm sorry. I have something related to teaching if you're interested."

"Well, then I'm all ears. What is it?"

He walked to his office and returned with a folder. "The mafia class just finished their first section on the Italians. Can I interest you in using the reference material in there to design the test?"

"Absolutely. When do you need it?"

"End of the week, please."

"You got it."

His eyebrows furrowed when I stood and gathered my things. "You're leaving?"

"You gave me homework, so I'm going home to work on it. Besides, there's no ice cream here. And I do my best work with a pint of something with chocolate in it."

"I see. Well, good night, Ms. Ross."

With my backpack over my shoulder, I headed for the door without another word. My hand was on the knob but stopped when his footsteps came closer. His warm breath on my neck caused my own to hitch. My heart slammed into my chest when I looked up and his eyes met mine.

"Would flowers have worked on you?" his voice husked.

I inhaled sharply and closed my eyes. The electricity crackled between us and kept me frozen in place. My skin prickled, anticipating his touch. When it didn't come, I wasn't sure if I felt disappointment or relief. One touch and I would've been lost. I dug my nails into my hand to break the spell. "Without knowing what you did, I can't say. But I wouldn't have sent any severed body parts."

I stumbled outside and the chilly air jolted me back to reality. Afraid he'd find me outside and get the wrong idea, I raced up the hill to my apartment. My backpack fell from my shoulder, but I ignored it and headed straight to my bedroom.

Thank god I bought plenty of batteries for Cosmo.

Chapter Twelve

Mi Famiglia

IT TOOK OVER AN hour to shower and... release the tension from our conversation in the office. Now armed with a pint of some triple chocolate fudge brownie ice cream concoction, I got comfortable on my couch and read through the reference materials for the test. The folder held information on each of the major Italian mafia families: Lucchese, Bonanno, Colombo, Gambino and Genovese. I saved the Genovese for last, almost dreading the family that had caused my life so much conflict.

They were the oldest of the families, dating back to the late nineteenth century when it originated from a gang formed by the Morello family. The group, founded by Giuseppe Morello, started as a small gang in New York City. By the early twentieth century they'd expanded and were soon involved with several illicit activities throughout Manhattan. When Giuseppe went to prison in 1909, several power struggles ensued. By the early 1920s, he was forced to flee to Italy but returned to the U.S. and reigned as boss of the organization for two years. He then stepped down to become underboss until his murder in 1930. When he died, he left behind his second wife and three children, including his youngest son, Calogero.

My maternal grandfather.

Calogero married my grandmother and had a son, whose name I never learned, and my mother, Serafina Morello. I'd never met the

Morellos; my mother had been long estranged from the family. They refused to accept my father, not only because he wasn't who they chose but also because he wasn't Italian.

Seamus Donovan was a hardworking Irishman whose devotion to my mom knew no bounds. They often danced around the kitchen; his arms held tight around her as they stared into each other's eyes. He called her his queen, and I was his princess. The memories faded over time, but one of falling asleep in his arms while he sang Irish songs was one I desperately clung to.

"Sera, may I live a hundred years and be no happier than I am right now here with the both of you," he often whispered to my mom when the three of us were piled on the couch. "For the two of you have shown that even a man like me is deserving of love and happiness."

It never made sense what he meant by that, but it didn't matter. My parents were warm, caring people who loved unconditionally. Until Gio Sardi shattered it all in one terrible night. It only made the pain worse when, at age fifteen, I discovered the connection between the two families.

The question of how my mom was killed by a family with ties to her own plagued me. Felton, ever the realist, explained the Genovese most likely didn't even know. The organization had alliances with several smaller families; the fights and squabbles between the peons were of no consequence to them unless it threatened their own members or bottom line. That knowledge only fed my resolve to make Gio and the rest of his associates pay for their crimes.

Bored, I tossed the folder aside and called Barton. Felton hadn't responded to my message, so it was unlikely there was any news from the CIA. However, it had been a few days, and he was bound to have something noteworthy on the pig's head.

"Please tell me you haven't gotten yourself in trouble again," he answered.

"Not so far. Just checking in. Heard anything?"

"Not a thing. The package was clean, and the address was a bust. Felton is following up with a surveillance team tracking Gio."

"Well, crap."

"Why? What's wrong?"

"Oh, nothing. I was just hoping for more info. Just feels like I'm spinning my wheels right now."

"There's been a lot of activity between Bari and Rome. Felton wasn't sure what to make of it, so he went to go check it out himself. He should be back in a couple weeks."

"So we twist in the wind until then?" I griped.

"According to Ginnie, the rumor is Winters was hooking Gio up with local contacts whenever he traveled to college campuses. No word on what those contacts were for. Could've been drugs, guns, or god knows what. She didn't know why they stopped working together, but that's more than what we had."

"I guess."

"We'll get to the bottom of it soon enough. You just continue to keep your eyes and ears open. I know this latest info isn't as exciting as you'd like it to be, but it's a start. And I'll know more once Felton can talk."

Deciding I'd done enough for the night, I grabbed my phone and sent texts to Jake and Nicole. Jake sent a picture of the engagement ring he'd bought for Sami and then told me his plan to pop the question. After Nicole and I agreed to meet up in the morning for breakfast, I grabbed my ice cream and turned on the TV.

Over the next few days, I swapped some of my office hours and classes with my fellow TAs. The library was my new hangout, both to study and get my work done. By the time Nicole came over for dinner Thursday night, she joked that I was avoiding the office on purpose. I'd laughed it off, telling her there was a hot football player I was trying to snag. In truth, I still needed distance from Caleb. At first it was easy to say it was nothing other than a physical attraction. When I found myself smiling about things he'd said or done earlier in the day, however, it was clear my focus had slipped.

No matter how I felt, he was still a man whose actions and associates attracted both the CIA and the FBI, the latter of which had sent me to watch him. That alone should have been a deterrent and the fact that it hadn't added to my already uneasy mind. I placed the picture of Caleb and Gio on my coffee table as a reminder that he'd been close to the man who killed my family.

Since the work he gave me was due the next day, my self-imposed exile was ending. I could've emailed it to him, but I had to get my ass back in the game. That was the plan anyway.

A deep despair made crawling out of bed a near overwhelming experience the next morning. I got ready as if in a trance, selecting a basic pair of jeans, a black mock turtleneck, and shoving my hair into a messy ponytail. Brushing my teeth, I tried to boost my plunging mood with no luck. The next day was the twentieth anniversary of my parents' deaths, a day I usually spent visiting their graves in Virginia. Ordering a bouquet while I ate my breakfast lifted my gloom only slightly, which was just enough to get me out the door.

He wasn't in the office when I arrived, so I left the test on his desk. I busied myself with organizing bookshelves and cleaning up the small kitchen area. We had office hours where students could stop by, ask questions, and get help on assignments. I was sitting on the couch with two students from one of the undergrad classes when he strolled in. Our eyes met for a fraction of a second before he greeted everyone and headed into his office, closing the door. He reappeared as the students were packing up to leave.

Once we were alone, he sat in the old brown armchair next to the couch. "Test looks perfect. Thank you."

"No changes?"

"Nope. It's a perfect mix of questions and covers all the content. Nice job."

"Thanks."

I carried my laptop and headed to my desk. We sat in silence while I read through some notes Trevor sent me. I looked up when I'd finished and found him pacing. I raised my eyebrows but said nothing. Lord knows I'd learned my lesson the last time.

"So, I'm going to go out on a limb and say the reason you made yourself scarce this week had to do with our last conversation," he paused. "When I crossed the line, made you uncomfortable, and also made a complete ass of myself."

"Well, I guess that saves me from trying to come up with an excuse."

"I could stand here and make excuses of my own, but the bottom line is we agreed to keep things professional, and I didn't keep up my end of the bargain."

"Thank you for your honesty, Professor. I appreciate it. But is this going to be a problem? If it is—"

"It won't be." His voice was firm. "I promise."

My shoulders relaxed. "This is the last conversation we have about this subject. From now on, the only things we talk about are history or history classes. Agreed?"

"Agreed."

"Glad we got that sorted, as Trevor would say. I'd hate to leave before I got to teach the mafia class."

He motioned to Nicole's chair and sat down after I nodded. "Yes, everyone loves me for my mob class. Rachele because she saw it firsthand, Karl likes it because there's so many areas to research. What about you? Which part interests you the most?"

"It was a no-brainer, really. Mob stories are everywhere. TV, movies, books, and so on. It's a huge cultural phenomenon, so that part appeals to me. But looking at it as a sociologist gives it a unique perspective." Also, the part where the professor has ties to the mob, I joked to myself.

"Okay?"

"Sociologically, the mafia is defined as a deviant group. They operate outside of a societal norm. In this case, the rule of law. So, you have this group that's incredibly significant in pop culture, but how do you think anyone who consumes all these TV shows and movies would react if they were to meet an actual mobster? Sure, everyone wants to have dinner with the mob boss who's on their favorite TV show every Sunday, but do you think anyone would want to have a beer with John Gotti? I don't think it would go the way most people think it would go."

"Good point," he said, suppressing a grin.

"What's so funny?"

"I came up with the idea for the class one night while I was watching one of those TV shows. But I can understand where some of the appeal comes from. Personally, I think it's because most mob families would do anything to protect their family, whether it be blood relatives or fellow members. So many everyday people have family issues, and then you see these mobsters who would do pretty much anything, including killing someone who's even perceived to be a threat to their family."

"That's a great point, too," I agreed quietly.

There it was again, the knot in my stomach that came every October whenever I thought about my parents. My chest ached and my skin felt scratchy. I shifted in the chair and his eyes widened a fraction. Jesus, in one week I'd gone from wanting to rip the man's clothes off to getting as far away from him as possible.

Nicole's tentative voice broke the rising tension. "Hey, Professor. Mind if I sit? Or, if you guys were talking, I can just grab a couple things and sit over there."

Trevor stood behind her and both looked uncertain. With a nod and a quick apology, Caleb stalked back to his office and closed the door. I hitched a plastic smile on my face as they both sat down.

Trevor glanced over his shoulder. "We weren't interrupting, were we?"

"Not at all. Just going over the test I put together for the mafia class. How were the freshman today?"

He shrugged. "Still freshman but marginally less whiny. Anyone show up during your hours?"

"A couple sophomores with questions. Nothing major."

We chatted for a while, long enough for my earlier tension to vanish by the time she told Trevor it was his turn to grab lunch. Irritation flitted across his face, but he left without a word. Shit, I knew what was coming. The door closed, and she pounced.

"Okay, what the hell did I walk in on?"

"Nothing. He asked me to make a test on the Italian groups. I turned it in, and after we went over it, we started talking about why people are so interested in the mob. Why?"

She pursed her lips. "Just curious."

"Nothing to be curious about."

"Everything okay? You're awfully quiet."

I nodded. "It's just been a long week. Looking forward to relaxing this weekend. Any big plans for you?"

"Nothing set in stone just yet. Might hang out with my friend, but I'm not sure. My mom's been making noise about me coming to visit, so I'm going home next weekend."

"Are you ever going to give me any details about this friend?"

"A lady doesn't kiss and tell." Within seconds she burst out laughing.

"Does he have a brother or a friend?" I asked between giggles.

We were still laughing when Trevor returned with a stack of Styrofoam boxes I recognized from the Thai food truck around the corner. As we ate lunch, we talked about our weekend plans. He'd never been to a pumpkin patch and was planning to go with a woman at the cafe who recommended one outside of town.

We got to work grading several assignments, but my concentration and motivation were gone. The work should have been a welcome distraction, but the unrest in my head refused to be ignored. I powered through, and by the time my stack was complete, I wanted to be alone. I packed up in record time, mumbled my goodbyes and headed for the door, thankful that Caleb had already left.

I usually called Felton when my emotions went to a dark place. Since he was in the field, CIA protocols made that impossible. The FBI had the same rules, which meant Karina and Georgia weren't options either. I trusted Barton, but we didn't have the kind of relationship where I felt comfortable spilling my guts and talking about feelings. In the end, I retreated to my bed and hoped watching some stupid comedy would take my mind off everything enough to fall asleep.

Sadly, the sleep I spent the day seeking was anything but restful...

Chapter Thirteen

That Night

Alexandria, VA
October 7, Twenty years ago

We had dinner at Uncle Cal's house, who was a close friend of my mom and dad. He didn't have a wife or any kids, but he had one of those small video game boxes. I spent hours playing, lost in solving the puzzles and moving the pieces so they fit together.

Tonight, they wanted me to play in the other room while they sat in Cal's office. I got bored and lonely after a while. They stopped talking when I came in, but nobody was mad or made me go. Instead, Mommy let me sit on her lap. While I played more puzzle games, she watched the guys talking at the desk. My dad said something, and she hugged me close to her. She looked sad. When I asked her what was wrong, she just smiled and kissed my forehead.

I woke up later and felt her arms wrapped around me as she softly hummed. Her long, black hair hung over both of us like a thick curtain. When I sat up, she did too, and wiped her eyes.

"Mommy, what's wrong? Why do you look so sad?"

She smiled even though tears fell from her eyes. "I just love you so much. I love snuggling you, and someday you're going to grow up and be too big for me to snuggle. And sometimes it makes me sad when I think about it."

I hugged her as hard as I could. "I love you too."

"Are my two favorite ladies ready to go home?" His smile faded when he saw her face. "Sera, love, why are you crying?"

"She's sad that someday I'm going to be too big to snuggle with her," I answered.

They laughed, and she kissed my cheek. Uncle Cal looked away for a second. When he turned to us, he said something but it sounded like funny words. My dad shook his head.

"I think it's past someone's bedtime," Cal whispered. "Six-year-olds shouldn't be up this late. Not even princesses like you, Lissi."

Dad nodded. "Aye. It's time to get home."

They spoke quietly while Mommy stood up, clutching me to her chest. Soon we were in the car. She insisted on sitting in the back with me, wrapping her arm around my shoulders and letting me sleep against her during the ride home.

Dad held me tight as he carried me upstairs. His stubble tickled when he kissed my cheek. I hugged him to me as we entered my room. "It's time to sleep, little one," he whispered and lowered me into bed.

"Will you read me a story?"

"Larissa, it's late. You need to go to sleep."

"Just one. Please?"

He sighed and ran his hand through his messy dark brown hair. "The fact I can't say no to either of you will be the death of me. All right, one story and that's it. I still have to run down to the market and grab more cigarettes."

"Deal."

He lay next to me in bed and read my favorite books about a boy with a long, silly name. Mommy made me read along with her, so I was happy it had been him. I was too tired to read. After a few pages, my eyes were heavy and wouldn't stay open.

"Sleep, mo dhóiteán beag," he whispered. His Irish accent always sounded so cool.

I heard their voices and then the front door closed. Mommy didn't like Daddy's smoking at all. Lately, he'd been doing it a lot, but she didn't get mad at him. The store was just around the corner from our house, so he wouldn't be long. As I fell asleep, the rumble of his car was the last sound I heard.

My eyes popped open when I heard a loud bang downstairs. I sat up in bed and clutched my doll, trying to be brave while wondering what was going on and when one of them would come upstairs to tell me everything was okay.

"Lissi!" My mom's frantic voice yelled.

I ran to the top of the stairs and found her standing in the doorway at the bottom. Her eyes were wide. We both jumped when we heard a loud thud by the front door, and she made a scared sound.

"Mommy?"

"Baby, there's no time for questions. You need to go in the bathroom and lock the door. Then I want you to climb out the window and run. Can you do that for me? I need you to run. Run as fast as you can and don't let anyone see you."

"I'm scared. What's going on?"

"There's no time, Lissi. Try to find Daddy if you can, but you need to go now!" At the sound of another bang, she gasped and held on to the wall.

I nodded and without another word she slammed the door. The lock clicked, followed by more banging and then loud voices. Remembering what she told me to do, I ran to the bathroom and locked the door. The voices downstairs were muffled, but I heard her yelling as I opened the window and peeked outside. The room was at the rear of the house, and thankfully there was nobody in the backyard. I grabbed a thick branch of the giant tree and climbed down.

My bare feet landed on the cold, wet grass. I hid behind the bushes and crept to the front of the house. Three big cars and a couple smaller ones were parked on the street, but it was quiet inside. I crawled through the hole in the neighbor's fence and took off in the market's direction. Once I found my dad, everything would be all right.

The market was in sight as I rounded the corner. I saw his car but stopped when I saw a black car that looked just like the ones parked outside my house. A man sat inside so I crouched down until I was close enough to crawl under my dad's green Volvo. It was gross under there, but it wouldn't matter when my dad came out and saved us.

The door of the black car opened, and a pair of feet moved to the sidewalk. The man wore black pants and shiny black shoes, which were now shuffling. Every now and then his right foot twitched and then the shuffling began again.

I crawled further back, trying to keep myself hidden when a sharp pain tore across my shoulder. Tears flooded my eyes, but I couldn't make a sound. I flattened myself against the ground and covered my mouth with my hand. Both the air and the man stood completely still. My shoulder hurt so bad I couldn't hold in the tears anymore. The hand over my mouth made it hard to breathe, but I was too afraid he'd hear me if I took it away.

The door to the market chimed and new footsteps came closer from the right. I was relieved when I saw my dad's sneakers and faded blue jeans. But then he stopped moving.

"Evening, Seamus," the man said in a low voice.

"Wish I could say it was a pleasant evenin' but it would be a lie."

He moved closer and leaned against the car. They started talking quickly. I couldn't hear much of what they said, but it was clear both men were very mad at each other.

"Did you really think—," the man yelled after he stepped back.

"I don't think. I know. And that's not how this is going to work. There are rules you're going to follow."

"Not if I just take what's mine."

My dad laughed. "Over my dead body."

"That's the idea."

A loud bang shattered the silence. My whole body jolted, and I did everything I could to keep from screaming. Everything was quiet again until a cigarette fell and rolled under the car.

The man said something, but I couldn't understand his words. My dad's feet turned sideways, and his legs bent. His body slid down to the ground and didn't move. After what seemed like forever, the man got back in his car and sped away.

I scrambled out from under the car and ran to the front. His head sat at an odd angle on the hood and didn't move. My foot brushed against his, and when I looked down, I saw the cigarette. With shaking hands, I picked it up and nudged his shoulder. His head fell to the side, and I tried not to scream when I saw the big red dot on his head. Blood dripped from his mouth; just like on the scary movie he'd let me watch when Mommy had to work one night. I didn't want it to be true, but I knew what that meant.

My dad was dead.

Someone was yelling from inside the market. Afraid of who might come out and find me, I turned and ran. My dad couldn't protect me anymore. I didn't know where to go, or who could bring this horrible nightmare to an end so I did the only thing I could. I just kept running.

My eyes snapped open at the realization the loud noises in the room came from me. I sat up in bed and tried control the bile rising in my throat. A minute later I raced to the bathroom and my stomach emptied. Again. Loud, dry heaves mixed with the hard sobs that racked my body echoed off the walls. Once everything calmed, I slumped forward and closed my eyes.

Two fucking weeks this had been going on. I couldn't sleep for longer than a couple hours at a time before my own brain terrorized me. Tears fell from my eyes, which I swiped away.

After splashing cold water on my face, I studied the zombie looking back at me in the mirror. My skin was pale, nearly ashen, which only made the dark circles under my eyes appear even darker. I'd gone through a ton of foundation and concealer to try to look human during the day. Once I removed it each night, however, my reflection showed how hollow I looked and felt.

I stumbled back to my bed and reached underneath to grab the dull green canvas knapsack that held my few personal possessions. My fingers searched the interior until they found my target: a small metal case. The pale blue scrollwork was faded in places and the silver octopus in the middle had long since dulled. I held it in my palm and ran my finger over the top, rubbing the rough spot where the tip of one of the tentacles broke off before easing it open. The inside still held a very faint smell of tobacco as I gazed at the cigarette tucked inside: my one memento from that terrible night.

After fleeing the market, I found my way to Felton's house. He found me in his backyard and called the police after he brought me inside. That was when he learned of the fire at my house. They found my mother inside tied to a dining chair with a single gunshot to the head. Felton told me very few details, but I later found out there was evidence of sexual assault by at least three assailants.

A single bullet casing found in the house's rubble led police to a Sardi foot soldier, who was questioned but never arrested. When a senior officer from another field office announced that Dad had been passing information about weapons deals in Italy to the CIA, it shocked everyone including Felton. The news did little to move the case along and it closed a few weeks later, not long after the Sardi minion was killed in a drug bust in New York City.

My father's killer may as well have been a ghost. Forensics were a bust; the bullet and casing were clean. The old man who owned the market was hard of hearing and literally heard nothing. His security system was a single camera pointed at the front door, which showed only comings and goings. And based on the account of the traumatized six-year-old hiding under the victim's car, all the police knew was they were looking for a man with shiny shoes.

Afraid to lose the only link I had to my old life, I hid the cigarette in a desk drawer in my bedroom at Felton's house. He found me playing with an old metal case, which had belonged to his grandfather back in Ireland. When he gave it to me, I hid the cigarette inside. There it stayed, only to be smoked once I'd avenged their deaths. After twenty years, I wanted nothing more than to stamp it out on the forehead of the ringleader: Giovino Sardi.

With each October seventh, however, the anger and need for vengeance grew. Doubt seeped in after a while, and now it felt like an overwhelming blackness that threatened to swallow me whole. Fuck, after all this time all I had to show for it was a borrowed metal case and an old cigarette. I refused to give up, but it was hard to not feel like a failure.

"Dad, I'm sorry." My voice sounded and felt like shards of glass were stuck in my throat. "I'm still trying to find them. And I will. I'll make them pay. I promise you."

Swiping the fresh tears away, I closed the case and returned it to my knapsack. Groaning, I stared at the clock and rubbed my eyes. It was four in the morning, I was wide awake, exhausted as hell, but terrified to sleep. Settling back in bed, I picked a channel showing what looked like a Brazilian soccer match. My eyes grew heavy as my brain tried to keep up with the commentary in rapid Portuguese. When my phone jolted me awake, I didn't know how much time had passed.

"What's up?" My voice was a croaky mess.

"You sound lousy. You okay?" Barton's voice was full of concern.

"I'm okay. Any news?"

"I'm afraid there was a setback in Italy, so Felton had to stay a little while longer."

"What happened?"

He sighed. "All the chatter in New York dried up. And all the activity between Bari and Rome stopped. It's almost as if they realized we were watching."

"God dammit! You can't be serious!" Clutching the phone to my ear, I didn't know if I wanted to send another, less than subtle message to Felton or chuck the fucking thing against the wall.

"This is a normal setback. You know these things happen. In a week or two, things will pick up again," he paused. "What's really troubling you?"

"Just a long, shitty week. I'm sorry for taking it out on you."

"Well, did anything noteworthy happen during this long, shitty week?"

"No, and why do I feel there's an underlying meaning by that comment?"

"The meaning is simple, Lissa. I've got the higher ups on my ass about this case. It's been weeks now and aside from the pig's head, we've got nothing."

I pinched the bridge of my nose and took a deep breath. "And that's my goddamned fault? I seem to remember telling you it felt like I was spinning my fucking wheels. We don't have enough evidence to wiretap, so there isn't much else I can do here. This may seem like a simple assignment, but today I'd much rather be back east doing something constructive."

"What do you mean—," he paused and was silent for several seconds. "Shit, Lissa, I'm sorry I forgot. Is there anything I can do? Do you need anything?"

Rationally, I understood the complaints and concerns. If it weren't for the pictures of the two of them together, the chances of opening the case would've been zero. Unfortunately, sleep deprivation and all the other emotional shit created a toxic mix of feelings that churned in my head, and I had little appreciation for rational arguments. Anger, sadness and everything between felt like salt poured into an open wound.

"I don't want your pity," I snapped. "What I *need* is Gio Sardi either in cuffs or a morgue. My parents died twenty years ago, and this asshole is still walking around. I need Felton to shed some light on why I'm holed up in a dorm room barely bigger than your office acting like some blushing coed when I could be back in Virginia paying my respects. You want to know what you can do? You can find some damn intelligence that will tell us what the hell is going on. Because your bosses aren't the only ones thinking I'm wasting my time here."

Silence settled between us. While he tried at least twice to speak, I grabbed the remote and surfed through the channels. When he still had said nothing by the time the soccer match reappeared, I sat forward.

His uneasy voice broke through. "Do you want to talk about it?"

"I'm not in the best mindset to talk to anyone right now, Barton."

"I know this can't be easy, especially with Felton out of touch. You probably won't reach out to talk about this stuff but know that I'm here to chat whenever you need to. And if you don't feel comfortable talking to me about it, please consider calling Yolanda. You know you can tell her anything and it'll be secure. I don't want you to think you're all alone or don't have anyone you can reach out to."

Yolanda, Barton's wife, worked as a unit chief for the NSA. When their son was injured in a car accident three years earlier, she quit her job to care for him. They moved into a farmhouse in nearby Annapolis, and by the time he recovered she'd fallen in love with life on the farm so much that she stayed at home with the kids permanently. She and Georgia were friends, so our paths crossed often.

"Thank you," I mumbled. "I need to go. We'll talk later."

I hung up before he replied and hugged my legs to my chest. The alarm blared from my night table, callously reminding me it was time to start another exhausting day. I slapped the off button and stood up, letting out a groan. These nightmares were temporary, I reminded myself. The beeping of the coffee maker in the kitchen reminded me time hadn't stopped or slowed despite how shitty I felt. Without another word, I shuffled to the bathroom to start yet another day of emotional hell.

Chapter Fourteen

Midterm Musings

MY NIGHTMARES STOPPED AND sleep returned a week later. I was thankful for the timing since it was now midterms. We were all busy as hell attending study sessions with the students or helping to write and grade exams. At the same time, lecture notes and all the other usual tasks had to be done.

Nicole and I spent the morning going through notes for the following week. The exams for Caleb's two freshman classes were that afternoon and had to be graded quickly to keep us on schedule. We planned to stay until well into the evening to finish up, which neither of us minded since the office would be quieter.

"What are we doing for dinner tonight?" Trevor asked, glancing up from his laptop.

"I don't care as long as it's not pizza," I answered. "The office smelled horrible after whatever that was Rachele ordered the other day."

She rolled her eyes. "Like I knew it was going to have that much garlic."

"Well, at least it kept the vampires away," Karl piped up.

We all laughed and made jokes, deciding to vote on dinner later. The room quieted, limited to the sounds of typing on laptops or murmured discussion. We were all distracted a couple minutes later by the sound of the door in the front office.

Caleb entered and placed two large bags on a nearby table. "I know it's only Wednesday, but it's already been a long and stressful week. So, I wanted to show my appreciation for all the hard work everyone has been putting in. Dig in, guys."

The unmistakable smell of Chinese food from everyone's favorite restaurant around the corner filled the room, and everyone perked up within seconds. The room filled with cheerful voices as we all piled food on our plates. I turned to thank him, but Rachele nudged Nicole and me out of the way to grab a pair of chopsticks. After shooting us a glare, she leaned against the table right next to Caleb.

"Just a quick bite before Trevor and I have to get to that freshman midterm," she practically cooed.

"Thanks. I appreciate it, especially since I have that department meeting and won't be there," he responded.

She waved her hand. "Oh, it's no problem."

Nicole pursed her lips as we headed to our desks. We sat down and I grabbed a pot sticker. Once she turned her back on the group, her eyes rolled. "Could she look any more obvious or desperate?" she whispered. "Of course, it's no problem. It's your freaking job."

"Hey, let her try. If he's dumb enough to fall for it, he deserves her."

She suppressed a giggle and turned around in her chair. Jake sent me a text, asking to get together for a drink soon. I was typing my reply when she nudged me with her elbow. Looking up, Rachele and Caleb were gone.

"What? Did they leave together or something?"

Her eyes were like saucers. "He kept looking over at you. Like three or four times."

"What is this, high school? He probably realized you were watching him, you snoop."

"If I didn't know better, I'd say he was looking to see if it bothered you that she was flirting with him."

I shrugged. "Then I'd say it's a good thing you know better. She's not the first woman we've seen make a fool of themselves and won't be the last."

"You're telling me you don't find him attractive at all?"

"I wouldn't say that. He was hot as hell when I saw him at that party you dragged me to."

She gasped. "Wait. He was at the party?"

"Oh, crap! I thought I told you! Remember Bathroom Guy?"

"That was him? And you didn't go for it? What the hell's the matter with you?"

"It's a damn good thing I didn't," I hissed. "It wasn't even eight hours later that I discovered he was our teacher!"

"But you felt nothing before you knew that?"

"He is… *was* tempting as hell. The only reason I didn't act on it was because I didn't want to be late for class the next morning."

She arched a brow. "Is? What kind of ship name would you two have? Jaleb? Calessica?"

"*Titanic*, there's our ship name. Destined to sink on its maiden voyage. Seriously, he's Caleb, I'm Jessica, and it's never going to happen. Nothing to ship, Nic. Sorry."

She leaned closer and peered around the room. Oh, dear Christ she was on a roll and not about to let up. "Did he ever say anything about it? Wait. Was that why he asked you to stay after orientation?"

"No, he wanted to ask a couple questions about my sociology degree. And really, what would there be to say? 'Hey, sorry I flirted with you at a party that I shouldn't have attended in the first place?'"

She narrowed her eyes. I said a silent prayer she'd let it go even though I knew this would be a topic she'd be obsessed about for a while. I was relieved when Caleb asked to speak to her in his office. He nodded, and I returned to my notes. When they returned, she scrambled toward me with a huge smile and grabbed her backpack. He stood by the door holding his bag.

"Trevor had to leave so I'm helping Rachele with the freshman exams!" she announced. "Are you good here?"

"I'm good. Almost done with the notes for this lecture, and then I can get started on the next one. I should be ready to grade tests when you get back."

"All right. Don't work too hard. And our earlier conversation isn't over."

"Yes, it is."

"No, it's not!"

"Professor is waiting!" I retorted, refusing to look at her.

After finishing, I decided to take a break and grabbed another plate of fried rice. Karl joined me, and we sat around and talked about the horrible state of his favorite New York teams. I wasn't a baseball fan, but my love of football dated back to watching games with my dad every Sunday. Trevor returned as the subject turned to soccer. Soon they were debating American versus English soccer, and it was time for me to get back to work.

Rachele, Nicole and Caleb returned a little while later. Rachele dropped the stack of exam books in her hand next to me and left, muttering that she was late to an appointment. I grabbed them while Nicole handed me one of the pink drinks in her hand. She sat down at her desk and began typing on her phone as soon as her ass hit the chair. A slow smile spread across her lips.

"Someone looks happy," I observed.

"Yeah. Do you promise not to kill me?"

"Depends on what you're about to say or ask me to do."

She bit her lip. "My friend wants to meet up. Now. How much would you hate me if I left?"

"I won't hate you, but you'll owe me. And you damn well better find out if this guy has a brother or friend you can hook me up with."

She drew a cross over her chest with her finger. "I'll owe you big time. I hate to even ask, but it's been a while since we've been able to get together."

"Well, far be it from me to stand in the way of your booty call."

"You're the best."

"Yeah, yeah, yeah," I grumbled. "At least one of us is getting some."

"Well, there's always Bathroom Guy," she whispered before racing toward the door.

"Not funny!" I called after her.

I shook my head and then tackled another booklet. There were no windows in the office, but the clock on my laptop showed it was just after six thirty. I drank my smoothie, appreciating it was my favorite triple berry flavor. She knew how to butter me up.

The office emptied as Trevor and Karl finished for the evening. They offered to stay and help, but I told them to go ahead. A quiet office would be the perfect setting to get a ton of work done. Rachele stopped by the office around seven thirty and grabbed a book she'd forgotten. Before heading out, she offered to help me finish up in the morning and told me not to work too hard.

My sleep deprivation and emotional state the past few weeks had turned me into a moody bitch, which caused everyone to approach with caution. I apologized to everyone several times and explained I'd had some personal issues. Rachele was the most sympathetic, offering to grab a coffee and chat. Her kindness was unexpected, but not unwelcome.

Caleb came out of his office just after eight carrying his bag and typing on his phone. When he saw the stack in front of me, he paused. "You know those don't all have to be graded tonight, right? I better not find you still reading these when I come back in the morning."

"You won't. I'm just finishing up this stack and then I'm out. The mafia test is tomorrow so I'm just trying to leave a smaller workload so we don't fall behind."

"Fair enough. Just remember there are four other TAs."

I smiled. "Yeah, but the essays in these books are just so riveting. I can't put them down."

He turned back to his phone, and I went back to reading. After a time, I noticed he was still standing there. As if realizing I had caught him watching me, he stepped back. "Can I ask you something?"

"Sure."

"This might be too personal, so you don't have to answer if you don't want to. But lately it seems like you've been distracted. I just wanted to make sure you're okay. Like I said, you don't have to tell me, but I wanted you to know I'm here if you ever need to talk."

My heart pounded in my chest. I'd felt his scrutiny more than once. Our eyes often met, only to look away fractions of a second later. It was yet another complicated layer to add to my feelings for the man. I'd pushed them aside, but they couldn't be ignored forever.

I lowered my head. "Sorry. Insomnia had been an issue for a while, but it's better now."

His eyes softened, and I suppressed a shiver. Maybe it was wishful thinking, but he looked concerned. Just then, I craved nothing more than for him to hold me in his arms and tell me everything would be okay. Afraid of the words on the tip of my tongue, I looked away and broke the spell. I had to remember who we both were and the danger of falling for his charm.

He crouched in front of me. "I mean it, Jess. This isn't some ploy. I can see when someone's hurting. We've all been there."

"I appreciate that, but I promise I'm better now."

"All right, but the offer still stands."

"Thank you."

He stood and headed toward the door. "I guess I'll leave you to it."

"I'll be done with these soon."

"One hour," he instructed. "Then go home."

I hung my hand over my brow in mock salute. "Aye, aye. Good night."

"Good night. One more hour, max."

With a nod, I turned back to the open booklet on the desk. His gaze lingered for a few moments before the door closed, followed by the click of the lock. The words on the paper blurred. I leaned back in the chair and stared at the tiles on the ceiling to refocus.

A jaw stretching yawn made my eyes feel like they were made of lead. The ugly red couch looked like a great place to curl up and take a nap. I rubbed my eyes. The closest pile was small, maybe three more. I took another drink of my smoothie and propped my head up on my fist, determined to finish. I yawned again, my eyes closing and then bouncing open. Just a bit longer...

Chapter Fifteen

Trespass

MY EYES OPENED IN an exhausted haze to find myself in a dark, unfamiliar room. After a few seconds, I realized I was still in the office. Apparently, I fell asleep long enough for the sensors in the office lights to turn off. When my stretches didn't trigger them to come back on, I stood to hit the switch. Taking a few steps, I froze.

I wasn't alone.

The person was behind me, close to Caleb's office door, and moving closer. Just as I reached my destination, a gloved hand grabbed my hair and yanked backward. Their other arm coiled around my right shoulder and over my mouth to silence my scream. Hot breath fanned across my neck and the grip on my hair tightened.

My left arm fell slack beside me, and I tried to lower my shoulder. When that didn't work, I struck low and tried to connect with any part of the body. A canvas-like fabric brushed against my hand. I brought my fingers together and pinched, causing a pained grunt. I reared my head back and connected with a hard, flat surface, most likely a chest. My attacker's gasp was small but satisfying.

I stepped forward and planted my foot. My body lurched to the side, and I slammed my head back even harder. The grip on my hands eased just enough for me to surge forward. Pain shot through my wrists as they were seized even tighter. I kicked my leg upward and when their knee buckled, my feet hit the ground.

Spinning around I thrust my fist into the darkness, hitting nothing. Pain exploded across my cheek when a gloved hand struck out of nowhere. Ignoring the tears in my eyes, I punched in the attacker's direction and felt my fist connect. A hand slammed into my face, and I stumbled. They grabbed me by the hair again, but when I thrust my elbow backwards, we both fell to the floor.

The wind was knocked from my lungs when I landed face down. My head was free, but my legs were tangled. I gasped for air and kicked against the obstruction, desperate to break free. An angry growl was all I heard before a hand gripped my neck and pulled me violently to the left. My face slammed into a hard surface. I heard a pained scream before my face collided again and everything went black.

$$\bullet \cdot \bullet \cdot \bullet \cdot \bullet \cdot \bullet \cdot \bullet \cdot \bullet$$

My head was pounding. Hot, blinding pain shot through my eyes when I opened them and glanced around the room. Where the hell was I? Trying not to panic, I tried to sit up, but my vision swam, and I fell back on the bed. A gentle hand on my shoulder made me jump.

"Ms. Ross, can you hear me?" The voice was soft and feminine. "Are you okay?"

I turned toward the voice, sore neck be damned. A tall woman with dark brown skin, short black hair and kind amber eyes smiled at me. She held my hand in hers and gently placed her fingers on my wrist.

"Who are you?" My throat was dry and scratchy.

She grabbed the pen from the breast pocket of her dark blue scrubs and wrote in the folder on the table. "My name is Willa, and I'm an ER nurse. You're at Portland General Hospital. Do you know why you're here?"

The pounding in my head only got angrier as I struggled to remember what happened. Darkness and an uneasy feeling in my stomach were my body's only responses. I shook my head and tried to rub my eyes. My cheek burned and throbbed, causing me to cry out. She placed my hand on my chest and went back to her notes.

"The left side of your face is severely bruised. Based on what your friend said, you were attacked."

Murky images floated through my head. A hand gripping my hair while another held me in place. Struggling to break free and falling to the floor. Pain, and then nothing. My stomach bottomed out. Who found me and brought me here? Were they attacked as well? Could they be trusted?

"Who?" I rasped. "Who brought me in?"

A knock on the glass door to the exam room ended the conversation. The curtain drew back, and a shorter woman entered. Between her lab coat and the horrible fluorescent lighting, her pale skin looked almost grey.

She gave me a tired smile as she approached. "Hello, Ms. Ross. I'm Doctor Cari Warner and I'm the doctor assigned to your case. May I call you Jessica?"

I nodded, wincing. The throbbing in my head felt like a steady drumbeat that made my eyes hurt. Willa dimmed the light above the bed. I mumbled my thanks and followed Dr. Warner's pen with my eyes as instructed.

Cari moved to a computer in the corner and began typing. "Do you remember what happened?"

"I fell asleep in the office and when I woke up, someone else was there. And now I'm here."

She nodded and continued typing. "It's okay. Memory loss and disorientation is common for head traumas."

I tried to bolt upright, but my head swam. "Did you give me any medications or take blood? I have a few medical issues. Was I... I mean, was this all that..." The monitor to my left let out a loud beep.

Willa nudged my shoulder, gently directing me to lie down. I tried to resist until the stern look from both women made me think better of it. Since I was on assignment, protocol had to be followed or I risked exposure. Undercover identities were flagged when accessed by medical personnel and their records systems were to instruct them to contact our "doctor," who was our contact from the local field office or handler.

"Jessica, you're fine," Willa said. "I spoke with Dr. Barton, and all precautions are in place."

"To answer your other question, yes, we performed an exam and there were no signs of sexual assault," Dr. Warner added. "We're just waiting for the results of a few more labs and your scans. It shouldn't be too much longer."

My shoulders relaxed. It was a relief she'd talked to Barton, but that was a phone call I wasn't looking forward to when I got back to my place. I blew out a long breath and told myself it was something to worry about later.

A loud voice in the hallway made me jump. Willa left the room to investigate. She returned not long after and pulled the doctor aside. They spoke in rapid sentences, but in low enough voices that I couldn't hear their words.

Dr. Warner cleared her throat. "Your friend who brought you in is agitated and insisting on seeing you. Are you okay to have visitors?"

"As long as they know my head hurts like a bitch so I won't be great company. And they should keep their voices down."

Willa headed toward the door. "I'll make sure he understands before I bring him back."

Wait. *He?* Who the hell brought me here?

"Jess? Oh my god! Are you okay?" Caleb's face was frantic as he burst into the exam room.

I raised my head and instantly regretted it. "Jessica, please lay down," Dr. Warner ordered in a soft but firm voice.

He sat in the chair next to the bed. "Are you okay?"

"I've been better."

His ran his hands through his hair and nodded, but his mind was elsewhere. When the doctor excused herself to check my lab results, I tried to relax. After several minutes, I couldn't ignore his fidgeting and placed my hand over his. He stilled but then watched my every move. I wanted to tell him to stop, but Willa's voice broke the tension when she asked me a series of questions. I sat up, breaking our touch, and focused on my answers.

"Excuse me, we were told we'd find Jessica Ross in here?" a voice asked from the door.

I recognized Detective Nelson from the mail incident. Behind him stood a tall, muscular man with close shaved platinum hair and piercing green eyes. Both men stepped toward the foot of the bed.

"Detective Nelson," I croaked.

"I see you remember me. This is Detective Jack Marlowe."

He tapped two fingers on his sleeve, and I tugged a strand of hair over my right ear in response. It was easy to figure out how he came to be in my room. But even with a head injury I knew my case was in danger of being shut down. Shit, this wasn't good.

"Ms. Ross, first of all, are you okay?" Marlowe asked. "Can you tell us what happened?"

I recounted the events of the evening. The memories were still fuzzy, but I remembered someone grabbing me. Based on where I hit the person when I reared my head back, I guessed they were at least six inches taller than me, and most likely male based on the sounds they made as we fought. They were strong, but not overly muscular based on the arm I tried to wrench away from.

As my story progressed, Caleb's agitation grew. He rose from the chair and paced the small room, gripping the back of his neck. After Willa stepped around him for a third time, he returned to his seat and fisted his hands in his lap.

"Are you the one who found her?" Nelson asked, turning to him.

"Yes. I left my cell phone at the office and went back to retrieve it. I thought it was weird that the lights didn't turn on automatically. When I hit the switch, I found her unconscious on the floor next to a desk."

My stomach plummeted. Why was he lying? His face stayed neutral, but his eyes refused to meet mine. My blood chilled, and I wrapped an arm around my waist. Agent Marlowe seemed to notice the awkwardness based on his raised eyebrows but remained mute. Shivering, I drew my blanket over my shoulders and moved closer to the wall.

Jack nodded at Nelson and placed a business card on the table next to the bed. "All right, I think we have all we need for now. If you can think of anything else, please call us."

The real detective and the federal agent pretending to be a detective left, and Willa helped me sit up on the bed. Caleb stood and held out a hand to help, but she shook her head. As she asked me to follow her finger with my eyes, I knew he was staring but I refused to let him distract me. He wasn't my attacker, but he was hardly innocent.

Dr. Warner breezed into the room with papers in her hand. "I got the results back from your CT, and you have a concussion. It probably doesn't feel like it, but it's a mild one. Since you aren't showing any other symptoms that concern me, I'm going to release you, but with restrictions. For starters, how are you getting home?"

"I'll take her home," he piped up.

He was the last person I wanted driving me, but my options were thin. Jake was visiting Connor in Washington and Nicole was probably still in the throes of her booty call. Resigned, I nodded. My mind tuned out after that, barely registering the list of restrictions on the sheet of paper in my hand. All I wanted was to retreat to the security of my apartment and wrap my head around everything that happened. After sleeping like the dead for a few dozen hours, of course.

His jacket slipped over my shoulders, jolting me back into the present. "I'll make sure she gets plenty of rest," he assured the doctor as he helped me stand. His hand clasped mine, tightening when I tried to pull away.

Apparently satisfied, Dr. Warner stepped back. "Take it easy, Jessica. I cannot stress that enough. Your body needs time to rest and heal. The bruises on your face should clear up in a couple weeks."

He walked me to his car, keeping a firm grip on my hand. I tried to stay calm, which was damn near impossible since my heart was beating almost as hard as my head throbbed. My body was losing every bit of energy, but I refused to surrender to the exhaustion. With no idea how dire my situation was, relaxing wasn't possible until I had my phone and could send a message to Jack or Barton to track me.

He placed my backpack at my feet as soon as my seatbelt was fastened, and I dug out my phone as he moved to the driver's side. Not surprisingly, I had about a dozen missed calls from Barton. I sent him a quick update in the hopes it would calm him down so he wouldn't be as hysterical when I called. My next message was coded and sent to the FBI relay. Less than a minute later I received a reply: my location was being tracked. If things went sideways, all I'd need to do is press a button, and they'd send the cavalry. Of course, by the time help arrived the agent was usually dead, but at least they'd be able to find my body.

Okay, I was being bitchy and cynical. But in my defense, it had been a shitty day.

Caleb was silent as he sped down the street, hopefully back to my apartment. He glanced over every few minutes but said nothing. When we turned onto the main street that led to the campus, the knot eased in my shoulders. The tension between us was stifling. Why did he lie? Did he know who attacked me? Or why?

I replied to the alert on my phone to confirm I was still safe and watched him for a moment. When we stopped at a traffic light, he caught me and raised an eyebrow, causing me to look away. A few minutes later, he parked in front of my building.

"Stay there," he instructed when I unbuckled my seat belt. He jumped out and ran around the side. His hand was warm and gentle when he helped me stand.

Since it was almost one in the morning, the lobby was thankfully deserted. He released my hand once the elevator doors closed but kept his arm on the rail behind me. I kept my gaze fixed on the floor for another awkward ride in a small metal box with the man. When the doors opened, he motioned for me to walk ahead of him, much to my relief.

He stopped a few feet behind me as I dug out my keys. "May I come in for a few minutes? Just to talk."

"Sure," I mumbled, unlocking the door and stepping inside.

I sent a message to the relay that I was home and safe. We were in my domain; I could defend myself despite my injuries. I slid my phone in my pocket and dumped my backpack on the couch. After grabbing a glass of water from the kitchen sink, I leaned against the counter and waited for him to say something.

"Are you okay?" His tone was soft and wary.

"No. No, I'm not. Everything hurts like hell and—." My voice cracked, and I blew out a breath toward the ceiling to keep the tears at bay. He moved closer but stopped as soon as my hand flew up.

He moved to the other side of the counter and watched me closely. There was no doubt I looked and sounded like a pathetic mess trying not to fall apart in my kitchen, but everything was a jumbled pile in my head that made no sense. After a long moment, the meltdown that threatened to burst free subsided.

"Do you need anything?"

"I need to know what happened, to remember. I was reading through the exams and felt tired," I paused, forcing my mind to focus. "He wore gloves. And some kind of uniform, like a coverall." My head throbbed again, and I stopped.

"Don't force it. You'll remember soon enough."

Eager to change subjects and lighten the mood, I tried to smile. "So does this mean I can sort the mail again? After this, the threat of severed animal heads doesn't seem so bad."

"Whatever you want," he replied with a small grin.

My phone buzzed in my pocket and I turned to check it as he brushed past. Barton replied to my earlier message that the Portland office had updated him on the situation, and I was to call him in the morning after a night of rest. The last word was in all caps.

Caleb opened the freezer door. "Do you have any ice?"

"Doubt it. I think all I have in there is ice cream."

"And also wine and old mac and cheese," he sniffed, looking at the contents of the fridge. "You need groceries."

"Yeah, I was going to do that but got beat up instead."

"It's good to know that not even a concussion can stop you from being a smart ass," he quipped, coming closer with a pint of mango frozen yogurt in his hand.

He held the container to my left cheek, which had the largest and nastiest bruise. The cold felt nice, but the pressure hurt like hell. Letting out a hiss, I pulled away until he cupped his hand to my right cheek and kept me in place. When the cold eased some of the pressure, I relaxed.

His brows furrowed. "You have ink on your forehead."

He grabbed the washcloth next to the sink and ran it under the faucet before lightly rubbing the spot. I tried to keep my eyes closed while my heart beat against ribcage, but I couldn't ignore the electricity I felt from his touch. Between his scent and the concern on his face, I found it impossible to focus on anything other than the warmth radiating from his body. My gaze went to his lips. They sure looked soft...

"All better." His voice was husky, raw.

He tossed the container back in the freezer while I took several gulps of water. I felt him behind me when the door closed and my heart stuttered. His eyes were dark and hungry when they met mine. I inhaled, trying to steady my shaky breath when his hands moved to my hips and drew me closer.

I closed my eyes. His head hovered over the top of mine as he held me close. A voice in my head whispered warnings, but the comfort I felt in his arms didn't want to listen. He brought the palm of his hand to rest on my upper back and I pressed closer to him.

He kissed the top of my head and my eyes opened. Entranced, I leaned closer, wishing my arms weren't pressed to his chest. He trailed feather light kisses across my right cheek, avoiding the bruises. His lips curved into a slow smile when he caught me staring at them. The war between my head and my heart ended when I refused to retreat, instead angling my head to welcome his approach.

His lips were soft, warm, and made me crave more the moment they gently touched mine. I kissed him back, and the world fell away. He wrapped an arm around my lower back while the other hand cradled my head. We stayed in our tight embrace and blood thrummed in my veins. His tongue teased and prodded me to open my mouth. For a split second I almost surrendered until a twinge in my cheek brought reality crashing back down like a bucket of ice water poured over my head. I opened my eyes and pushed against his chest. "Stop," I whispered. "Please stop."

He stepped back and held up his hands. "I realize this is the worst possible time to do that. I'm sorry."

I took a deep breath before heading to the freezer. The blast of frigid air should have brought me back to my senses. Closing the door, I turned and was relieved to see he hadn't moved closer. My feet remained welded to the floor as he watched me.

After an uncomfortable silence, I cleared my throat. "So, that's a yes on doing the mail again."

"Jess."

A weight dropped into my chest and my fingers felt numb. I grabbed the rag he'd thrown in the sink and started wiping down the counter. His hand grazed my shoulder, which I sidestepped until he placed it over my hand.

Taking both hands in his, he examined the bruises striped across my wrists. "Jessica, stop. You have a concussion and you need to rest."

"You're right," I whispered. "I should get some sleep."

"The doctor said it would be a good idea if someone stayed with you tonight as a precaution. Can I stay? I promise to behave."

"I appreciate the offer, but I'll call Jake and have him come over." Thank god my brain stopped letting my hormones run the show.

"Ah, yes. Saint Jake."

"Caleb—"

He released my hands. "When I walked into that office and found you like that," he whispered. "Bleeding and unconscious. It scared me. I can't even imagine what could've happened to you if I hadn't gone back for my phone."

The weight in my chest dropped to my stomach. "Caleb, you need to leave. Right now."

"Why? What's wrong?"

He tried to pull me closer, but I pushed his hands away. "Stop touching me."

"Jess, I—"

"No. This isn't happening. Now or ever."

"Are you worried about getting caught? Because no one would have to know."

"Because there's never going to be anything for anyone to know. I appreciate you taking me to the hospital, but at the risk of sounding ungrateful, you need to go."

He straightened to his full height and stepped closer with his hands raised. "What the hell just happened?"

"We both know you lied about your phone. You were typing on it when you left the office." His face paled. "I don't know why you lied, and I don't care. You clearly have some shit you need to sort out, so I recommend you go deal with that and whatever other secrets you've got. I refuse to be another one."

He hung his head as I opened the door. Moving slowly, he paused in front of me but kept going when I jerked my head toward the hall.

"Good night. I'll let you know when I'm cleared to come back to classes."

He'd barely crossed the threshold when I clicked the lock in place. Watching through the peephole, he slapped the wall and cursed. With one last peek in my direction, he disappeared into the stairwell.

I exhaled and returned to the kitchen for another drink. Barton had sent a ton of messages because he hadn't heard from me, so I typed a quick reply to call if I hadn't called him by noon. After that, I trudged to my bedroom, stripped out of my clothes, and slid under the covers so I could get some damn sleep. It had been one hell of a day.

Chapter Sixteen

Prodigal Return

MY PHONE RANG AT one minute past noon. By then I'd stopped cursing the sun and the fact I forgot to close my curtains. My hands were so sore I could barely grasp the evil device that wouldn't shut up despite my groans of protest.

I brought the phone to my ear and burrowed under the blanket. "Yeah."

"I'd give you shit for being so cranky, but I can't say I blame you," Barton replied. "How are you feeling?"

"I think the only thing that doesn't hurt right now is a couple toes."

After telling him everything I remembered from the night before, he grudgingly told me the police had very few leads. The only physical evidence found at the scene was my blood on the side of the desk they found me next to. Both Caleb's office and the common area had been ransacked, so it was hard to figure out a target or motive. It was possible Caleb was the target, but Barton wasn't convinced.

"All we have to go on right now is a severed pig head and a phone call where he was pissed off at someone," he was quick to point out. "Unless you've got anything else for me, I'm just not sure."

I waited to see if he brought up the fact Caleb was in my room at the hospital. Jack's eyebrows were sky high when he took down his name, and I'd prepared myself for thirty million questions about that bit of information during the call. When he said nothing else, I was curious but found no need to bring it up if he wasn't going to. Either Jack didn't mention it, or he didn't find it important.

"I'd have to agree," I replied. "That said, I don't think it's safe to call the case a bust just yet. There's a reason this is all happening. Regardless of the target, why the hell would someone break into a college professor's office?"

"Well, the spy who helps teach History 101 would be a good reason."

"All right, fair point," I conceded.

"I have some good news, though. Felton is stateside. He said to tell you he'd see you soon."

"It's about damn time. How much does he know about last night?"

"All of it. I called Ginnie as soon as I heard."

"God," I groaned. "He's going to be insufferable when he gets here."

"He had to meet with a couple associates in New York before coming to Portland. And to be an even bigger pain in my ass, he refused to meet with me until after he talks to you. Once we talk, I'll decide if there's enough to continue this case."

"You're thinking of pulling the plug?" My head knew this was a possibility and partially agreed. My heart screamed in protest.

"Of course I am. I'm surprised that you're even questioning it. But I'm not deciding until I talk to the asshole and get some damn information. Now I want you to call Marlowe and then get some rest. Rest and take it easy until your check-up. Think you can do that?"

"I can try," I groused, ending the call.

A text message arrived from Barton with the date and time for my check-up with a doctor the following week. Since Jack wouldn't give me any details about the attack, our call was brief. He agreed to send over a stylist to come to my apartment and fix the hair extensions that were ripped loose during the attack. After repeating several times to call him if I needed anything, we hung up, and I slowly climbed out of bed.

Anything that went over my head hurt like hell, so I opted for a soft gray zippered hoodie and sweatpants before dragging a blanket out to the couch. Most people considered bedrest to mean watching countless hours of TV, but it only made my headache worse. Finding myself tired again, I curled up and fell back asleep.

I woke to a soft knock at the door a while later. After wobbling across the floor to answer, I found Nicole with a large bag in her hand. Her eyes widened as soon as they landed on my face.

"Oh my god!" she cried, her voice cracking.

"I'll be fine. You should see the other guy."

She rolled her eyes as she followed me inside. "Hilarious. Go sit down and I'll bring the food to you."

I returned to the couch and burrowed under the blanket. She placed a container in front on my lap before sitting to my left. To my extreme delight, it was a burrito bowl from one of my favorite food trucks on campus. We ate in silence, but her constant stares made it tense.

She set her food down and eyed my bruises. "Are you okay?"

I nodded. "It could've been worse."

"I am so sorry. I never should have left you last night."

"Nic, you didn't know it would happen. Nobody did. Please don't blame yourself."

"I'd hug you, but I'm afraid I'll hurt you," she sniffed.

I laid my head on her shoulder. "This works for now."

She gave me a warm smile until a buzz from her pocket caused her to sit up. Her jaw clenched at the screen, and she leaned forward with her elbows resting on her thighs. What followed looked like a heated exchange, furiously typed messages, glares at the screen and more typing. After the third or fourth reply, she finally tossed it into her purse. She then grabbed her food and stabbed it so hard with her fork, it surprised me it didn't break through the bottom.

I gestured to the floor. "Everything okay?"

"Just someone getting on my last nerve." At my confused look, she shook her head. "As soon as Professor Winters heard I was your neighbor, and that I planned to stop by, he's been bugging me non-stop."

"Sorry."

"He's not handling it well and even though he's driving me nuts, I get it. Finding one of your TAs like that would mess anyone up."

"Being at the hospital until well after midnight with me probably didn't help either," I added with a grimace.

"No doubt he's tired, but I think the fact that you were the one that got hurt makes it worse."

"Ugh, don't start. My face hurts too much to roll my eyes. It could've been you or Rachele and he'd be just as upset."

She shrugged. "Something tells me that's not the case, but fine. I'm just glad he found you and got you to the hospital. I can't even imagine."

"Trust me. You don't want to."

"Security was all over the office this morning. They're having one officer patrol each floor while they figure out something long term."

I opened the container of beans and rice, thankful she dropped the subject of Caleb. The kiss was still fresh in my mind. Every time I went into the kitchen, my cheeks flushed as I remembered his lips against mine and the calm I felt in his arms. The reminder that he'd lied for reasons I still needed to figure out challenged those feelings. The bottom line was Caleb was an issue I'd need to figure out once my head stopped throbbing.

She stood up and gathered the empty containers. "All right, missy. You looked tired. It's time to lay back down and rest."

The blanket was warm and soft when I pulled it over my shoulders. "I'd argue but I'm too comfy."

"And I'd win, anyway. When you wake up, text me what you want for dinner and I'll bring it by, okay?"

I mumbled my agreement as she continued cleaning up. After promising several times to call or text, she locked the door behind her and left. I looked around the room to make sure everything was in order and then nestled further under the blanket. With thoughts of intense brown eyes and a warm embrace, I fell asleep.

The next few days were spent camped out on my couch either sleeping or staring at the walls of each room. It was boring as shit. Food was delivered either via Nicole, or from various delivery people, and I found myself way too excited about interacting with them as a break from the isolation and boredom.

Jake came over Friday night with groceries. His jaw clenched when he saw my bruises, and I had to remind him to be gentle with my produce. He cooked dinner and stayed to watch a movie, but I was a terrible host and barely made it an hour before falling asleep. I woke up the next morning in my bed with a note telling me to send him my next grocery list and he'd be back in a couple days.

That weekend the stylist Jack hired stopped by. She removed the extensions, leaving my hair shoulder length. By Monday morning, I felt well enough to watch a couple talk shows. Felton still hadn't shown up, but I figured I'd deal with it once I was cleared to go back to work at my check-up in a couple days.

There was a sharp knock on my door at noon on Wednesday and, to my surprise, I found two men in the hallway when I glanced through the peephole. The younger man appeared average sized with light blond hair and brown eyes. He shot the occasional glance at the older man behind him. He stood taller, his back ramrod straight. His dark gray hair was perfectly styled, and his piercing blue eyes seemed like he was staring straight through the door at me. I knew that face all too well.

Felton.

The younger man looked relieved when I opened the door. "Jessica Ross? I'm Dr. Robertson. I'm here to examine you?"

"And I'm Detective Brooks, Portland Police," Felton greeted, showing me his fake badge and credentials. "I had a couple follow-up questions about the events from the other night. After you finish with the doctor, of course."

Felton's eyes were laser focused on the other man as I let them both inside. His eyebrow quirked as he walked past, and I gave a small nod. Jack sent me the information about the doctor, including a picture. His gaze darted around the apartment before he stood next to the island in the kitchen. I turned my attention back to the doctor, ignoring his scrutiny. He could bitch about whatever was pissing him off later.

Dr. Robertson conducted the exam in my bedroom, asking about my symptoms and checking my reflexes. Even though both the headaches and dizziness had improved, he ordered another week of bedrest. At my groans and whining, he smiled, told me the delay was nothing to worry about, and he'd be back the following week. He shot an uneasy glance at Felton and made a hasty exit.

Felton locked the door and pulled me into a gentle hug. "When they find the bastard who did this to you, I'm going to rip him apart."

"Where have you been? I sent you at least three messages through the black box app. What the hell?"

"I'm sorry, Lissa. Some of the intel we got out of Rome concerned me, so I went to check it out myself. It's rare Gio Sardi travels that far out of his territory, but it turns out he was traveling there to schmooze several new officials at the port. He's looking to buy a few properties, which is bound to start a turf war with some of the smaller groups.

I'd just landed in London on my way back home when I heard what happened to you."

"Did Barton tell you if there's any leads on the break in?"

"Do you really think the FBI is going to tell me anything?" he scoffed. "I'm lucky that bean counter saw fit to tell me what happened to you."

I pushed myself away from him. "Oh, Jesus Christ. Enough with the snide comments. I've had enough headaches to last several lifetimes."

"I don't mean to put you in the middle. You know I'm not supposed to give you any details, but I know you're not going to let me out of here without them."

"Damn right I'm not. Let's hear it."

He pointed toward the couch. "Not until you sit. You're still on bedrest for at least another week."

I made an unladylike sound and flopped on a cushion. "Start talking."

"The Sardis are keeping tabs on Professor Winters. It's unclear if they're planning any actions against him, but he's definitely being watched."

"Why?"

"According to our sources in Italy, they had an agreement and Winters didn't fulfill his part. That pissed off Gio, so he's been keeping tabs on him for the last eight months."

Ice filled my veins. "Are you saying there's a chance we could have some mob shit go down on this campus?"

"Doubtful. If they decide to take any action, he'll just disappear."

"That's comforting," I muttered.

"Have you seen any drug activity or anything else suspicious around him?"

"Nothing drug related, and I've already reported the few suspicious incidents. It makes me think something was there, but it's gone. Which makes me wonder why the FBI didn't get this case when those pictures were taken?"

"They were ready to open the case but needed more evidence. The pictures were taken around the same time Winters walked away from their deal. We'd heard rumors they'd been in contact again, so they opened a case and try to get ahead of them this time."

I sighed. "Based on what I've seen, more to the point, what I *haven't* seen, I'm not sure there's a case."

"We'll see what Barton and I come up with when we meet. The trip to Italy wasn't a waste. I found out a few things that are still classified but might move things along. However, it's still up to him. I know he has a lot of doubts, and your attack did nothing to change that."

"He's not convinced Caleb was the target."

"And he may be right. We have no way of knowing right now. All I know right now is the more I see your bruises, the angrier I feel."

I nudged his shoulder with mine. "Don't go getting all soft on me. I'm fine. The doctor is just being too cautious. I'll be cleared to go back to work next week. Assuming you two decide to continue."

"I promised Karina a couple days at home with her since I was in Italy much longer than planned. But then Barton and I should be able to meet and decide by the end of next week."

"He'll be pissed about the delay but it's not like I'm busy doing anything else in the meantime," I muttered.

"You know these things take time. What's the rush?"

"I don't know. Maybe I'm just getting stir crazy since I can't do anything aside from sit around here and watch TV."

His eyes narrowed, scanning my face. "Is that all?"

Shit. Apparently, I wasn't completely healed if I so easily stumbled into one of Felton's traps. He read people like a fifth-grade book report. Even though I was trained to beat polygraphs, he'd been gifted with some weird magic that sniffed out any form of deception. I rubbed my temples feigning a headache to buy myself an escape. If he saw my eyes, he'd know every conflicted feeling I had about both the case and my target.

Maybe using a smidgen of truth would work. "It's rough every year, but this time it felt a hundred times worse."

"Lissa," he whispered, putting his arm around my shoulders. "I'm sorry. Why didn't you call the private line?"

Felton had a private cell phone for Karina and me to use for emergencies. Most situations I found myself in were ones I could solve myself. I couldn't even remember the last time I'd used it.

"It was hardly an emergency. I'd just started to feel better when all this happened, so maybe I missed something because I was exhausted and off my game. Being on bedrest has sucked, but I can't say I'm not well rested now."

"You've never been one to stay idle, so I know how much you've got to be hating this. And I know you'll hate it even more when I say that there's no shortcut here. You need to let your body heal. I'm going to head out now so you can do that."

We both stood, and he gave me a gentle hug. "Promise me you'll be careful. I'm hoping to be stateside for a while, so I'll do a better job about keeping in touch."

"I was being careful," I scoffed.

"That wasn't a promise."

"Fine. I promise. Happy?"

He gave me a stern look and pointed to the couch. As I settled under the blanket, he brought a glass of water and placed it on the coffee table. After making sure I was comfortable, he showed himself out.

I sighed and stared at the ceiling. It wasn't much, but he gave me some useful information. And I couldn't do a goddamned thing with it other than let it bounce around in my head. For at least another week. My frustration must have been exhausting because the next thing I knew, I opened my eyes to a darkened living room and a knock at the door.

"Just a minute," I grumbled, stumbling off the couch.

My visitor was looking around the hallway when I checked the peep hole, but seemed to sense I was looking based on his nervous smile. At least someone was happy since it shocked the hell out of me. The smile fell when I leaned against the door frame and crossed my arms.

"Good evening, Professor."

Chapter Seventeen

Confessional

THE BAG IN HIS hand shifted, but he caught it before it fell. "I couldn't find a place that delivered decent Italian around here, so I decided to just bring it by. Hope you don't mind."

"Thanks," I murmured.

"I also wanted to see how you're feeling."

He looked like shit. His skin was pale, which highlighted the dark circles under his eyes. I mentally scolded my body's reaction to his mussed hair. No, he did not look vulnerable and sexy at all. I shifted my attention to the unzipped blue hoodie and black t-shirt that clung to his chest. Not that I was checking him out. Who was I kidding? I was. Dammit.

"Jess?"

I turned my face up to his. "Sorry. Still foggy at times."

"It should get better soon. May I come in? I promise to be a gentleman."

"Okay, but only because you have food that smells really good. And if you agree not to talk about what happened in my kitchen the last time you were here." I stood back to let him inside.

I was still recovering from a concussion, I reasoned, so that would've been insensitive on his part. Using pity was a crappy way to avoid the topic, but I didn't care. Bottom line, it shouldn't have happened, no matter how good it felt. And it felt good. Too good. Fuck, I was doing it again.

"Deal."

"Please excuse the mess," I muttered, moving toward the kitchen. A week of bedrest had left my apartment cluttered, and that was putting it mildly.

"Don't worry about it." The door closed, and he pointed to the couch. "I haven't heard how your check-up went, so as far as I know you're still on bedrest. Sit."

I flopped ungracefully onto the couch and pulled the blanket over my legs. He joined me a moment later and handed me a plain white food container. The smell of sage filled my nose, and I almost squealed when I found gnocchi covered with butter sauce inside. Thankfully, he ignored the moan I let out after the first bite.

We talked as we ate. I filled him in on my week of shitty television while he brought me up to speed about some of the security improvements. When I tried to ask how things were going with the students, he reminded me it was none of my business until the doctor allowed me to return to work.

I dropped my fork into the empty box and leaned back. "So, am I safe to assume that you're the one responsible for food magically being delivered to my door when Nicole couldn't bring it?"

"You can't recover from a head injury with just ice cream and wine."

"Fair point. Thank you. It was very much appreciated."

He nodded, focused on the hospital armband on the coffee table. I hadn't moved it since sliding it off my wrist the day after the attack. He looked around the apartment and then back at me, his jaw tense.

"Caleb, would you like to tell me why you're really here? Something is clearly on your mind."

"You don't beat around the bush, do you?"

"Subtlety has never been my strong suit. Let's hear it."

He sat forward, resting his elbows on his knees. He stared at a spot on the wall above my TV and took a deep breath. "What I'm about to tell you isn't something I tell many people because it's personal. But you have the right to know, and the right to judge me all you want. All I ask is that you keep it to yourself. Can you do that?"

"Yes."

"When I was in college, my friends and I spent most weekends in Atlantic City. At the casinos. It was harmless at first, just hanging out, drinking way too much, and playing a few games here and there. After a while, it became not so harmless. I tried to keep it under control, but the debt spiraled. About a year ago, I got treatment. However, I still owe quite a bit of money, and to some less than reputable people. Everything that's happened, the phone calls, the pig's head, all of it is because of them."

I stared at him. "Wow. Not sure what to say to that."

Did I believe this new story? Absolutely not. However, I was curious to learn his reason for showing up with tasty food and an impressive line of bullshit. He wasn't the one who attacked me, but my gut told me he knew there was a lot more to the story than the fairy tale he'd just spun. There was a reason he came back that night, a reason worth lying about.

"I know this makes me a shitty person, and I wish I could do more than just apologize or somehow make it all better. The fact that I can't kills me. And I'm fucking embarrassed that I let 'my shit,' as you called it, hurt you."

I looked away. "I could've been less bitchy about it."

"Don't be. That's what it is. If I knew then what I know now, things would've been done a lot differently."

"Please tell me this was a wake-up call and that you're going to get this resolved."

"Oh, it's already been taken care of," he muttered.

The way his face darkened was curious, but I didn't press it. Not yet. Secrets and lies were the currency of my world, and something told me I was on the verge of a jackpot. With the new information Felton gave me, all I could do was hope there was enough to keep the case alive so I could keep digging.

He went to the kitchen and started cleaning up the food containers strewn everywhere. Knowing just how gross the contents of my sink were, I tossed the blanket back and stood up. Too quickly, as it turned out. I gripped the arm of the couch to allow the dizziness to pass.

"I can do that," I protested, moving closer.

"Please, let me help. There's a lot I should do to make this up to you."

"But—"

"Jessica, stop!" he barked, his eyes blazing. "Just let me do this, please. If you want to do something, tell me where you keep your kitchen towels. You can keep me company, but you have to sit down. Don't think I didn't see you almost fall over just now."

Resigned, I pointed to the correct drawer and grabbed the chair from my desk. We both remained silent until he saw the name of a restaurant on one container and asked if they were any good. After that we talked about the food trucks around campus, both agreeing that the egg roll place by the science building was probably the grossest food ever. As we continued to talk, I propped my head up on my hand on the armrest of the chair.

"So, you like Italian food," he began as he dried the dishes and put them away. "Have you ever been to Italy?"

"I spent the summer after high school in Europe, which included two weeks there."

"I have family outside of Verona, so I visit pretty often. Where did you go when you were there?"

"Not everywhere I wanted to. All my friends wanted to hit the touristy spots as you can imagine. They couldn't wait to get to Venice, so we wound up speeding through most of the cities until we got there."

"Ah, yes. Everyone can't get to Venice quick enough when they're up north. Bit of a shame, really. There are plenty of other places to see in the region."

"Venice was nice, but to be honest I got seasick from riding around on the water all the time. Turin was my favorite city in the north if I had to pick."

"Turin doesn't get as much attention as it should," he agreed with a nod. "The architecture alone is amazing. But everyone would rather see Venice or Rome."

"You can't hold that against Rome, can you? That's thousands and thousands of years of architecture, history and culture. It's a scholarly nirvana. The fact it sucks at night is a whole other story."

He quirked an eyebrow. "Sounds like there's a story behind that comment."

A fake laugh burst from my lips, and I launched into a story about a night of partying gone awry and a nasty hangover. In truth, I'd spent almost two months in Italy chasing down a group who kidnapped a congressional aide's son from a nightclub. It took weeks undercover at the club to discover he'd been sold to a human trafficking ring. I'd needed my longest break afterward, and it was during that break that his body was discovered outside of St. Petersburg.

"You look tired," he said as he wiped the counters.

"It's been a long day." Thanks to the check-up and two exhausting men visiting me, my energy was spent.

"I'd offer to stay with you until you fell asleep, but I'm pretty sure I know the answer."

"And you'd be correct."

"Can't blame a guy for trying, right?"

Ignoring his comment, I walked him to the door. His hand brushed against my lower back, but vanished before I could react. I allowed my gaze to linger on his face for several seconds before he stepped closer.

"You'll call and let me know how the next check-up goes? I'd prefer not to hear it from Nicole or anyone else. I mean, I am your professor and technically your boss."

"Of course."

"And you promise you'll lock this door as soon as you close it?" His voice was stern and low, giving me goosebumps.

"I promise."

"Thank you. Good night, Jessica."

"Good night, Caleb."

His hand covered mine over the doorknob, and I froze. Smiling, he placed a gentle kiss on my forehead. "At some point, there's going to be a conversation about what happened in the kitchen," he whispered.

My mouth snapped closed as I fought the temptation to pull him close and kiss him until we were both breathless. We stared at each other for a few more seconds before he left. I locked the door and headed to bed. It was after midnight in Virginia and I was done talking to people. Barton could wait.

My phone rang at six the next morning, and I didn't even need to look at the display to know the caller. "Have you even sat down at your desk?"

"Good morning to you too."

"Sorry. I know I was supposed to call you after Felton left. I fell asleep and then the good professor stopped by."

"Is there a reason he was visiting someone he believes to be a student at her dorm room?"

"He dropped off food and supposedly wanted to see how I was doing. And to give me an explanation. A dramatic one."

"Oh, do tell."

"According to him, he's a recovering gambling addict and everything that's happened is because of these shady people he owes money to."

"You believe that?"

"What do you take me for? A few weeks ago he said it was because of some crazy ex-girlfriend."

He sighed. "I don't even know what to believe anymore. What did Felton have to say?"

"Caleb was supposed to introduce family associates to local drug contacts. He stopped a year ago, and it pissed Gio off. He thinks nothing will happen on campus, but who knows? I've learned not to trust anything when that family is involved."

"Wow, you're actually questioning info from Felton?" His voice was more than a little smug.

"Don't you start, too. You two are worse than a couple of teenage girls who like the same boy. He's on his way home and said you guys would meet and come to a decision by the end of next week."

A loud bang, as if a fist slammed on the desk, rang out. "Jesus Christ, seriously? He was in New York last week! Did he stop by then? Of course not. He had to take another goddamned week to make it out to see you and gives you information you're not even supposed to know. Now you're telling me I have to sit around and wait until he deigns it worth his time to meet with me?"

What the hell? Always the rational one, Barton's outburst was not only surprising but also hypocritical. I pushed down my first response that would've probably gotten me fired. "What's that supposed to mean? Why was I not supposed to know anything?"

"You haven't been cleared to work yet, Agent. I know he likes to flout the rules just for you, but the rest of us must keep them in mind."

I bolted upright. "Now, you just hold it right there. You gave me details about the attack less than twelve hours after I was discharged from the hospital. Now it's a problem because Felton did it?"

"Lissa—"

"No, I've had enough of this immature prick waving. I've been stuck in the middle almost since this arrangement was made, and I'm goddamned tired of it. Do you think I like the idea of two men sitting in a room and deciding the future of my job without having a say in any of it? Just sit around and twiddle my thumbs while the adults figure it all out for me?"

"It doesn't matter if you like it or not," he bit out. "Because those are the rules, Agent Donovan."

"Do you think I enjoyed getting the shit beat out of me? That I enjoyed having my fucking face slammed into a desk enough times that I still don't remember how many? I sure as hell didn't force you to tell me anything about the case. That was your choice and yours alone, just like it was Felton's choice to tell me."

Silence. I wondered if he'd hung up until he let out a slow breath. "I was out of line. I'm sorry. For all we know, you're still in danger, and the time he's spending to get out of the doghouse with his wife is time we could use to get this figured out."

"Well, since you're such a stickler for the rules, I guess I don't need to point out that you're the Special Agent *in Charge* and that gives you the authority to cancel this case at your sole discretion if it's in the best interest of the Federal Bureau of Investigation to do so. But I'm pretty confident you didn't need some low-level field agent to point that out to you."

I didn't want to be the bitch who questioned his authority, but I'd reached my limit. He knew Felton would be a thorn in his side when he agreed to the deal. In five years, he'd never discussed any problems or involved me. I wondered why that suddenly changed.

"It's a joint case," he grumbled as if hearing my thoughts. "The CIA is investigating in Italy. I can't pull you unless both agencies agree."

"If that's the case, then why am I here and not in Italy?" That made no sense. Felton knew how important it was to me to be the one to bring down Gio Sardi.

"I wasn't involved in the decision. All I know was that they selected you for the domestic part. That might be a question for you to ask Officer Lynch."

My wrist throbbed, and I relaxed my grip on the phone. Apparently, my body had reached its limit as well. "Will that be all, Agent Kane?"

"Lissa—"

I needed to get off the phone before the conversation went any further downhill. "I said will that be all?"

"Yes."

"Thank you. I shall keep you updated of my medical condition, including when I can return to active duty. I trust you will let me know the status of my case once a decision is made. Until then, goodbye."

His response was muted with the press of the button ending the call. The phone rang within seconds until I turned it off and shoved it under my pillow. It was then that I realized my whole body had turned into one giant ball of tension. Not only was my wrist sore, but so were my jaw, neck and shoulders. When my head throbbed, I groaned and climbed out of bed.

I took some pain meds and downed the glass of water. It wasn't often Barton and I argued, but this time it felt different. He wasn't out of line when he pointed out Felton broke the rules, and it was something I wasn't proud of at all. What bothered me the most was my indecision about how I felt about the case.

The deeper I followed Caleb down the hole, the deeper the mystery grew. I knew there was something buried under it all; I just needed the case to stay open long enough to prove it. The best part was that I'd convinced myself that was the whole reason. In reality, I was a goddamned liar.

My previous flings, including Jackson, never influenced my work. This time was different and I knew it was because Caleb was under my skin. After ignoring and refusing to admit the truth, his visit forced me to admit that my feelings were much deeper than they should be. It was such a cliche; the cold-hearted spy falling for their target. It was a tale older than shit with an endless number of shitty outcomes. At best, I'd be found out and my integrity would be destroyed, forcing me to slink off into retirement. At worst, I'd get myself killed.

I trudged back into my room and crawled under the covers, opting to take a nap. Maybe Barton and I could speak like adults after I woke up. If not that, perhaps Jake or Nicole would come over. I needed to hang out with people unrelated to the mess I'd made for myself. However, as I drifted off to sleep my thoughts went to Caleb once again, and I knew I was still lying to myself about what I genuinely wanted.

Chapter Eighteen

Turn Around

I WAS CLEARED TO return to class two weeks later. By then I wanted to strangle someone if for no other reason than going to jail would've meant leaving my apartment. Barton kept the case open but reserved the right to close it without Felton's input. I celebrated my return to class by bringing a giant box of donuts to the office to share with my fellow TAs.

The building's new security system was impressive. Video cameras watched every hall, door and lobby. Everyone had to use their student ID to enter the outer office, and access to the inner office required a special badge issued only to faculty and staff. Caleb's office didn't require a badge for entry, but a new lock was installed.

Nicole spent the morning catching me up on everything I missed. We'd just started going through lecture notes when Caleb entered. My stomach fluttered when our eyes met, and he smiled. I turned back and glared at the smug look on Nicole's face. Karl sat down next to us and whatever snarky comment she wanted to make was forgotten.

"Ms. Ross, can I talk to you for a couple minutes?" Caleb's voice broke through our conversation.

Her eyebrows were sky high as I followed him. I was barely inside, and the door closed with a soft click. We both stood frozen, staring. I laced my fingers together to stop my hands from trembling. "What's up?"

"It's good to see you again," he replied in that low husky voice that gave me chills.

"Thank you. It's great to be back. Which reminds me that I need to give you the release form from my doctor."

The door nearly hit him in the shoulder when I tore it open. Nicole watched with interest as I rummaged through my backpack and then raced back into the office. She winked, causing me to roll my eyes, just as he closed the door a second time.

"No restrictions," I announced, handing him the folded sheet of paper. "So as long as the Trojan army isn't hidden in another package, I'm ready to do the mail again."

He chuckled and leaned against the front of his desk. "That's good to hear. I wanted to let you know that the office now closes at five. Campus Security will be coming by each night to kick everyone out."

"Understood. Anything else?"

"Don't let those pit vipers guilt you into taking their classes for them for at least a week."

"Rachele won't be happy to hear you say that," I chuckled. "I'm expecting an epic sob story once she gets here."

I moved to the door but froze when his hand brushed my shoulder. He moved closer, close enough to feel the heat radiating from his body. As my hand grasped the knob, I tried not to gasp when I realized he'd moved even closer. His lips hovered over mine as if daring me to close what little distance remained between us. Thankfully my sanity returned, and I opened the door.

"It's good to see you all healed up," he murmured.

"Thanks. It's great to be back. One can only watch so much day-time TV."

I sat at my desk in the now empty office and got to work sorting through hundreds of unread e-mails flooding my inbox. As expected, Rachele showed up an hour later with an epic tale of her suffering while I was gone. I read through the messages and uttered the occasional comment as she outlined how no TA helped her. By the time Caleb came out of his office in time for his next class, I grabbed the materials out of her hands and announced I'd cover just to get away from her whining. He opened his mouth, but merely shrugged when he saw my glare. Better to let him think what he wanted rather than know I was close to ripping her goddamned throat out.

The rest of the week was less dramatic. By the next day I was back up to speed and did my best to resume my workload before midterms. Nicole and Trevor caught me up on the gossip that circulated about the attack, and even Karl had a good laugh about some of the wild stories. Rachele alternated between a fake, saccharine smile and a nasty sneer whenever our paths crossed, which I ignored.

Since the school was closed the next day, the mood in the office was relaxed when I arrived Thursday morning. Trevor was scheduled to present a lecture to the mafia class, so Karl and I helped him with last minute practice. My phone rang just as he was gathering his things together. I smiled at the caller's name on the display.

"Well, hello, Mr. McGuire."

"Hey there," Jake replied. "How does it feel to finally be out in the world again?"

"It feels amazing. Of course, I have to get used to people not confessing that they're in love with their sister's roommate's third cousin or anything like that, but it's been an easy adjustment so far."

"Damn, you watched way too many talk shows. How do you feel about venturing out of your apartment tonight?"

"That depends," I drawled, waving at Trevor as he headed off to class. "What did you have in mind?"

"Just a beer and a bite to eat, somewhere around your place. I wanted to catch up now that you're feeling better."

Jake refused to even entertain the idea of me walking by myself to meet him somewhere else and told me he'd meet me at the office at five. I asked if Sami would be there, but she was sick and wouldn't make it. After telling him to give her a hug from me and confirming that I wasn't to leave until he arrived, I joked it was a date and hung up.

"A date, huh?" Caleb's voice asked behind me.

"Yeah. Jake is coming by and we're going out." The dreamy smile on my face was probably a bit much, but I needed to sell it. Plus, I was genuinely excited to see my friend.

"Well. Sounds fun."

His flat tone told me he was as excited as a root canal, but that was the point of letting him think Jake was my boyfriend. The hurt in his eyes felt like someone carved a hole in my chest. I forced the same smile reserved for Rachele all week and bounced back to my desk. After the door slammed, I placed my head in my hands and took a deep breath. I wanted him; after dancing around it for the past few months I'd admitted it to myself. My need to bring my parents' killer to justice was greater, however.

I got back to work, immersing myself in the Russian bratva for a few hours until everyone filtered back into the office to finish up for the day. My phone buzzed as I slid my laptop into my backpack, and I went to the door to let Jake in. The security guard stood in the outer office and reminded me we had five minutes to clear out. Jake opted to sit on the couch while I finished. Karl joined him, and they promptly started chatting about football. Caleb stomped out of his office, slamming the door, and locking it. I tossed my backpack over my shoulder and froze at the sour look on his face.

"Jess, you ready? This guard looks like he's going to storm in there any second!" Jake yelled.

Caleb's jaw clenched for a fraction of a second. "Have fun on your date."

"Thanks. Enjoy the long weekend." Without another word or peek in his direction I grabbed my coat and strolled out to my fake boyfriend.

"Finally," Jake muttered, glancing up. "How's it going, Professor? Long time, no see."

"Hey, Jake. How have you been?"

He draped his arm over my shoulder and smiled. "Can't complain. Just taking Jessie out to celebrate the end of her captivity."

"That's a good reason to celebrate. She gave us all quite a scare."

Karl stared at the two of them glaring daggers at each other before mumbling a hasty goodbye and retreating down the hall. Lucky bastard. Why didn't I follow him? The guard cleared his throat and gave an impatient look at Caleb, who nodded and held up his finger.

I tugged Jake toward the door. "Well, gentlemen, Jessie is hungry. So if we could stop talking as if I'm not standing right here, that would be great."

Jake took the long black coat from my hand and held it open so I could slide my arms through. The weather had been cold and rainy, so I'd worn a red sweater dress and black suede thigh-high boots. I turned to thank him, and he pressed a gentle kiss to my forehead. Based on the loud huff behind me, I knew his action had the intended effect.

He ignored my narrowed eyes and smiled. "You ready?"

"Yep. Let's go." In my mind, I'd already shot him in the ass. Twice.

With a nod to both Caleb and the guard, he led the way to the elevator. I heard voices behind us and saw the two men talking as we stepped inside. Once we were alone, I spun out of his arm and put my hands on my hips.

"Jacob Jonathan McGuire, what in the fuck was that?"

The easygoing smile vanished. "I don't like that guy at all. There's something about him that rubs me the wrong way."

He was too perceptive for his own good. I'd never told him the details of the case, but with that comment he'd figured out more than he should have. He'd never blow my cover or ruin the case on purpose, but his aggression was a complication I couldn't afford.

"And that's why you need to stay the hell away from him. I'm serious," I said in a stern voice. "No more coming to the office. It's too dangerous."

"Shit, I'm sorry."

"There's nothing to apologize for. I know you'll always have my six, and I'll always have yours. That's why I'm telling you to stay away. But tonight, let's forget about all of that and have some cheap beer and greasy bar food."

The door opened with the sound of scraping metal and he crooked his arm toward me with a grin. "To the Bullfrog, my lady?"

A light mist hung in the air as we trudged up the street to my building. Ever the gentleman, he ordered me to wait in the lobby while he dropped my backpack off upstairs. Several ladies stopped and stared as he returned, causing me to snicker. He shot me a mock glare and dragged me through the revolving metal door, not stopping until we stepped into the Surly Bullfrog. The sports bar was a popular hangout across the street from my building.

"So enough about me and my bullshit," I began, taking a sip of beer. "What's new with you?"

The wide grin on his face told me he'd been waiting for me to ask. "She said yes."

"As if she wouldn't. Congrats!"

"We also found out that she's pregnant."

My eyes widened. "Was that planned?"

"No, but we're both excited. She doesn't want to waddle down the aisle, so we're waiting until after the baby is born."

"So that's why she wasn't feeling well?"

He nodded with a frown. "Her nausea has been brutal. She's almost three months, so hopefully it gets better after the first trimester or whatever it's called."

"I sure hope so. Oh my god! I'm so happy for you! You guys are going to be amazing parents!"

Our food arrived, and we continued to talk as we ate. After telling me about his craziest bookstore customers, he told me all the details of his proposal. He then told me about how they learned of her pregnancy a couple weeks later. I was so overjoyed for them that my cheeks ached from the smiles and laughter we shared. They'd been through so much together and deserved a happily ever after.

He smirked after we toasted to their happiness. "So enough about my love life. Aside from Professor Winters, are there any other admirers I need to warn off?"

"I'm on a job, so it's not even an option," I replied with a dramatic sigh. "As for Winters, he should know better."

His eyes shifted. "Are you sure about that?"

I followed his gaze and cursed under my breath. Less than twenty feet away, Caleb sat in a small booth eating. Well, stabbing the hell out of a plate of pasta was a more accurate description. I let out a disgusted sound and turned back to Jake.

"Fuck my life," I sighed. "Let's go."

When Sami's ringtone blared from his phone as we stepped outside, I leaned under the awning while he answered. His face was grave when he tucked the phone back in his pocket. "She needs ginger ale and crackers. She feels awful."

"Go," I instructed and pointed over my shoulder. "My building is right there. I'll be fine."

"You sure?"

"Positive."

He hugged me and jogged toward the parking garage. Passing by the front door of the bar, I headed for the crosswalk. I'd just crossed the street and started typing a message to Jake that I was home when I felt a presence behind me.

"Jessica."

Shit. That one word from that one voice. A battle between my head, heart and hormones raged inside. Turning around was the worst idea in the world, but I wanted to. So damn bad.

"Can I talk to you?" His voice sounded closer.

Crap, crap, crap. My feet remained rooted to the small ramp under the pedestrian signal, earning strange looks from people passing by.

"Please."

Fuck. The only sound that echoed in my ears was my heart thundering in my chest. I closed my eyes and turned around. "Yes?"

The tension in his eyes eased. "Five minutes. Please." His hand grazed my elbow as he turned left and led us up the street.

"Where are you taking me?"

"Somewhere a little more private. I promise I won't hurt you."

His red Audi gleamed in the parking lot, the only car that remained. When my steps slowed, he released me. Numb, my brain urged me to follow. He stopped on the passenger side and watched me approach. Drawn to his scent, I stepped close enough that I had to crane my neck to see his face.

I shivered and drew my coat tighter around my body. "What did you want to talk about?"

"I think you know."

"Are you serious right now? Jake has to leave, and you swoop in not five minutes later to, what? Chat about something that doesn't need to be talked about?"

"Tell me it meant nothing. That you didn't feel anything." At my silence, he loomed closer. "You can't, can you?"

"Why does it matter? It can't—"

"I want to know why. Why can't I stop thinking about you? How were you able to get under my skin so damn easily? I want to stay away from you, but I can't. And I'm sure you feel the same way."

My blood heated at his words, but I found myself unable to force another past my lips. In less than five minutes, he'd shaken me to the core by revealing the same feelings I'd battled and tamped down for months. My fingers strayed to the base of my throat and rested on my collarbone, a common reaction when I felt stressed.

"I'm trying to do the right thing. For both of us," I replied, stepping back. He had no idea.

His arms pulled me closer, and his face hovered above mine. "I've tried, but I can't. The truth is, I don't want to fight this anymore. Can you? Can you keep pretending?"

His touch flooded my body and mind with warmth, overwhelming my senses. I pressed my forehead to his and when his arms tightened around my waist, my defenses shattered. Should I fight my attraction? Absolutely. I should have punched him in the throat and raced to the safety of my apartment. Did I want to fight anymore?

"No," I breathed. "I can't."

I felt the car against my back a second before his lips crashed against mine. The kiss was desperate, bruising, and felt like I'd been reunited with a missing piece of me. My arms pulled him closer, and a hungry sound came from his throat. We broke apart and his lips moved to my neck. I shivered and gasped when his teeth grazed the skin.

"Caleb—"

Breathless, I kissed him again. He cradled my head as his tongue teased mine. His other hand pressed my body closer, and I felt his erection against my stomach. He gripped my hair tighter when my hands reached under his jacket.

His eyes gleamed when we broke apart. "Do you trust me?"

"Yes."

After several more kisses, we stopped long enough to climb into the car and speed from the lot. I kept my hand on his thigh, teasing him and earning several promises of what awaited me once we got to our destination. We parked in a small underground garage and when he opened the door, I whispered in his ear that he had exactly two minutes to get me somewhere private before I combusted.

Ninety seconds later we stumbled inside an apartment. He turned toward the door and paused. My heart sank until the click of the lock broke the silence. His lips devoured mine a second later. Hands fumbled and pulled at sleeves until we tossed our coats to the floor. My dress followed not long after. His hands gripped my hips and pulled me flush against his body.

I trailed kisses along his jaw, drawing a long moan from his throat. My hands roamed the soft fabric of his shirt until they stopped in the middle. His heartbeat thundered, nearly matching my own. Wrapping my arms around his neck, I brought my lips to his.

The kiss was tender but heated quickly. A dull throb started low in my core as he cupped my ass and set me on the island of his dimly lit kitchen. I wrapped my leg around his waist and the growing bulge in his pants rubbed against my panties, teasing me. Impatient, I gripped his shirt and yanked it open, sending buttons flying. He slid the fabric from his shoulders and placed both hands on the counter, caging me in.

"That was my favorite shirt."

I crooked an eyebrow. "Shall I hop down and sew the buttons back on?"

"Don't you dare."

With a gentle tug, both boots fell to the floor, and he stood between my legs. His hands explored my heated skin as I trailed my tongue over his collarbone. When I bit his neck, he growled and unclasped my bra. My nipples hardened under his gaze.

"Fucking beautiful," he breathed before taking one into his mouth.

I gasped at the first lash of his tongue and my panties were soaked within seconds. He released it with a loud smack and turned his attention to the other one. I ran my fingers through his soft hair as he continued his torture. My head fell back with a loud moan when he rubbed his cock against my now throbbing heat.

"Feels so good," I breathed, finally able to form a coherent sentence.

"I haven't even begun to make you feel good."

My panties disappeared. The few seconds of regret at missing my last wax appointment were dashed when his fingers skimmed the area my body begged for his touch. His fingers gently flicked my clit as he silenced my loud moan with his lips.

He broke the kiss and moved away. The only contact between us was the finger that slid through my wetness and moved lower. Cold and confused, my skin heated at the hunger in his eyes.

"What—"

"Shh." His gaze held mine as his finger slid inside.

"Fuck!" I cried, grinding against his hand.

He added a second finger and kept the pace slow. I wrapped an arm around his shoulder and buried my face in the crook of his neck, kissing every bit of his heated skin I could reach. He sped up the motion, causing me to shudder at the sensations and building pressure.

His fingers slowed and then stilled. With a gasp, my head shot up. He smirked before kissing me, slowly at first. I ground against his hand, but it remained motionless. My hand moved from his shoulder and caressed his chest, drawing a soft moan from him. I deepened the kiss and my hand moved lower. Two could play that game.

My hand arrived at the waistband of his pants and moved to the bulge straining against the fabric. I traced the outline of his cock, earning a harsh groan when I reached the tip. His fingers moved in response, causing me to shudder when they curled and pressed against my walls. He sucked my breast into his mouth, attacking the nipple with his teeth. Just as my body teetered over the edge, he moved away. My eyes snapped open and found him watching me with scorching eyes.

A low hum came from his throat when he licked his fingers. "I look forward to feasting on this sweetness."

"Nothing stopping you now."

"Oh, but there is," he chuckled, his lips hovering over mine. "The first time you come is going to be with my cock buried deep inside you."

I closed the distance between us and brushed my lips against his. He held me close, but I was tired of playing. Breaking away, I slid off the counter. His eyes widened and he tried to kiss me, but gasped when I bit his lower lip. I turned my attention to his chest next, kissing and nuzzling the warm skin under my fingers. He threw back his head and moaned when my teeth grazed his bronze nipple. My hands moved to his belt buckle. He grabbed them and pressed a kiss to both palms.

"Keep that up and I can't promise I'll be gentle," he whispered.

"So, don't be. And that's a lot of empty talk for someone who still has their pants on."

Setting me back on the counter, he winked. "Just saving the best for last."

He pulled a condom out of his wallet and placed it in my hand. His black pants and boxer briefs slid to the floor, freeing his monster sized cock. I took it in my hand and stroked him. He closed his eyes as his breathing sped up. My finger swirled around the tip and collected the pre-cum. When I brought it to my lips, he let out a low growl.

"Jessica."

I tore open the wrapper. As soon as he was sheathed, he slid my body to the edge of the counter. Gripping my thigh, his gaze held mine as he slid inside with one hard thrust. Feeling stretched, I gasped and moved my hips to meet his. He moved hard and fast, giving me everything I wanted and more. My arms wrapped around his neck and I kissed him as if my life depended on it. His hand gripped my hip and he thrust deeper. I gasped at the new sensations rocketing through my core. My arms clung to his back, desperate to feel as much of his skin against mine as I could.

"You feel so goddamned good, baby," he panted.

He buried his head in the crook of my neck, kissing and biting the skin below my jaw. This was crazy, dirty fucking; the kind that left you completely spent and begging for more. The pressure in my lower back built higher and higher, reaching a fever pitch when he swiveled his hips, dragging his cock against my clit for several strokes.

"Fuck, don't stop!"

He moaned and his motions became erratic. My skin ignited, and the orgasm exploded through my body. The scream from my throat sounded foreign and the shudder that came with it was almost painful. I was still seeing white and gold stars when he slammed his body against mine one last time and shouted through his own release. My eyes were closed as I stroked his back while we caught our breath. I opened my eyes and kissed him.

"Wow," I rasped out.

He smiled and nuzzled my ear. "Are you okay? I didn't hurt you, did I?"

"No."

"Good."

He slid my body off the counter and held me to his chest. After carrying me upstairs, he placed me on his bed. I felt cold the instant he pulled away and disposed of the condom in a nearby wastebasket. He then crawled across the bed and pulled me to him.

"Because I am nowhere near done with you."

As his body covered mine, I knew it was going to be a very long night.

Chapter Nineteen

Breach

THE ROOM WAS FULL of soft light and the sound of rain tapping against glass. There was something about rainy days that always made me want to stay in bed hidden under multiple blankets. The soft, warm bed made moving the last thing I wanted to do, so I watched the droplets slide down the window before nestling into the pillow and letting the sound lull me back to sleep.

An arm pulled me against a wall of muscle, pinning me to him. I shifted my hips, wincing at the tenderness between my legs. Leaning my head back, I inhaled his intoxicating scent. His stubble tickled my neck before I heard a low chuckle.

"Way too late to escape now." He trailed kisses down to my shoulder, causing me to shiver.

I spotted a stray condom wrapper on the floor, and my cheeks flushed at the memories of every filthy, naughty, and mind-blowing thing we did. All night and all over each other. The man was a goddamned beast, a sexy beast. His arm relaxed and I slowly, gingerly, rolled to face him. He bent forward and gave me a tender kiss.

"Morning," I murmured.

We held each other and laid in silence, his fingers strumming against my arm. In the daylight, I took the opportunity to fully appreciate his sculpted chest. My fingers danced over his warm skin until they settled on his abdomen where they traced over the ridges of muscle. I snuggled closer against him and sighed.

His fingers stopped on a large, puckered mark on my upper left arm. "Where did all these scars come from?"

"I could ask you the same thing," I quipped, tracing my finger over a thin white line near his right armpit, a spot that I'd learned over the past several hours was quite sensitive.

"That one is from the days when I was a less than upstanding citizen and got into a bar fight. Met the wrong end of a switch-blade." He gestured to his right side where several smaller marks dotted the skin. "Those happened when some asshole knocked me down and I fell on a bunch of broken glass during the same fight. And the spot on my leg is a burn from a dirt bike when I was thirteen." He cocked an eyebrow. "Your turn."

My eyes closed. Emotional scars were easy to hide by immersing my mind elsewhere. The physical ones were impossible to ignore. Most of the marks, including the one that piqued his interest, were from Iraq. The rest were thanks to various jobs over the years: a few knife slashes on my forearm and a bullet graze on my left thigh. The advantage of hooking up with fellow members of the intelligence community meant they knew talking about injuries and scars was taboo. It was only those rare times a civilian saw them that I dreaded.

"When I was twelve, my friends and I snuck into an abandoned house," I explained, reciting my cover story. "I was looking around upstairs and didn't realize the floor was almost completely rotted out. I stepped down, and the floor collapsed. Landed on a broken glass door outside the dining room."

"Ouch."

"The doctor said I was lucky it didn't impale me. I thought my dad was going to skin me alive when he got to the hospital."

"I would've definitely given you a spanking," he teased, pulling me onto his chest. His fingers moved to the scar on my left shoulder blade and my whole body tensed.

Of all the marks on my body, the jagged wound extending the length of my shoulder blade to my underarm held the most emotional pain. Another reminder from the night my life changed forever. Countless times I studied the bumpy white line and wondered how my life would've been if the skin was smooth. It was more a dream than a question with no answer.

He moved his hands to my hips and watched me closely. "Is it time for the awkward morning after talk?"

"Probably."

"All right. I'll go first," he paused and took a deep breath. "This wasn't just about getting you into my bed for a night. I want more."

I blinked. "Um, okay. I wasn't expecting that."

"I've been drawn to you for a while, that's no secret. I've tried to fight it, ignore it, anything and everything I can think of. But when I saw you two last night, I just couldn't take it anymore. I wanted to be the one walking down the street and making you laugh." His hand slid up and rested between my shoulders. "Kissing you. Feeling your skin against mine."

"Caleb."

"I know this… complicates things with him—"

"He's not my boyfriend." I blurted. "He's just a really good, extremely overprotective, friend. He didn't know if you were someone who could be trusted when he met you at the store, so he faked you out."

"And you went along with it?"

My cheeks heated, and I lowered my head. "You weren't the only one trying to fight this. I thought you'd stay away if you thought I had a boyfriend."

"What was last night then?"

"Since the attack he doesn't trust you, or anyone else. He picked up on your... interest in me, and well, it was just too easy for him."

"Wow. He's kind of a dick. But I get it. I'd do the same thing if it were someone I care about, too. Under different circumstances we'd probably be friends."

I bit back my first response. Jake would shoot Caleb in the throat before they ever cracked open a beer and watched a football game. I didn't even want to think about the body parts he'd shoot if he found out about last night.

"Not a good idea."

"Fair enough." He swept a lock of hair away and kissed my cheek. "But I meant what I said. I want to see where this goes."

The conflict in his eyes lasted maybe a second, but it was unmistakable. What worried him? The fact he was my teacher? Doubtful since his ethics were, at best, malleable, but I was in no position to judge. I put a joint case in serious jeopardy the minute my clothes fell on his floor. There had to be something else, but what?

"This violates so many rules. If we get caught—"

"We'll keep it under wraps. We'll make sure we're careful. I'll control myself on campus and around other people. We won't get caught. And if we do, I'll take full responsibility."

"It would be a disaster for your career," I pointed out.

"Then we'll just make sure it doesn't come to that."

"So, when you say you'll 'control yourself'," I made air quotes. "Does that mean you won't follow me into a bar and out on the street from now on?"

"I can control myself in front of other people if I know I don't have to when we're alone."

I lowered my head to his chest, angry at the mess I'd gotten myself into. How many times had I told myself to stay away? Reminded myself about his connections? I'd tried to keep a distance, threw as many obstacles as I could in the way, and all for nothing. Because no matter how much distance was between us, an almost constant unease lingered in my mind that refused to be silenced. Lying in his arms was like a balm, providing peace and comfort. I'd officially lost my goddamned mind.

His fingers traced my spine and stopped at my lower back. "Jess?"

My eyes met his. "If we do this, if you really want to see where this goes, I have to be able to trust you. And I can't if we aren't honest with each other. No more lies. Period."

"I promise."

Barton and Felton would probably join forces and have me exiled to some god forsaken corner of the world, but I couldn't bring myself to care. This new "thing" between us, whatever it was, put me closer to Caleb and his secrets than ever. If Felton's intel was correct, the man in my arms was an enemy of the Sardi family and most of their enemies wound up dead. I'd be damned if I'd let that happen.

I traced my fingers over the light dusting of hair on his chest. "All right."

A slow smile spread across his lips before rolling me onto my back. His face hovered above mine. "Are you sure?"

I brought my hand to his face and caressed the stubble on his cheek. "Positive."

We spent the morning in bed, talking about nothing important and fucking like we couldn't get enough of each other. We fell asleep and woke up in a tangle of arms and legs. By then the rain had stopped, and the light was less gray and hazy.

"I'd love to stay in bed with you all day, but I'm going to need some food before we play again."

After sliding on the black sweatpants at the foot of his bed, he told me to help myself to the clothes in his closet or dresser before heading downstairs. I came down a few minutes later in a pair of blue boxer briefs, white tank top, and a dark gray hoodie. My pace slowed as I took in the rest of his place that I didn't pay any attention to the night before. The furniture was in neutral colors with bright and colorful accents. My eyes tracked the trail of clothes near the door, and my core throbbed.

A sound to my right brought my attention to the kitchen. He stood at the stove, his muscular back to me. When I was close enough, I embraced him from behind, pressing my hands to his chest. A low moan came from his throat when I pressed a kiss to his back. He turned and brought me around his side, tucking me under his arm. Bacon sizzled on the back burner as he poured batter into the skillet in front of him.

"Smells delicious," I said.

He flipped the pancake and smiled. "Thanks. So do you."

With an eye roll, I asked what else was needed and got to work. Once he finished cooking, we sat at the breakfast nook on the far side of the kitchen. Climbing onto the barstool was a bit of a challenge thanks to our earlier activities. At the smirk on his face, I narrowed my eyes.

I glanced around the room again as we ate. "This place is gorgeous."

"I'd like to take credit, but it was already furnished when I rented it."

"Well, it's a hell of a lot nicer than my crappy dorm room. Even with all the clothes on the floor."

"That mess was worth it," he replied, caressing my thigh.

"Can't argue with that."

After breakfast, I insisted on cleaning the kitchen while he went into his home office to do some work. I was wiping down the counters when he strolled back into the room. I smiled and leaned against him when his lips grazed my neck.

He kissed the tip of my nose. "So, what do you have planned today?"

"Sadly, not what's on your mind. I still have a ton of crap I need to do to catch up my other classes."

It wasn't a lie. To make the identity believable, I'd opted for a full graduate course load. Barton joked I was the only agent who'd wind up getting another degree while on a job, to which I'd shrugged. Given my history in some regions of the world, it was interesting to learn more about them from a more objective point of view.

"I'd be glad to help you study," he offered, tracing the outer shell of my ear with his tongue.

I giggled and ducked out of his hold. "Unless you want to read about three hundred pages of text, I think your time is better spent working on your own classes."

"Oh, all right. How about a shower?"

That took no convincing at all. After pulling him into a kiss that curled my own toes and left me breathless, he tossed me over his shoulder and carried me upstairs. My legs were still wobbly thanks to his many talents afterward. I dressed slowly, jumping at the chime of his phone. His brow furrowed as he read the screen and then tossed it on the bed.

He pulled a plain black sweatshirt over his head. "How about I drop you off a couple blocks from your dorm?"

"Sure. Is everything okay?"

"Security asked me to swing by the office. Something about an irregularity. I needed to grab some papers anyway."

He dropped me off north of the bookstore and I walked the three blocks back to my place. I had a voicemail from Barton, so he was my first order of business. The call was quick; he wanted an update and

I told him there was nothing to report. Because he sure as hell wasn't going to know how I'd spent the evening.

Afterward I grabbed my laptop out of my backpack and plugged it into the charger at my desk, yawning as I walked back to the couch. My eyes closed almost as soon as I laid down, only to snap open at the sound of my phone. My annoyance vanished once I saw Caleb's name.

"Hey," I yawned. "How'd it go at the office?"

"Oh, fine. I just wanted to make sure you got back to your place okay."

"I'm lying on my couch as we speak," I answered, noting the edge to his voice. "Why?"

"What I'm about to say has to stay between us. While the police were investigating your attack, there were two other breaches. And then this morning the system alerted them to an entry into the building and into our office."

I hadn't been in that building for nearly three weeks after the attack, so it wasn't me they were after. The questions lined up single file in my mind. Was Caleb the target? If so, why? What were they after? And more importantly…

"I thought they locked the building up every night?"

"They do. Unfortunately, I can't share too many details right now. All I can say at this point is that the investigation is ongoing, and there are a lot of leads that are being looked at."

"So, nobody knows anything," I muttered.

"Nothing they're comfortable acting on yet. For now, I'm just glad there are measures in place to keep everyone safe. We just have to trust they'll catch this fucker."

I bit back the nasty words that nearly broke free. If leads were still being chased almost a month later, the chance for a solved case was practically zero. I cursed Barton to the depths of hell for his continued refusal to give me updates. Apparently, none of this was important enough to tell the field agent assigned to the case.

"Jess?" His voice was uneasy. "You know you have nothing to worry about, right? Security is watching everyone coming and going into the building. But if you ever don't feel safe, tell me. Okay?"

I smiled, my heart warming at his words. "Okay."

"So, how's the homework coming along?"

"Haven't started it yet. I planned to take a nap for a couple hours since I didn't get much sleep last night."

"You weren't complaining at the time, I'd like to point out. I was going to ask if you wanted to come over. I'd be willing to read all those pages to you."

"And we both know how that will end," I replied with a grin. "I'd love to, but I really need to get this done. Rain check?"

"Of course, but only if it's sooner rather than later. I already miss you."

"Miss you too. And I promise it'll be sooner rather than later."

We said our goodbyes, and I fell asleep on the couch in no time. The daylight was fading when I woke up. The clouds had cleared, and I watched the sky change colors as I placed a takeout order from my favorite restaurant down the street. Ten minutes later I settled onto the couch with a box of fried food and a book on modern European cultural history.

I'd just started the chapter on Germany's reunification when my phone chimed. My eyes were bleary when I saw it was just after ten. The text message was a picture of Caleb's bare chest, his legs covered by the dark blue blanket on his bed with the caption "wish you were here." Smiling, I typed out a quick reply which turned into a back-and-forth conversation until midnight. Resigned to the fact that I wouldn't get any more work done, I crawled into bed. Sleep didn't come right away. Instead, I stared at the ceiling and wondered just how much of a mess my case had become.

Chapter Twenty

Rough Seas

I POURED TWO GLASSES of wine and set them on the table as Caleb pulled the baking dish from the oven. He'd made macaroni and cheese but based on the mouthwatering aroma he'd put his own twist on the recipe. As he spooned up bowls for both of us, we resumed our conversation about vacation spots.

He pushed my chair in and sat next to me at his small dining table. "Where did you always want to go, but haven't gone yet?"

Everywhere. My parents took me to the beach every summer until their deaths, and that was the end of my travels until I went to college. Felton's work took him all over the world but left him with little desire to go anywhere past his front door once he returned home and Karina's idea of a vacation was spending a day at the spa.

"Somewhere tropical. Anywhere I can drink something out of a pineapple and get sand between my toes."

He let out an appreciative hum. "You'd look spectacular in a bikini."

We'd been seeing each other slash sleeping together for a few weeks, and while my guilt and conflicted feelings lessened every day, the lack of movement on the case brought added concerns. Every morning I expected a call from Barton telling me the case was over. One way or another, I knew it would end at some point and it was all

I could do to hope my heart survived. Until then, I vowed to enjoy our time together.

I couldn't help the snort that slipped out as I sipped my wine. "You offering to take me some place so I can wear one?"

"Maybe not anywhere tropical, but how would you feel about going away with me this weekend?"

"Are you sure? I mean—"

"The beach is only about an hour from here. I'll rent a cabin," he took my hand in his. "We can walk around in the open, maybe build a fire on the sand, drink some wine, see where the evening takes us."

"That doesn't sound too crazy."

"Is that a yes?"

"Yes," I paused. "But there's no way I'm wearing a bikini in November."

We worked side by side on the couch after dinner; Caleb read through our TA journals while I made notes for an upcoming paper in another class. The trip didn't come up again until we were brushing our teeth before bed and he asked if he could persuade me to wear a bikini if the rental had a hot tub. It turned into a hell of a negotiation and in the end, I agreed in exchange for breakfast in bed.

He curled his body around mine as he did every night. It felt wonderful to fall asleep in his arms, but the challenge was getting my brain to quiet long enough to fall asleep. Sex and the exhaustion afterward were a blessing. The intimacy we'd found without it was a blessing as well, but also a curse.

On those nights I went through all the lies told that day, as if keeping a ledger of it all would somehow lessen the pain and guilt when the case ended. Guilt. In my world, the only time that word was used was in terms of the law. Instead, it turned into an emotion that threatened to drown me every night.

"Can't sleep?" his gruff voice rasped in my ear.

I rolled to face him. "Yeah."

"Want me to tell you a bedtime story?"

"Does that mean you're going to tell me something boring so I'll fall asleep?"

"Close your eyes, smartass," he laughed. "Let me tell you how we're going to spend our day at the beach."

"Are you gonna buy me one of those red lifeguard hoodies everyone wears?"

"Maybe."

He told a tale of walking along the beach looking for shells and watching the waves until it got too cold. After warming up we'd go into town and hit all the cheesy tourist shops. He enveloped me in his arms and described the house, complete with a fireplace he planned to ravish me in front of. When my eyes became heavy, I let the dream of a romantic weekend with him free of deception and guilt carry me away.

· · · ● · ● · ● · ● · ● · · ·

Lying to the TAs about my weekend plans made me feel like a teenager, one who felt a rush as I strolled the few blocks off campus to our meeting spot. A pistol was hidden in my knapsack, and I'd installed a tracking app for my cell phone on the laptop. As one final precaution, I left a note with all of Caleb's info in my apartment. With one last glance around to make sure nobody recognized us, I tossed my bag behind the seat and we set out.

As his car sped through the tunnel leading out of downtown Portland, he placed a gentle kiss on my hand and smiled. It was always fun to talk about just about anything with him and I soon discovered this was even more entertaining on a long road trip. From exchanging random facts about killer animals in Australia to our most embarrassing high school stories to laughing at road signs, the conversation was never dull.

We turned off the highway and onto a narrow road with a stunning view of the beach, only to make a sudden left at a hidden driveway. He parked in front of a large three-story house with dark gray clapboard siding and red shutters on the windows. It was gorgeous, but too big for just the two of us. He turned off the engine and fidgeted with his keys.

"So, it turns out that beach rentals are in high demand on the coast even when the weather is crummy," he explained. "It was sheer luck that I found this place. The original renters canceled when they found out there was a storm this weekend. The hot tub is broken, but it has a fireplace, lots of space as you can see, and access to the beach."

"How many bedrooms?"

"Five."

"Well, I'm sure at least one of them has a comfy bed that will fit both of us," I replied, opening the door. "Only one way to find out, right?"

I followed him up the steps while he unlocked the front door. Once inside, I took in the robin's egg blue walls with white wainscot trim and crossed the light hardwood floors to the nearest floor lamp. The room was bathed in warm light, a welcome contrast to the gray cast outside. A gas fireplace with a white mantel sat on the far wall to our left, a feature not lost on him based on his wide grin. Walking past the denim blue couch, we found a kitchen with black granite countertops, white cabinets and stainless-steel appliances.

"Well, this will be perfect for you to cook me breakfast in bed tomorrow morning," I quipped, hopping on the center island.

"I believe the agreement was only if you wore a bikini in the hot tub, which is broken. Unless you plan on wearing it on the beach?"

With a scoff I spun away from him. "Fine. I'll make myself breakfast and eat it in bed. You're on your own."

He pulled me closer and stood between my legs. "I'm kidding. Besides, I'm sure you're going to be sleeping late after I'm done with you tonight."

I hopped off the counter and followed him through the house to pick a bedroom, deciding on the largest room on the second floor. The room was decorated in a kitschy beach theme, complete with a rattan headboard and a seashell print comforter on the king-sized bed. The large bay window facing the beach sweetened the deal. I watched the waves, vaguely aware of his movements around the room until he nuzzled my ear.

"You look like you can't wait to get down there," he said, taking my hand. "Let's go."

We followed the stone path in the backyard to cement steps that led down to the beach. The ocean churned and battered everything in its path. A thin veil of fog blurred the row of trees lining the area, as well as the cliffs in the distance. I slipped off my shoes and skipped across the sand, stopping short of the waves. When the icy water slid over my feet, I screeched and ran back to Caleb, who doubled over laughing.

His hand was warm as it held mine and we walked along the shore, stopping to look at shells or watch the waves. He led us to a large rock in the sand and leaned against it, holding his arms open. We kissed before I leaned my back against his front.

"This feels good," he said after several seconds of quiet.

"Damn near perfect."

We watched the surrounding scenery, laughing at the seagulls battling over the French fries a little girl tossed their way and nodding at a couple riding their horses on the beach. The mist in the air thickened and the wind gusts grew stronger. By the time we headed back to the house, the drizzle in the air had escalated to a downpour.

He turned on the fireplace and after we stripped out of our wet clothes, we huddled together on the floor under a blanket. Shivering, he pulled me into his lap and rubbed my arms. His warm lips trailed across my shoulders, and when my eyes met his, I wrapped my arms around his neck. Our embrace heated, and it wasn't long before he made good on his promise to ravish me in front of the fire.

"That's one way to warm back up," I panted, leaning against his chest. "I wouldn't be opposed to doing that again."

"We could, but that wouldn't leave much time to go into town." He helped me stand. "Let's go get you a hoodie."

Dressed in a pair of black jeans, a green flannel shirt, and the jacket I'd left in the car, we drove into town. The rain stopped, so we strolled along the promenade by the beach before he led me across the street to a row of stores with a rack of red sweatshirts in the front window. We emerged with my hoodie, and a hat with a large crab on top that I insisted he buy.

A round of bumper cars followed with Caleb swearing the reason he got stuck in the corner was because the cars were too small to accommodate his longer legs. Unsympathetic, I told him he had to wear the crab hat as an added insult to the loss. His sullen mood improved after two scoops from the ice cream parlor around the corner. As we sat on a bench to eat our treats, I leaned my head on his shoulder.

If I could put my finger on the moment his mood changed, it was after we kissed on the bench. His body tensed for a fraction of a second and his eyes moved to something over my shoulder, but there was nothing when I turned around. I studied his face, but it stayed stubbornly blank.

"I think I saw an arcade by the kite store," he said. "Let's go check it out."

His arm around my lower back was firmer than earlier as we continued to our destination and his demeanor sharpened. I caught him scanning our surroundings more than once, but he stayed mute. After playing several games, his heightened awareness caused my own alarm bells to clang.

After a round of air hockey where he watched the snack bar more than the puck, I'd had enough. "Why are you so distracted?"

"Sorry. All this talk about the storm has me keeping an eye outside." His gaze stayed fixed on something in the distance.

We cashed in our tickets for a small plush whale, which I joked would look adorable in his office. As we passed a candy store that claimed to have the largest selection of saltwater taffy, I dragged him inside. Memories of my dad's obsession with the green and yellow candies drew me to fill a bag with both flavors. When we lugged all our purchases back to his car, I had way more candy than any rational person could eat.

He drove up a winding hill and parked in front of a restaurant on a cliff. The clouds were dark gray, black in the distance, and the wind masked the roar of the waves below. His hand clutched mine as we walked inside and got a booth with windows overlooking the water. Our conversation was relaxed after we ordered appetizers and drinks. He'd almost returned to normal.

Almost.

"We need to go," he barked, shattering the comfortable silence. The edge to his voice chilled my skin. What was going on?

"What? Why?"

"The wind's getting pretty wild out there. I want to get us back to the house before things get worse."

"I'm sure it'll be okay long enough—"

My words were lost when he motioned to the waiter and asked for our order to be boxed up. He was less than thrilled to hear it would take five minutes, and even more annoyed when I said that gave me plenty of time to visit the restroom before we left.

"Stay," he ordered, grabbing my elbow. "I mean, can it wait?"

Refusing to wince at his fingers digging into my skin, I tried to pull my arm away. "Take your hand off me. Right. Now."

His eyes followed me through the bar and I felt instant relief once the lock clicked. What the hell was he running from? Was it the same threat that spooked him outside the ice cream shop? I cursed myself for not bringing my gun, but there was nowhere to hide it since my purse was so damn small. Washing my hands, I decided to try and find the source of his stress on my own. Otherwise, he owed me one hell of an explanation once we got back to the rental.

Trying to look for suspicious people in a bar full of tourists on a Saturday night proved to be impossible, especially when everyone was watching a raucous basketball game. I bumped into several patrons on my way back to the table and found Caleb looking like he was about to explode.

"Let's go." The grip on my hand was tight as he led me to the exit. Several people watched us, drawing even more attention to our retreat.

I tried to jerk my arm free as soon as we were outside. "What the hell is your problem?" I yelled over the wind.

"Later." He shoved me into the passenger seat and raced around to his side.

The tension in the air made it impossible for me to focus. Refusing to acknowledge both his existence and the angry tears in my eyes, I watched the scenery fly by in the dark as he drove like a bat out of hell. He parked in the driveway but remained at the wheel until I finally looked at him. His jaw was tight, but his eyes weren't angry. His face was uneasy as he took the food bag from my lap.

"Let's go inside." His voice was barely a whisper.

"Only if you're planning to give me a damn good explanation for what just happened. Because I'm about to call Nicole and ask her to drive out here in a storm and take me back to Portland," I snapped before grabbing my bags from the back and storming up to the front porch.

A steady flow of curse words erupted from his mouth until he got to the door. After damn near breaking off the knob, he wrenched it open and stomped inside. He lowered his head and gripped the back of the armchair while I headed toward the kitchen. I'd just passed the dining area when his keys sailed past my head and hit the wall, followed by an angry yell from behind. Heart hammering, I whirled around and met his wide-eyed gaze.

"Fuck, I'm sorry. I didn't mean—"

I set them on the counter without a word. He raced toward me with his hand extended, but I raised mine and stepped back. "I'm not going to freak out over you throwing your keys, but I want to know why the hell you've been acting so strange today. We both know it isn't because of the weather, and it's insulting that you think I'd believe that."

"I... I can't even begin to tell you how sorry I am for today. As for what's going on, I can't really explain it. Something doesn't feel right to me."

"Explaining by saying that you can't explain won't cut it. In fact, if I didn't know better, I'd swear you didn't want to be seen with me. That's the only thing I can think of. So, who is she? Another campus conquest?"

"No!" He slapped his palm on the counter. "That's not it at all. I just... I can't," he broke off and took a deep breath. "I can't tell you."

"More like won't," I sighed, shaking my head. "I don't know what more to say if you won't tell me the truth."

"I wish I could explain."

"Yeah, me too." I dug through the drawers, found a fork, and then grabbed my food container. "I don't know what your plans are, but I'm going to eat my food and listen to the storm. There's four other bedrooms you can occupy. Cheers."

I grabbed my bags and stomped upstairs. He tried to follow me but stopped after the look I shot him. Once I got to the room, I tossed my hoodie in the corner and put my bag of candy next to the bed. After tripping over his bag, I grabbed his toiletries from the ensuite and tossed everything in the hall. With a smile on my face when I heard it fall down the stairs, I slammed and locked the door.

The trees bent and bowed to the wind as rain lashed the windows. From my view I saw plenty of branches and other debris fly by the light posts near the beach. I turned off the lights and watched the ocean churn and crash against the cliffs. The tide was higher, looking as if the sand had been swallowed up. Taking a seat in the bay window, I opened the styrofoam container in my lap and ate my fish and chips, annoyed that my potato wedges were cold.

Pro tip: warm up your food before storming upstairs.

I also realized I'd slammed the door before grabbing towels from the linen closet in the hall. Padding across the floor, I made my way to my destination. I headed back to the room but stopped when Caleb's voice filtered upstairs.

"Fuck, man, I don't know what to do. She locked herself in the bedroom."

Who was he talking to? What part did this person play in today's events? Was I in danger? I rubbed my throbbing temples and grabbed my knapsack before heading into the bathroom, locking the door.

After taking a couple painkillers, I sat on the edge of the clawfoot tub for a time to try to make sense of it all before turning on the taps.

Outside, the wind wailed like a banshee. I sank into the steaming hot water and sighed as I pondered an explanation for his... fear? Paranoia? There was someone he had to have seen in both locations that set him off. Who? My secret agent intuition told me it was connected to the family, but I hadn't heard of anyone in the area.

I forced myself to think of every single possibility, but the voice that had been whispering in the background grew louder with each passing minute. Slowly climbing out and toweling off, it wasn't until I looked at my reflection in the mirror that I acknowledged it.

It hurt that he couldn't even come up with a convincing lie to explain his behavior. That it was just easier to push me around physically and verbally. Scoffing, I turned away from the mirror. I was no better. How many lies did I spew each day? After brushing my teeth and changing into pajamas, I stared at myself in the mirror. I needed to stop wasting my time with guilt and wounded pride. Who the hell was I? I was the federal agent investigating the moody prick downstairs, I reminded myself. There was no room for something like hurt feelings.

I looked at the bed we'd joked about a few hours earlier, and my resolve and remaining energy abandoned me. My body felt like it was made of lead as I crawled under the covers. The mattress was like a cloud and the blankets felt heavenly. We'd found the perfect bed for the night he'd planned for us. A night that was ruined. I swiped the annoying moisture from my eyes before curling into a ball. The last sound I heard was the bellow of the waves before another gust of wind drowned them out.

My eyes snapped open when the bed dipped and relaxed only slightly at his familiar scent. When he placed his hand on my back, I tensed. Of course he had a goddamned key for the door.

"Jess?" His voice was low, soothing. "Baby, I'm so, so sorry."

I shut my eyes tight, but not enough to keep the fresh wave of tears from falling. Groaning, I rolled away. His arm curled around and held me close to him like it did every night. I cursed my traitorous body for relaxing against his but refused to react when he pressed a kiss to my shoulder. I went to sleep, relieved the miserable night was finally at an end.

The next morning, my eyes felt like they were full of sand. Tears and contact lenses never mixed well, I reminded myself as I tried to blink away the salt and grit. The light in the room was muted thanks to the gray skies I saw through the windows. I shifted to get a better look until his arms tightened, imprisoning me.

"Bathroom," I muttered, pushing against him.

Once I was free, his hand splayed over my pillow. I studied his face, wondering why it looked so troubled. He mumbled and his brows creased briefly before calming. I crept to my knapsack and grabbed a change of clothes before heading to the bathroom.

The cool water soothed my eyes but did nothing for my scattered emotions. I dressed on autopilot, pulling on a pair of sweatpants and a t-shirt. To my relief, he was still asleep when I returned so I grabbed my hoodie and crept to the stairs. He'd picked up his bag and the stairs were immaculate. I glanced at the coffeemaker, desperate for a cup, but resisted since the smell would no doubt wake him. I wasn't ready to deal with another strained conversation just then.

Instead, I put on my shoes and went through the French doors in the dining room. The wind was gone, and a heavy mist hung in the air. Twigs, leaves, and even strips of seaweed littered the porch. I kicked a tangle of weeds and brush from the steps and made my way to the stone path.

The sand was a mosaic of rocks and broken shells as the now calm water lapped against the shore. I watched the seagulls comb through the bits as I hopped and climbed around the obstacles until my destination was in sight. The large rock was covered in long strands of kelp and several chunks of wood, which I spent several minutes clearing away before climbing on top.

I inhaled deeply, letting the salt air fill my lungs, and let it out. Closing my eyes, I let the sounds of the wind and water filter through and calm the internal battle that now raged in my head. Caleb saw at least one person who spooked him, and I intended to get to the bottom of it. I still needed to figure out how to get the info without arousing any suspicion, but the choice was clear.

Despite my resolve, there was a part of me that felt like I was betraying him. There was bound to be an explanation for what I discovered, but it was a lead I had to follow. The fact it felt like I was wronging him bothered me, posing a hard question to my conscience. A lead was a step closer to bringing my parents' killer to justice. Why should it matter if it put him in a difficult position?

"Jessica!"

I turned and Caleb was running toward me with a frantic look in his eyes. My head swiveled back toward the water and my fingers played with the metal ties on my hoodie. His steps slowed and stopped a foot to my right, close enough to touch but he hesitated.

"Hey." His voice sounded shaky.

"Hey."

"I was going to make you breakfast in bed, but that's hard to do when you're not in bed."

"I didn't fulfill my end of the deal."

"Look at me," he begged. He placed an arm on my shoulder, but my back remained rigid even after I saw the turmoil in his eyes. "I woke up, and you were gone."

"Sorry. I was restless, so I came out here to think."

"About?"

I rose to my feet, stepping to the side to keep the rock between us. "Whether I'm in too deep for my own good."

He held out his hand, and after a moment I allowed his fingers to twine with my own. My tense shoulders showed him that an arm around me was a step too far. He squeezed my hand as we headed toward the stairs, which made my chest ache and throb. With each step on the cold concrete, the truth of my situation was clear. I wasn't just in too deep, I was drowning and had to figure a way to pull myself out before it was too late.

Chapter Twenty-One

The Assignment

MY PHONE LET OUT a long buzz and moved across the table. I checked the display and placed it face down on the towel next to me. It was the fourth call from Caleb that afternoon, and the fourth one that was ignored. After another drink of coffee, I rolled my neck and turned back to the chapter detailing Oregon's path to statehood, promising myself a break after I finished.

Two days had passed since the weekend of disaster. After our conversation on the beach and a tense breakfast, the drive back to Portland was silent but filled with plenty of unspoken accusations. I kept my face staring out the window and refused to acknowledge his presence. Not even waiting for him to drop me off near campus, I hopped out of his car near a grocery store while he was stopped at a traffic light. The last words we exchanged were my mumbled thanks and him shouting my name as I slammed the door behind me.

Closing the book, I leaned back in the chair and yawned. Sleep had been scarce, and I was too stubborn to admit it was because of him. That said, there was only so much coffee a human should drink before their heart rate and blood pressure hit an unhealthy level. My stomach rumbled, and I went to the kitchen. At least my appetite was handling this upheaval just fine.

Another call came as I scooped spoonfuls of cold mashed potatoes into my mouth. Rolling my eyes, I pressed the decline button and glared at the voicemail notification that popped up. Oh goody. I put the message on speakerphone and resumed eating.

"Jessica, it's Caleb. If I don't hear from you in the next hour, I'm coming over there and pounding on your door until you answer. I don't give a shit who sees. Call me."

No matter how badly I wanted to keep a distance and squelch my feelings for him, I had to put on my big girl panties and get back to work. I put the first part of my plan in motion that morning with a call to the Portland field office and a request for the records of the three cell phones I found in his bedroom. It was pure chance I made the discovery before the trip, and after overhearing part of his conversation that night, it was a decision I struggled with. I knew I'd made the right choice, but that didn't make it feel like I'd betrayed him any less.

He called again, and I checked the time. Fifty minutes. "Hello, Professor."

"Jess, hi." He sounded surprised. "Are you okay?"

"I'm fine. Busy with assignments. Is there something you need?"

"I need to see you."

"I don't think that's a good idea."

"We have class business to discuss, so yes, it's a good idea. And mandatory. I expect you in the office by nine tomorrow morning." His voice was hard, authoritative.

"As you wish," I replied and ended the call.

I scrolled through the pictures on my phone, avoiding all images with him. My heart hammered in my chest, but there was no going back. Once the pictures were sent, I dialed.

Barton answered on the second ring. "What's up?"

Our conversations were strained when I first came back from medical leave and had only slightly improved in the past couple weeks. Before I was cleared to return to duty, we had a lengthy talk and put our issues aside for the good of the case. I still suspected he was withholding information but couldn't prove it. Until then, I had no choice but to rely on him and the Portland office.

"I just e-mailed you several pictures. I need you to run them through facial recognition."

"Why? What's going on?"

"I know you ran checks on the other TAs in the program, but I'm guessing you didn't run them through facial recognition?"

"We did. The results were inconclusive." He paused. "Why?"

"We've fallen into a rut again. I'm just trying to see what I can dredge up. You'll be receiving a package from Field Post tomorrow morning with a few items to have the fingerprints checked."

"I'm guessing that's also why you're going after his phone records?"

Shit, nothing got past him. I'd routed the request through Portland because I was afraid he'd ask how I found the phones. Explaining that Caleb kept the phones in the same drawer as his condoms was the last thing I wanted to do.

"Yes and no. There were multiple cell phones in a drawer in his office, which I found odd."

"It's definitely strange," he agreed, but then his voice sharpened. "Is there a reason you're not asking Portland to run the prints and faces? They'd be able to get it to you quicker."

"Portland is running the prints too, but I was hoping you could get McCray to run the faces since I'm guessing she wasn't around to do it the first time?"

Mia McCray was one of the top forensic technicians in D.C. who was an expert in facial recognition. She'd been a consultant and developed two software platforms, including the program recently deployed by Interpol. She'd been on maternity leave when I left for Portland. The original analysis was good, but I needed the best.

"Yeah, she was still out when we ran everything the first time. Anything else going on? Tell me you're being careful."

"Who, me? I'm always careful. Have you heard anything from your friends across the Potomac?"

"Not a thing. Felton's off the grid back in Italy and Ginnie didn't have any intel."

Felton made good on his promise to keep in touch, but that wasn't saying much. He sent at least one message every two to three days but offered nothing more than microscopic crumbs of information. His most recent passage led me to believe he was back in Italy, but for all I knew he was guzzling limoncello at the cafe a few blocks from his house.

"I guess no news is good news," I sighed. "There isn't anything noteworthy other than these phones and a simple curiosity. Like I said, both could be nothing, but we won't know until we check."

"Your intuition has a habit of being pretty dead-on, so I'm not going to question it. I can't guarantee results this week because of the holiday, so try to be patient. Don't go doing anything crazy."

"Wouldn't dream of it," I quipped and hung up.

• • • ● • ◆ • ● • • •

I strolled into the office at two minutes to nine the next morning with two drinks and a bag of pastries for Nicole and me. No classes were scheduled as it was the day before Thanksgiving, but the plan was to work until noon to get caught up on all assignments and grades to prepare for the last stretch before finals. We grabbed a stack of essays and I'd just read the front page of my first when the door behind me swung open.

"Ms. Ross, can I have a word, please?"

Nicole raised her eyebrows at my blank face as I stood and grabbed my coffee cup. Taking a slow sip, I ignored the flare of his nostrils and took my time crossing the room. His fingers were white as they gripped the door. Once I finally crossed the threshold into his office he tried not to slam it shut.

"Please take a seat." The iron in his voice was unmistakable.

"I'll stand, thanks. You said we had class business to discuss?"

He pursed his lips and stalked behind his desk. "It's your turn to lecture a class. I have you scheduled for this coming Monday for the mafia class. Is that enough time for you to prepare?"

"Yes, that should be fine."

He handed me a folder from the stack on his desk. "Here's the topic and some of the research. You know the drill."

"Thanks. I'll make sure it doesn't suck." I headed for the door.

"Jess?"

His voice was soft, disarming. I took a deep breath before turning around, which did nothing to calm the butterflies in my stomach. His eyes met mine, and I realized the dark circles underneath mirrored my own. Just then I wanted nothing more than to crash into his arms and ignore it all: the case, the bullshit, all of it.

"Yes, Professor?"

"I fucked up, and I'm sorry. I owe you an explanation. Can you please come over tonight and hear me out?"

I mentally cursed the pressure behind my eyes. "You had your chance to explain, and you said you couldn't. What's changed in three days?"

"Not falling asleep with you in my arms. Not waking up with you," he answered in a gruff voice. "You want to know what's changed? The idea of losing you."

A sharp inhale escaped my throat as a knot dropped into my stomach. He stepped forward but stopped when I shook my head. I blew out a slow breath, thankful for the ability to calm my emotions. Most of the time.

"I'll give you an hour," I said and left the room without another word.

• • • • • • • • • •

The smell of basil filled the hallway when I got to his place later that evening. I stuffed my hands into the pockets of my jeans to keep from tracing them over the dark gray thermal shirt stretched across his chest. My eyes sought his, and he smiled.

He opened the door wider to let me pass. "Hey."

"Hey."

He bent down to give me a kiss, but I deflected, and it landed on my forehead. Sidestepping his arms, I moved through the door and stopped at the kitchen island. He caressed my lower back as he rounded the corner, and tried to take both my hands in his, only for me to place them flat on the surface.

"You want some dinner? I made chicken and pesto noodles."

"No thanks. Look, you told me you'd explain yourself if I came over so here I am."

"Right to the point as usual." He paused and took a deep breath. "Do you remember when I said I owed money to some people who were less than reputable?"

I groaned inwardly and prepared to hear another tall tale. "Yes, and you said it had been taken care of. In fact, you were adamant about it."

"I didn't lie. I paid them back and then some. So you can imagine how concerning it was when I saw a guy that looked just like their enforcer when we were walking around on Saturday."

What the hell? Alarm bells blared in my head. I'd taken the whole gambling story with a grain of salt, but there was someone in that city who scared him. Thinking back, I remembered how closely he watched me and our surroundings at the arcade. I knew him well enough after the past few weeks to know for certain that none of it was an act.

"Are you sure it was him? And what about the restaurant? I thought we were having a wonderful time and then you turned into this crazed lunatic."

His eyes went to the floor. "That was me being a fucking idiot. A couple guys at the bar were watching you way too close for my liking. I was already keyed up and paranoid because of earlier, and I knew if we'd stayed, I would've made a bigger fool of myself than I already did that night."

I glanced at the dark gray countertop and wished I'd picked another spot that didn't hold such vivid memories. Without a word, I moved to the armchair in the living room. Leaning my head back, I said nothing until he crouched next to the chair. At the feel of his hand caressing my cheek, I turned and saw the unease on his face.

"What was the first thing I said to you when you told me you wanted to see where this goes?" I murmured.

"No lies."

"No lies," I echoed. "You could've just told me the truth that night. I wouldn't have judged you. It's not like I didn't already know."

The hypocrisy wasn't lost on me, and I felt like absolute shit. Here I was throwing that promise back in his face, and almost every word out of my mouth from the moment we'd met was no less false. As we watched each other in silence, the fact it bothered me wasn't a good sign. How much farther into this hole would I go to see this through to the end?

He took my hand in his. "I didn't want to tell you because you've already been on the wrong side of these people. That night in the office still haunts me."

I said nothing. This was my chance to walk away. I was positive the items sent in for analysis would reveal something that would turn the case around. The dangerous game I was playing would end with minimal atonement for my lies. When I turned and looked into his eyes, however, I knew the hole was only going to get deeper.

"Me too," I rasped. There were still nights I woke up in the dark and felt eyes watching my every move. On more than one occasion, he'd held me in his arms and helped chase those dreams away.

He held out his hands to help me stand. My arms wrapped around his shoulders when he crouched down and laid his head against my stomach. After several minutes, my fingers twined through his hair. He exhaled slowly and placed his hand on my hip.

His eyes were hopeful when he looked up. "Stay with me tonight?"

"I would, but I still need to get caught up on my other classes. On top of that, someone assigned me a lecture to give on Monday. And don't you need to be at Dr. Wheeler's place early?"

The History Department chair invited Caleb and a few other people with no plans for the holiday to his house. I'd already committed to spending the day at Jake and Sami's before we started seeing each other. Canceling wasn't a possibility, mostly because of Jake's immediate suspicions, but I also hadn't seen either of them in a while and wanted to celebrate their engagement and pregnancy.

"I can show up late. Grab your stuff and work on it over here."

I was close to caving but had to hold firm if for no other reason than to prove it to myself. Being away from him and his touch for three days was painful, making me realize how deeply I'd fallen for him.

Christ, the whole situation was well and truly fucked. All I could hope for was the end to come quickly, even if my heart would be ripped out in the process.

"The more I get done tonight and tomorrow means less time spent on it this weekend," I pointed out.

"Hey." He stood and kissed my forehead. "Are you okay? Are we okay?"

I wrapped my arms around his neck and pulled him closer, inhaling his scent. "We're fine. I just have a ton of work to get done before I can play. But I promise to come over Friday night. Deal?"

"Sorry for pushing. I've just really missed you."

"I've missed you, too." The lump in my throat grew.

"Get your work done so I can have you all to myself Friday." He pressed his lips to mine. "And all weekend."

After several kisses and promises that everything was fine, I left. Arriving back to my place with several cartons of food, I moved everything to the couch and changed. Now dressed in sweats, I grabbed the folder.

My topic was The Westies, considered the last Irish gang in New York City. After several high-profile raids, the government all but obliterated the group in the late 1980s. At the height of their glory, they were known for racketeering, illegal gambling and contract killing. They eventually partnered with the five mafia families, but not before engaging in a bloody rivalry with the Genovese in the late 1970s.

I thumbed through the articles in the folder, arranging them in chronological order. With a mozzarella stick in my mouth, I went through the pictures until the fourth image shocked me so much I choked. After several drinks of water, the coughing stopped.

My hands shook as I examined the picture, trying to stop my chest from tightening. I didn't recognize the people loading boxes into a white van, but the man walking out of the warehouse was forever etched in my memory. The old green jacket, the messy dark brown hair and pale blue eyes, the smirk coupled with the cigarette dangling from his mouth. It was the face of my father, Seamus Donovan.

Chapter Twenty-Two

Hard Truth

I STARED AT THE picture, dumbstruck. My dad informed on the Sardi family gun deals to the CIA, but his own involvement in the Irish mob was news to me. How the hell was he never arrested? Did he rat out his own gang?

My laptop was on and logged into the FBI database within minutes, searching for his file. It took some time thanks to the remote connection but then a single line appeared in the results. I hesitated, unsure if I wanted to see where this new rabbit hole led. When the screen dimmed, I prepared myself for the worst and clicked on the link.

NAME: Donovan, Seamus Conor

MARITAL STATUS: M (Morello Donovan, Serafina Lacole)

CHILDREN: Donovan, Larissa Ann

OCCUPATION: RESTRICTED

KNOWN ASSOCIATES: RESTRICTED

The file was a sea of black bars and the word "RESTRICTED." My security login was rejected, causing me to click on the restriction code for more information. The added layer of security was ordered and authorized by Lawrence Sullivan from the CIA. The name didn't ring any bells, and a search of the directory showed he'd retired almost five years earlier.

I clicked on my name and viewed my birth certificate, impressed that neither the Department of Justice nor the Department of Defense detected it was fake. My real birth certificate was a mythical document, one I'd never seen. Before my parents died, I overheard my dad tell Uncle Cal he'd used "the Irish one" to register me for school and nobody had been the wiser. It was strange to me that my dad wanted people to think I was born in Ireland rather than New York City, but he was adamant that it stayed a secret and said he'd explain when I was older.

The document didn't come up again until I was getting ready to enlist in the Marines. Felton came home in a panic, asking a million questions about my birthplace and my original certificate. After twelve years, I barely remembered the strange middle name my parents yelled when I got in trouble. He'd ground his teeth when I told him about the conversation with Cal and then shut himself in his office for several hours. Not long after, he brought home a new certificate, one that said I was born in Fairfax, Virginia and my middle name was Ann. He was quick to point out we'd both go to prison if it was ever discovered that neither were true.

Distrust churned in my stomach. The file wasn't fully blocked, which meant Barton knew. Did he know what hid under the bars and restricted access? My knuckles were white as I dialed. It didn't matter that it was after midnight in D.C. I needed some goddamned answers.

His voice was heavy with sleep. "Lissa?"

"How long did you know my father was in the fucking mob?"

He sighed. "This wasn't the way you were supposed to find out."

"And how the fuck was I supposed to find out? I'm guessing the fact his file was sealed a month before I joined the CIA isn't a coincidence."

"It was a condition of the agreement between the agencies when the Asset program was reinstated. And I'll be the asshole and admit I was the one who insisted on it."

"You've read it?"

"No, but I knew the temptation would be too great for anyone to resist. I can tell you that the director read it and had concerns you could be compromised by your dad's former associates. Felton plead your case. Since he raised you, he could prove you never had contact with anyone connected to your parents. He also told us that by the time the feds were building the case that brought the Westies down, Seamus was looking for a way out."

"Why?"

"He had a wife and daughter and wanted to make sure he made it home to the two of you each night. The FBI already had plenty on the Irish, so he agreed to pass along information on the Italians to the CIA. How did you find out?"

My eyes watered as I held up the picture. "The lecture I'm giving on Monday is on my dad's old gang. There's a picture of him in the reference materials."

"How much info were you able to view? As I understand it, most of it's redacted."

"Nothing I didn't already know." Enough to make the pain in my chest almost unbearable.

"Listen to me carefully." His voice was calm, and I knew his next words would not be what I wanted to hear. "I know you're going to call Felton and rip him a new one. And I agree you should; he should have told you a long time ago. But this is where I point out that this wasn't his case."

"You and I both know what a slippery son of a bitch Felton is. You don't believe any more than I do that he hasn't seen this file in its entirety. And how is this the one time you defend him?"

"I'm not, and I'm not saying any of this for his benefit. I'm saying it for yours. You're knee deep in a case, and all it will do right now is distract you if you scream at him and let it run wild in your head."

"You say that like I don't have other things going on that aren't a distraction," I blurted out. At the realization of my words, I hung up before he could respond.

After several deep breaths, I called the phone number I'd dialed less than five times in my life. A secure message would've sufficed, but I wasn't in the mood for secret codes and black bag bullshit. After four rings, Felton's stern voice introduced himself in Irish and directed callers to leave a message.

"I just saw my dad's FBI file. Call me."

He'd call me back, I told myself, and there'd be a reason he'd kept it from me. Their murders were no secret, so there was bound to be a logical explanation. He knew I was no shrinking violet, though my current emotional entanglements made me question that more than once over the past couple weeks.

Curious, I typed my mom's name into the database. The screen turned red and a message in all caps telling me access to the file was denied. My heart sank when I saw the CX denial code. All information about Serafina Morello came from the CIA, who had restricted her file. I'd officially hit a dead end.

No longer angry, fatigue set in and I yawned. I stacked everything in a pile, keeping the picture of my dad on top, before shuffling to my room. My phone buzzed, startling me. Part of me was relieved it wasn't Felton. I had no energy just then for the confrontation. Instead, my lips stretched into a smile at the text message.

CALEB: Waiting until Friday is torture.

ME: No, torture is poor Jake having to listen to me practice this lecture.

CALEB: Ha. I'm sure he'll survive.

ME: And I'm sure you can survive, too.

CALEB: Just gives me more time to think of all the naughty things I'm going to do to you.

ME: Good night. Looking forward to Friday.

CALEB: Me too. Good night.

The feelings of warmth were unavoidable as I put the phone away and snuggled under the covers. My emotions ran the gamut that day, and while things between the two of us weren't fully on solid ground, being with him for whatever amount of time was left was something to look forward to.

• • • • • • • • • •

Caleb rubbed my arm. "Everything okay?"

Thanksgiving was a productive and eye-opening day. I woke up to an e-mail from the Portland office. The three phones I found in his drawer were disposables bought just across the Oregon border in Vancouver, Washington. One phone had yet to be used while a second called and received three calls from phone numbers traced to disposables phones bought in Detroit.

The last one called a satellite number near Verona every few days and received a call from the same number every Monday night, which was the same night I slept at my place because of an early class the following morning. He'd mentioned having family in Italy, which led to a new set of questions I wasn't sure I wanted answered.

"Yeah, sorry. My mind's just elsewhere right now."

"Everything okay?"

My dad was a mobster, my mom had a secret CIA file, my guardian and sometimes boss was MIA, and my professor who I was investigating and banging made mysterious phone calls to Italy on the regular. Nothing was okay.

I leaned against him, letting his scent calm me. "It's better now."

It wasn't a lie. I'd felt content from the moment he pulled me into his arms when I arrived. If I hadn't needed more proof just how much I'd fallen for him, all doubt was erased. He eyed my purple tulle maxi skirt and cropped black sweater and grinned. After a kiss that made me want to rip his clothes off and repeat our first night together, he held me close and whispered how much he'd missed me. We then settled on the couch for a candlelit dinner and a basketball game on TV.

He kissed my temple. "I know we agreed not to talk about school, but if you're nervous about Monday, I'm willing to bend that rule."

"You? Bend the rules? That would be a first."

"Smartass," he retorted, motioning me to move closer.

I gathered my skirt and crawled into his lap, straddling him. "Maybe I'm a little nervous."

"I'm sure we can think of other ways to take your mind off it."

"Something tells me you have plenty of ideas all on your own. You and that one-track mind of yours."

"I haven't felt your skin against mine for almost a week." His hands slid down and stopped at my hips. "All I've had is my filthy, one-track mind to get me through."

My lips brushed against his, igniting my blood with the simple touch. I cupped his face with both hands and kissed him long and deep. A hungry groan erupted from his throat before he crushed my body to his. I moved to his jawline and kissed lightly along the stubble as his hands gripped me tighter.

"God, this week without you was hell," he breathed.

"It was for me too," I admitted. Being away from him cast a pall that left the world dark and colorless. My face hovered above his, and the words tumbled from my lips before I could stop them. "Let's never do that again."

He pulled my sweater over my head and trailed kisses across my collarbone. I gasped and then let out a soft moan when his teeth grazed my neck. My skin was on fire and a dull ache sparked between my legs. His eyes blazed with desire. I held his gaze and slowly moved my hips. A low sound came from his lips before they slammed against mine.

My bra unclasped, and the straps fell down my arms. He tossed it aside and cupped one breast, filling his hand. My nipples puckered at the heated gaze he gave me before moving his mouth lower. He suckled for several minutes before grazing it with his teeth. I moaned loudly and ran my fingers through his hair. When he turned his attention to the other nipple, I rubbed my aching pussy against his cock, which strained against the zipper of his jeans.

He gripped my ass and sat up. "Not wearing any panties when I haven't been inside you for a week is dangerous. I think it's time I take you upstairs and bury my face in that sweet little pussy of yours until you beg me to let you come."

Heat flooded between my legs. I wrapped my arms around his neck as he stood and carried me up the stairs. He tossed a pillow in the middle of the bed before setting me down at the edge.

"Head on the pillow," he commanded before pulling his dark blue sweater over his head. "And hands above your head."

I complied but wanted to throw the damn thing in his face when he grinned at my obvious confusion. He stripped off his jeans, leaving him in black boxer briefs that did nothing to hide the massive cock inside that threatened to peek over the waistband.

"Fuck," I whispered.

"All in good time." He crawled onto the bed and took both my hands in his. "So to answer the question you haven't asked yet, we both know how well you direct me when I'm... tasting you. But you're not in charge tonight. I am, and you don't get to come until I say so," he paused and kissed the back of each hand. "I know you're not a fan of having your hands tied, so be a good girl and keep them above your head. It would be a shame if you were naughty and had to go to bed with no dessert."

I swallowed and extended my arms as far as was comfortable. "Yes, sir."

He lifted my skirt as if unwrapping a present, smiling when the last layer exposed my bare skin to the cool air. I shivered as he settled between my legs. He gently spread them wider and kissed the top of each inner thigh before pressing a chaste kiss above my clit.

"Look at me," his husky voice commanded.

I watched as he closed his lips around my inner folds and sucked. Gasping, my head rolled back when my body shuddered. He alternated between slow licks and suckling the sensitive flesh several times before moving lower and thrusting his tongue deep into my entrance. I moaned and my hand flew toward his hair. His eyes narrowed and his movements slowed until it returned to the original position.

"Good girl."

"Evil man," I panted.

He slid a finger inside, thrusting it slowly while sucking my swollen nub into his mouth. The pressure built and my grasp of coherent thought and language skills evaporated. I arched my back and yelled out several expletives and mumbled words. His finger stilled, but I bucked my hips against his hand, desperate for more friction.

He gave my clit one last teasing lick and removed his hand. "Not so fast."

"Can't blame a girl for trying."

He slid the skirt down my legs and tossed it on the floor before grabbing a condom from the drawer. After placing a kiss just above my belly button, his lips traveled north until they closed around my left nipple and sucked. He rubbed the other nipple with his thumb, flooding my already desperate pussy with more heat.

My hand gripped the sheet as his tongue continued its torture. "Caleb."

He latched onto the right nipple before meeting my gaze and raising his eyebrows. I squeezed my legs together and squirmed to ease the ache between them. Releasing my nipple, he removed his boxer briefs. His cock looked painfully swollen and absolutely mouth-watering.

"Is this what you want?" He stroked himself before sliding the condom down his shaft.

"Please," I whined. "I need you inside me right now."

He hooked my legs over his arms and sank in deep. We both moaned as he eased back and thrust hard several times. I rocked my hips against his, only for him to slow his pace. He shifted our bodies to a different angle, which felt divine. My head rolled back as he teased the spot that I was desperate for him to touch. He released one leg to tease just above my clit but stopped when I tried to sit up. I let out a frustrated groan and flopped back on the bed.

The smug bastard let out a breathy chuckle. "What's the matter, baby?"

"Please. I—," I lost my thought when he rolled his hips.

"What was that?"

"Caleb, please." I hated the need in my voice. "I need to come."

"Your wish is my command."

Caressing my leg, he leaned it against his shoulder and slammed his body against mine. My skin ignited as his free hand kneaded my breasts before moving lower. I sat up, leaning back on my hands, and when his finger flicked my clit, my eyes rolled back. My hips met each of his thrusts as the room filled with the sounds of our breathless moans and bodies colliding.

"Don't you dare fucking stop," I cried.

Mindless from the pressure coiling deep inside, I moaned his name over and over. We were both barreling toward our respective climaxes at breakneck speed. I cried out when my orgasm ignited. He slowed his movement as waves of pleasure rocketed through my body. Once my climax slowed, his thrusts increased with a new wave of urgency. With a loud groan he slid out and pulled off the condom, stroking his cock until he covered my stomach and breasts with his cum.

I gasped for air as he pressed a kiss to my forehead and excused himself. He returned with a warm cloth and wiped me clean, kissing my still heated skin with each pass. My body shuddered when his lips touched my nipple, and he smiled before lowering his mouth to it again. Our bodies came together in a frenzy and moments later he was inside me once more.

He laced his fingers with mine and held both hands above my head as we moved together slowly. His lips touched every square inch of my bare skin he could reach. We climaxed together and when my eyes opened, he had an unreadable look on his face. I ran my fingers across his back as we laid there breathless. After a few moments he put his weight on his elbows and gave me another deep kiss. When we broke apart, I saw the same heated look. Lust and desire were there, but something else that I couldn't quite define. Need? Longing? I didn't know, and I wasn't sure I wanted to.

My body felt cold when he rolled away and disposed of the condom. He crawled into bed and tossed the covers over both of us. I wrapped my arm around his waist and hugged him close, placing a kiss on his chest. He ran his fingers through my hair and kissed the top of my head.

The look in his eyes played on an endless loop in my mind and with it a feeling of unease. I was prepared to deal with the fallout when the case ended, no matter how painful. I felt like the most selfish bitch in the world for not considering the hurt and betrayal once he learned of my lies. He meant more to me, more than he should, and the thought of telling him the truth brought a sharp pain to my chest.

"Can we just stay like this forever?" he murmured, kissing my forehead, nose and finally my lips.

"I'd love that." It was the god's honest truth.

His arm moved to my waist and soon his breathing slowed. When he pulled me closer and buried his nose in my hair, the ache in my chest throbbed. It was then that I knew I'd be the one left bleeding on the floor when it all fell apart, and that day was coming sooner rather than later.

Chapter Twenty-Three

Pesky Russian Migraines

MY FEET WERE KILLING me, but I continued to pace across the dais. "The Westies were broken up as a result of the federal raid, but there have been reports in the past few years about renewed activity by the gang. The validity of these claims, however, depends on who you ask. According to the FBI, there are several pending cases against current members, but that remains to be seen. Are there any questions?"

Caleb gave a warm smile from his seat a few rows away where he observed and graded the lecture. He glanced around the room to see if anyone raised their hands. Seeing none, he tapped his pen on the desk and gave me a thumbs up. "All right, if there aren't any questions for Ms. Ross, we'll bring things to a close for today. Just a reminder that the rough draft of your final paper is due next week."

There was a flurry of activity as the students packed up and left. I gathered my papers, allowing time for any stragglers. When nobody sought me out, I cleared the dry erase board and stuffed everything into my bag.

I'd added some little-known facts about the group that I'd gleaned through additional research, and then Jake helped me rehearse on Thanksgiving Day. He asked about my sullen mood during one of our breaks, and it was then that I told him about my dad. We talked through it over a couple beers and way too many snacks. By the time Sami dished up the pumpkin pie, I felt a lot better.

The TAs usually waited for Caleb in case he needed help carrying things back to the office, but students still surrounded him. He shook his head, so I gathered my backpack and headed to the vending machines for a celebratory candy bar. Afterward, I walked into the office and found Rachele rifling through Caleb's desk drawers. When the inner office door closed, she froze and turned around. Her eyes narrowed.

"Hey there," I said as if I hadn't just caught her red handed.

"Jessica." She closed the drawer and stalked toward me, a deadly look on her face.

"I'm just here to drop off a couple things and then I'm off to class. Don't mind me." I breezed past and headed for my desk.

She grabbed me by the shoulder and spun me around. "Leave. Turn around and walk out the door right now. I'd hate for something... bad to happen to you. Again."

"You know, it almost sounds like you're threatening me. But you wouldn't do that. Right?" The smile on my face was pure saccharine. Undercover or not, I refused to let the bitch intimidate me.

With one last glare she pushed past me and left, slamming the door behind her. I exhaled the breath I'd been holding and pulled open the drawer she'd been picking through. To my surprise, two more disposable cell phones were inside. Unsure who or when someone else may arrive, I closed the drawer and exited before anyone caught me.

A direct threat was definitely a "call Barton ASAP" situation, so I headed to my dorm. After no movement on the case, her actions were sudden and alarming. I needed to figure out what the hell was going on. I'd barely closed my door and locked it when my phone rang. To both my relief and dread, it was Barton, hopefully with news that wouldn't make things worse than I feared they were already.

"Lissa," he barked before I had time to speak. "Where are you?"

"My apartment, and I was just about to call you. I caught one of the TAs snooping in Winters's desk. She threatened me when I confronted her but left soon after. I checked the drawer and found two more disposable cell phones."

"Shit. I'm not sure exactly what, but something is brewing. We got most of the facial recognition results back. We're still waiting on one, but what we found already is bad enough."

"How bad?"

"I'll start with the good news. Nicole Turner came back clean. As far as Mia could tell, she's just your average grad student. The guys are a lot more interesting. Karl Fischer, whose real name is Dima Domnikov is a freelance spy who last stole weapons intel for the Chinese. Trevor Grigsby, real name Thomas Scott, is a former MI6 agent who went rogue and disappeared ten months ago. According to Ginnie, the latest CIA chatter had him roaming around South America, but he didn't stick around anywhere for long."

"Jesus. Dare I even ask about Rachele? She's the one I found in his office."

"Mia was hoping to have results back on her by the end of the day, but I'm not waiting. I'm sending Marlowe to escort you to the field office. He's working on a warrant so we can bring Winters in as a material witness."

"Do we have enough?"

"The two incidents you saw should be. Let's just hope finding out multiple spies have infiltrated his class is enough to loosen his lips."

I sat forward and cradled my forehead in my hand. "How the hell did we miss these guys?"

"Like I said, everything came back clean or inconclusive. We had no reason to suspect anything was out of sorts. It's a fuck up and I take responsibility for it. Let's get you out of there so you can kick my ass the next time you see me."

"Yes, because I beat you up on the regular," I quipped, rolling my eyes. "I'll settle for a round of drinks at Lulu's the next time I'm in D.C."

"Deal. Marlowe should be there soon. Sit tight."

Keeping my phone in my hand, I went to my dresser and picked through the plain black jewelry box on top until I found my dad's rosary. The large gold cross decorated with diamonds and one ruby in the center gleamed in my hand. His good luck charm when my mom and I weren't around, he often called it. He hardly ever took it off, keeping it in his pocket when the chain broke a few days before his death. It was because of that I had a love/hate relationship with the damn thing, but in that moment, I needed all the luck to be gathered.

A buzz broke my reverie, and I tossed the new chain over my head before accepting the call. "Hey handsome."

"Why did I come back to an empty office?"

"Sorry about that. My head started pounding about halfway through class, and by the time I got to the office it was a full-blown migraine."

"Are you okay? Do you need anything?"

I sat at the foot of my bed and palmed the cross on my chest. "I'm okay. I'm going to just take it easy and see if it goes away."

"Okay. Let me know if you need anything."

"I will." I ducked my head down and willed my eyes to stop watering. The day I dreaded had arrived.

"Miss you."

"Miss you too."

He ended the call, and I dropped my phone on the bed while wiping the moisture from my eyes. The thought of grabbing the box hidden inside my closet evaporated when a loud knock echoed from the front room. I glanced down at my white blouse and long black skirt and groaned; I hadn't even changed clothes.

Agent Marlowe wasn't alone on the other side of my door. A flash of curly blond hair moved past as he gave a nod and followed at a slower pace. I turned to find a tall, slender woman in a black pantsuit.

She extended her hand and offered a kind smile. "I'm Agent Becky Overland."

"Overland is a recent graduate," he explained. "She's going to stay here and keep the place secure while we go to the field office. Ready?"

After making sure Agent Becky was settled on the couch and flipping through channels, I grabbed my purse hanging on the desk chair and followed Jack to the door. I stepped into the hall just as Nicole rounded the corner from the elevator. Her eyes lit up and her pace toward us quickened.

"I was just about to see if you wanted to go grab a beer to celebrate your lecture, but I see you have plans," she said when she was a few feet away.

"Yeah, sorry about that. I'll need to take a rain check on that one. This is Jack. Jack, this is Nicole, my neighbor."

She beamed as they shook hands. "Pleasure. You better treat Jess right, or you'll have to deal with me. Are we clear?"

"Perfectly clear, ma'am. Now, if you'll excuse us. I owe this lady some dinner."

"Of course. Have fun!"

She caught my eye as I turned toward the hall and mouthed "oh my god." At her thumbs up, I smiled up at Jack as his hand hovered over my lower back. Once the elevator doors closed, I leaned my head against the wall and chuckled.

"She's, uh, energetic," he declared, shaking his head.

"She can be over the top, but she's pretty great. I'm actually going to miss her once this is over."

"Maybe take her up on that beer before you bring Winters in?"

I shook my head. "One outing at a time. Which reminds me, is dinner on my per diem or yours?"

We both laughed and crossed the lobby once the doors opened. What should have been a ten-minute drive to the office took almost half an hour thanks to early afternoon traffic, which only worsened my already frayed nerves. By the time he showed me to a vacant office to do my report, my head really was pounding.

Recounting the case was like trying to cross a minefield. I worded every sentence with care to avoid digging my hole even deeper. Most incidents were already documented, but that didn't stop my stomach from churning as I added the rest. When I finally clicked the button to upload the report to the server, my throat was so dry I guzzled the bottled water on the desk beside me.

The U.S. Attorney found a federal judge to hear the request for a warrant by the end of the day. Jack chattered with her non-stop on his cell phone as he led me back to the parking garage. My heart sank at the text message from Caleb asking how I felt. I ignored the message, choosing instead to enjoy what little time I had left before he learned of my betrayal.

Jack ended the call and pulled off his headset while we were stuck in traffic a block from the building. "Did you want to stop anywhere and grab some food before I take you back to your place? I know this was probably the worst date on record, but it's the least I can do."

"There's a Chinese place in my building. Excellent fried rice if you're interested." My mouth quirked upward. "And the award for my worst date still belongs to the patent lawyer in D.C. who got drunk and challenged our waiter to a fight."

He pursed his lips but was unable to hold back his laughter. In the interest of fairness, he told me his worst date involved a woman who chose the restaurant because she knew her ex-boyfriend would be there with his new girlfriend. The women wound up in a screaming match in the parking lot which later turned into a brawl until the police arrived and arrested them both. He and her ex watched everything from the bar as they bonded over beer and college football. Almost a year later, the two men were still friends.

We parked in the underground garage of my building just as sunset gave way to darkness. Apparently, my stomach recovered from my earlier guilt as it growled loudly when we entered the restaurant. While Jack ordered chicken chow mein, I decided to drown my sorrows in pork fried rice. And crab wontons. And fried chicken skins.

He carried both bags down the hall with his other arm around my shoulders in case Nicole saw us returning. We found Agent Becky sitting on the couch watching some reality show. After exchanging pleasantries, he told me he'd call as soon as he heard about the warrant and they left.

I dragged my food bag with me to the bedroom and ate the wontons and chicken skins before deciding to change out of my clothes. Finally comfortable in my pajamas, I tucked the rosary under my black tank top and devoured the entire box of rice in record time. After cleaning up, I decided to spend the rest of the night on the couch doing as little as possible.

Even though I had no interest in either team, the football game on TV proved to be a welcome distraction. I replied to Caleb's text, telling him I still didn't feel well, which wasn't a lie. When Barton's custom ring tone sounded just before halftime, my heart sank.

"Rachele Tulo's real name is Galina Polakoff. She's with Russian intelligence," he announced.

I rubbed my forehead and groaned, knowing what was next. "Great."

"It gets better. There are rumors Gio is headed stateside, so that could be why she was going through Winters's desk."

"I'm shut down, aren't I?"

"Marlowe just left the courthouse with the warrant so, yes, it's time we brought the esteemed professor in."

My heart collapsed into my chest and I released a shaky breath. "All right."

"Lissa, I know there were times it didn't feel like it, but you worked your ass off on this case. Let's bring it home and see if we can't bring that psychopath down. You should be hearing from Portland soon to work out the logistics. Call me when you have Winters in custody."

"Will do."

We hung up, and I called Marlowe. He gave me an hour to pack up and then rendezvous with the team. The plan was to keep Caleb in a safe house until he could be transported to D.C. When he asked me to accompany the transfer, my mind screamed in protest, but I agreed. My need to see the case through to the end would be worth the heartache, I told myself.

I went to my closet and pressed my thumb against the hidden sensor next to the fake electrical panel. It slid to the right and the four green lights on the outside of the black metal box glowed brightly. I placed the safe on my bed and pressed my finger to the small yellow square. The lid sprang open, revealing two Colt pistols. The black 1911 with custom scrollwork engraved into the slide was a gift from Felton when I graduated from sniper training. I splurged and bought a smaller model with the same scrollwork for my twenty-fifth birthday the previous Christmas.

Packing was a simple task since I only had to grab my knapsack and a few other items. Dressed in jeans and a black t-shirt, I grabbed the wallet at the bottom of the gun safe with my badge and ID with the name Agent Erin King. My secret identities had secret identities I'd always joked. Sadly, it was the only humor I found in the situation. I should have been almost giddy; a material witness was another step toward justice for my parents. Instead, my feet felt glued to the floor and my heart full of dread. Forcing myself to move, I slid both guns into the holsters on my waist and ankle. Grabbing my knapsack, I breezed through my front door without a backward glance.

Two black SUV's and a white cargo van were parked on the fourth floor of the structure across the street from the office. Marlowe came from the passenger side of the SUV parked next to me. I glanced through the window and saw Agent Becky seated behind the wheel. Scolding myself for being so dismissive of her as an agent, I offered a friendly wave.

"I got it," he declared, opening his briefcase. "Actually, two. One to search his office and the other is the material witness warrant. This will force Campus Security to give us access without contacting him."

I nodded as I glanced through the documents in my hand. "What's the plan?"

"Forensics is going to sweep all the vehicles here for tracking or listening devices. From there, we'll move to the office. Do you think you could get him to come here if you called and asked him to?"

"I can say I left one of my textbooks in his office or something." My lips numbed as each word fell out.

His brows creased. "Are you all right?"

"Yeah. I think I'm just coming down with a cold."

Satisfied with my answer he nodded and turned to the other SUV. Both doors opened as if on cue and two men who could've easily played linebackers stepped out.

"Agent King, I'm Agent Jason Waverly," a tall, bulky man with a gray buzz cut said as he offered me his hand. He pointed to the younger man who had the same tall, muscular build but with black hair and gray eyes. "This is Agent Tom Jennings."

"Nice to meet you." I shook both agents' hands before turning to the three people in blue windbreakers.

"Forensics team at your service," the young woman replied. "I'm Sylvia Goodlake, and this is Scott Byers and Ted Walsh."

The techs got to work scanning all three cars, and as soon as they were cleared, we parked outside the building that housed the History Department and all its offices. Jack led our group to the security booth with the search warrant in hand. The guard tried to argue but backed down when I threatened him with an obstruction of justice charge. Once the office was unlocked, Waverly escorted him back to the security booth to keep an eye out for any suspicious activity.

It didn't take long for Sylvia to find a listening device behind the coffee maker. Ted found two more in Caleb's office, which were placed in a cup with the first device and hidden in the refrigerator. She remained with me as I cleaned up my desk while Scott and Ted continued to scan the other desks.

Tom and Jack searched his office, bagging up the cell phones in the drawer and a few flash drives. My heart sank when not one but two pistols were found: one inside a hollowed-out book and the other in the false bottom of a desk drawer. After loading several file folders into an evidence box, it looked like they had plenty to make a case.

"Call him in," Jack instructed as Jennings sealed the box.

My fingers were almost too numb to dial. I sat on the couch in the common area and did my best to look calm. Each ring felt like a small dagger in my skin.

"Hey," he greeted warmly. "How are you feeling?"

I blinked, ignoring the sting in my eyes. "Better. Hey, I'm sorry to ask, but I need a favor. Can you meet me at the office?"

"Why don't you come over here instead? I think a nice quiet night of TV and snuggling is just what the doctor ordered."

"I would, but I'm a dumbass and left my Oregon history book in your office. I'd wait until tomorrow, but I need to get my paper done. How quickly do you think you can get over here?"

"What do you mean 'get over here'?" His voice was sharp. "Are you already there?"

"I knew Security was going to call you anyway, so I headed over and figured I'd call you myself."

"Dammit, Jess, I told you not to go over there alone! Is the guard with you?"

"He got called back to the booth by his commander. I told him I'd call you, and you'd let me in."

He cursed under his breath. "I'll be there in about ten minutes. But you're staying with me tonight. You need to rest, not work on that damn paper all night and make your migraine worse."

"Fine. Just hurry. I'll see you soon," I blurted before hanging up, swallowing down the sob in my throat.

We moved to Caleb's office. The two agents stood like sentries behind the desk and Tom and Sylvia sat down while I paced the floor in front of them. Waverly's text several minutes later alerting us to the professor's arrival broke the oppressive silence in the room. We all exchanged glances and prepared for what came next.

"Jess?" His voice traveled through the outer office. He appeared in the doorway and stilled. "What's going on?"

Exhaling slowly, I moved to the middle of the room. "Caleb, I'd like to introduce you to my associates. We'd like to have a little chat with you."

"About?" His voice softened, almost sounding resigned.

"Giovino Sardi."

Chapter Twenty-Four

Blackout

HE EYED THE TWO agents behind his desk and stepped closer. Tom's hand flew to his holster, but Jack held up his hand and they stilled. I stopped pacing and watched as confusion, followed by annoyance crossed Caleb's face. The tension in the room eased but stayed at an uncomfortable level.

Caleb's mouth curled into a smile that didn't reach his eyes. "Sorry for my lack of manners. When you told me to come down here, I didn't know you'd brought friends." His eyes narrowed. "Let's start with you telling me exactly who I'm speaking to."

"Erin King, FBI. Like I said, we'd like to talk to you about Giovino Sardi."

"So all this time you were nothing but a dirty fed sent to fucking spy on me?"

Jack nodded to both Ted and Sylvia, who left the room. Caleb's mouth curled into a sneer when his eyes scanned my body and stopped on my hoodie. The same green hoodie I'd borrowed from his closet almost twelve hours earlier before kissing him and racing out of his apartment. My stomach felt like I'd swallowed an anvil, but I stood firm and held his gaze until the sound of footsteps broke the silence.

Sylvia set a paper cup on the desk and reached a gloved hand inside. He cursed under his breath when she held up the first listening device. When his mood shifted from anger to unease at the other two, however, my skin prickled. Did he know who they belonged to? What were we missing?

"Judging by the look on your face, I'm guessing you're just as surprised as we were."

"I'm not saying another word to you fucks."

"You don't have to," Jack piped up. "When we executed our search warrant, your office told us plenty. Agent King, I'll let you do the honors."

I grabbed my handcuffs from my belt and shackled his wrist. "Caleb Winters, you're being detained as a material witness. You will be allowed to contact an attorney and request a hearing to seek your release."

"Such a shame we didn't have these cuffs the other night. That would've been hot as hell. Are your friends aware that you're a screamer?"

Once his hands were cuffed in front of him, I pushed him against the side of the desk. "My colleague here is going to scan you for any tracking devices while Agent Jennings conducts a standard pat down. It would be in your best interest to cooperate."

"And who knew you were so bossy, too?" He turned to Tom. "She's the complete opposite when she's begging for my," he broke off and winced when Jennings's finger poked his inner thigh before patting down the leg.

I pursed my lips. "Told you it would be best to cooperate."

When Tom unfastened his belt, he straightened. "I think I'd much rather have Ms. Ross, King, or whatever her name is do that. Lord knows she's a pro."

The smirk on his face disappeared when Sylvia's scanner buzzed over his belt. She held up a small circle before tossing it into the cup with the listening devices. After a few minutes, the scan was complete.

Marlowe led our procession down the hall while Tom and Caleb followed behind. I couldn't blame Ted and Sylvia for not joining us on the elevator ride. It was a tense, awkward endeavor that made me wish I'd taken the stairs. Caleb nodded at the guard and wished him a Merry Christmas as we filed past the booth. When Agent Waverly joined us, he asked who would provide musical entertainment for the evening. I shook my head and remained behind the group until we rounded the corner to our cars.

After a quick discussion about logistics, Jack and Agent Overland left for the field office, and the forensics team drove away. I dragged our witness to the lone SUV that remained, and Jason held open the door to the backseat. His hand hovered over his holster as we moved closer.

Caleb's feet came to a sudden stop. "Listen to me." His voice was low but urgent. "This isn't a threat, it's the truth. You do *not* want to bring me in. I'm *begging* you not to do this."

"Mr. Winters, this is my job. You know some bad people and we need information about them. If you cooperate, you'll be released before you know it."

"You have no idea what you're getting yourself into."

I shoved him into the seat and slammed the door. The tinted windows made it impossible to see inside, but I knew his eyes were on me as the car pulled away. I waited until it rounded the corner before my stomach lurched painfully. The guard in the booth gave me a strange look as I raced to the trash can across from him and retched. My head hung over the filthy cement for several minutes before I felt well enough to stand. Passing by the booth, I gave him a casual nod and walked to my car.

The water bottle in my center console was a godsend. I drained every last drop and tossed it in the back before dialing Barton. Since we detained Caleb without incident, our conversation was brief, and we agreed to talk more in the morning. After shoving two sticks of gum in my mouth, I drove off and a short while later parked around the corner from a small yellow house in the suburbs west of Portland.

"How is he?"

Jason rolled his eyes. "Pissed off. The first thing he told us was he won't speak to anyone unless it's you. Apparently, he also thinks he's a comedian. He then demanded a trial by combat and complained there was no TV in his room. I was just about to grab some food. Did you want anything?"

"Something plain for me. Grab a pepperoni pizza or something for the pain the ass in the other room."

A loud bang against the wall, followed by yelling caused us both to grab our guns. The door behind us opened and Tom appeared, looking murderous.

"I see he's started with the bullshit again," he grumbled. "Let me go shut him up."

I stuck up my arm to block him. "And then his lawyer says we abused him, and he gets released. You sit down and cool off. Jason, food sounds perfect right now. I'll talk to him."

With a nod, Jason left. Tom glared at the closed door before flopping on the couch and grabbing the remote. Caleb continued to yell and bang on the wall until I responded with my own bangs against the wood.

The door opened, and he leveled me with an icy stare. "Ah, Agent Lying Bitch. Please come in."

"Just say what you need to say."

"No. You're going to come in here and we're going to chat."

"Erin, I'm right here," Tom called from the couch. "I'll hear everything this shithead does. I'll gladly come in there and put a bullet in him if I need to. You're safe."

"Yeah, *Erin*. You're safe."

"God, I wish I really had a migraine now," I muttered, following him into the room. "What did you want to talk about?"

The door closed behind me and from nowhere his hand clutched my throat. When I struggled, he yanked me against his chest. He tightened his grip, and I froze. "Too bad he won't hear anything." His voice was low and deadly.

"You think I need him to protect me?" I snapped, pulling at his wrist.

His lips hovered just above my ear. "I don't know whether I want to rip your throat out or throw you on that bed and fuck you until you scream my name so that prick who's been staring at your tits all night knows exactly who you belong to."

"I sure as hell don't belong to you."

"Really?" His lips trailed down my neck and latched onto the skin over my pulse. At my gasp, a low, sinister chuckle filled my ears. "Who slept in my bed last night and woke me up with their lips around my cock? And whose back did you scratch when I fucked you senseless afterward?"

I shivered at the memory of his words and cursed the tingle between my legs. His scent invaded my senses, making it impossible to stomp my hormones back into compliance. When I tried to break free, an angry sound came from his throat and he sucked even harder. I bit my lip to stifle the moans he tried to coax from me. Closing my eyes, I was finally able to shut him out and bring my body under control.

"Get your goddamned hands off me. Last time I checked, assaulting a federal agent is a felony."

His grip on my throat tightened a fraction as he twisted my other arm against my lower back. "Decisions, decisions. Which one should I choose?"

"Either will have you bleeding out in less than a minute."

"That's a pretty bold statement for someone in your position."

My fingers closed around the handle of the small push dagger hidden in the waistband of my jeans. His arm stiffened when he realized what I was doing, but it was too late. I slid the blade free and held it to his abdomen.

"I like my chances."

He raised his hands and stepped back. I lowered the knife to my side but kept a firm grip on the handle. We stared at each other, not moving, for what felt like an eternity. My heart thundered in my chest as I tried to predict his next move. Sensing the impasse, his posture relaxed, but I stayed alert.

"Look at me being all kinds of rude tonight. I didn't properly greet the feds waiting for me in my office and here I am intimidating the lying rat bitch who pulled a knife on me. Guess you can't blame me. I have one question for you, though."

"What's that?"

"Was fucking me part of the job? Or was it just a perk?"

My throat felt like it was closing. "Does it matter?"

"Oh, it matters to me. For all I know you've ridden every cock in that room tonight. Are you weak, or just a whore?"

"You fell for it, so I'd say it's a moot point."

"Sounds pretty whorish to me. Always willing to do anything, or anyone, to get ahead. Fuck me and then report all the dirty details back to your superiors, right? Did you file the report about that time I fucked you in my car in triplicate?"

"Yeah, and Tom notarized the yellow copy before I sent it over to Accounting so they could reimburse me for my panties," I snapped. "I figured blowing him in return was the least I could do. Anything else you want to know?"

"Is Erin even your real name?"

"Is Caleb yours?" His eyes widened a fraction, confirming my suspicion.

"Look, I—"

"*Non sono l'unico bugiardo di merda qui, vero?* (I'm not the only lying sack of shit standing here, am I?)" I bit out in Italian. "Go ahead. Get pissed off because I lied. You conveniently forget that you've been less than honest yourself, *Professor*. You can act like what I did was some great betrayal. Go right ahead. Just remember the bullshit you peddled didn't smell any better than mine."

His shoulders slumped. "Was any of it real? I need to know."

"Why?"

"Because it was real to me."

"How do I know that? You've been lying from the beginning just like me. And, well, I'm just a whore who fucked you to get ahead and reported back to my bosses about it. In triplicate."

He reached forward. "Jess. Sorry, Erin. Can we—"

I slapped his hand away and moved toward the door. "We're done here, Professor. One of the other agents can handle anything you need. Agent Lying Bitch is taking the night off."

The door slammed behind me and Tom looked up. "How'd that go?"

"Someone else will have to deal with him tonight. Or I'm going to shoot him."

"Jason can do it. I can't guarantee I won't shoot him, either."

Jason wasn't thrilled about his new task when he returned. After a brief exchange where he told Caleb to get his food and Caleb told him to go fuck himself, he joined us on the couches. Tom put on some loud, cheesy action movie and both men were engrossed in the film while I picked at my food and tried to calm the adrenaline coursing through my veins.

Still wired from the confrontation, I volunteered to take the first watch while the other two agents slept. After changing into a black t-shirt and sweatpants, I threw a blanket over myself on the couch before finding a documentary on serial killers. My stomach growled after a while, and I was heading back to the couch with my reheated food when the bedroom door opened.

He waited until I sat down before moving closer and opening the pizza box. "Want a slice?"

I pointed to the container in my hand. "No thanks. I've got my beans and rice here."

"Mind if I sit?"

I shrugged and kept my gaze on the TV. A few seconds later he sat at the opposite end of the couch, shooting me a look when I turned and crossed my legs at the ankles. He placed the box between us and helped himself to a slice.

He nodded at the screen. "Did you catch any of those guys?"

I took another bite of food and stared straight ahead.

"Would you tell me if you did?"

At my silence, he exhaled loudly and grabbed another slice. We sat in silence, the TV making the only sounds until the credits rolled. When I reached for the remote, he grabbed it away. Tossing the pizza box on the floor, I snatched it back and called him an ass under my breath before changing the channel.

"I'm sorry I was a dick," he whispered.

I nodded, not taking my eyes off the sports news program. His words from earlier rang through my head and with them an ache settled into my chest. I changed the channel again, hoping the auto race would help clear all the bullshit he'd piled into my head, but I couldn't escape the painful throb. Grabbing my food, I stood up and tried to escape to the kitchen. Once I was alone, I braced my hands on the counter and took a cleansing breath.

I tensed at his footsteps and prepared for another verbal assault. When I felt his presence, but not his touch, I turned and he stood a foot away. "Can you at least tell me your real name?"

"As far as you're concerned, my name is Erin King. What about you?" When he refused to meet my eyes, I shook my head. "Jesus, aren't we a pair?"

"I wasn't kidding when I warned you earlier. You have no idea the shit storm that's going to happen if you bring me in. The less you know, the better."

I rolled my eyes. "And if I had a dollar for every time I've heard that, I'd be retired in Fiji. Look, Tom will be awake soon, and it would be a good idea if you were back in your room when he came out here."

Without a word, he stood and moved closer. My feet shuffled backward before I could stop myself. His hand rested on the counter behind me, close enough to reach out and touch my bare arm. I watched his eyes rake over my face before he brushed a tender kiss on my forehead.

"I'm sorry," he whispered. "For everything."

I waited until his door closed before slinking back to the couch. Nothing on TV held my interest, but Tom was none the wiser when he came into the living room just before three. With nothing to report, our conversation was brief before I headed to bed.

My body was exhausted and my brain was numb, but I couldn't sleep. The bed felt cold, and it had nothing to do with the low temperature outside. I ran my hand over the empty side next to me and the familiar ache in my chest returned. His scent, his warm body pressed to mine, and the sweet words whispered in the dark were gone and all I felt was emptiness in its wake. The darkness outside my bedroom window was thinning when fatigue finally won out and I fell asleep.

It was way too goddamned early when Tom banged on my door a few hours later, but the large cup of coffee in his hand made up for it. Jason was on the phone and staring out the window overlooking the backyard when I entered the kitchen while Caleb sat at the small table and sipped from another large mug. He showed a keen interest in the phone call, barely paying any attention to anyone else until I sat across from him at the table. Our eyes met briefly before he then stared out the window.

"Marlowe will be here in twenty minutes with breakfast," Jason announced as he sat next to me.

We fell into a guarded silence. Tom sat down, earning a glare from Caleb. A couple minutes later, I caught Tom staring at my chest and gave him my own nasty look when his eyes met mine. A knock at the back door thankfully broke the tension. Tom went to the door while I covered him from the back hall.

My posture relaxed, and I holstered my gun when Jack appeared in the doorway with several paper bags. Behind him stood a slim man who was several inches shorter and carried another bag. He nodded to both of us and followed into the kitchen.

"This is Agent Kevin Orosco," he explained. "He's going to watch Mr. Winters while we meet and go over a few things."

"I'm flattered that you had to bring another agent just to babysit me," Caleb retorted, digging through the bag.

Jack narrowed his eyes but didn't reply. Instead, he grabbed the bag from his hands and passed it around the table. I pulled what turned out to be a breakfast sandwich from the wrapper and dug in. Kevin and Tom made small talk about the football game the previous night, causing Caleb to grin.

"You like football, too, don't you Agent King? I seem to remember you talking about it a lot with the other TAs."

I narrowed my eyes. Fucking asshole. I should've known at some point he'd start with the bullshit again. He smirked before moving to the counter to grab another cup of coffee. Kevin glanced over his shoulder at me and raised his eyebrows.

"What was that about?"

"He likes to run his mouth," Jason interjected. "I'm sure by the time we're done here, he'll have some wild stories to tell about you, too."

Jack cleared his throat and stood. "All right, we've had enough chit chat. Agent Orosco, would you mind showing Mr. Winters to his room?"

The bedroom door closed, and we all gathered around the table. Kevin received a tip that several known Genovese associates had arrived in Portland and Seattle over the past two days. Based on the info, he estimated between four and six men were in the area with an unknown purpose.

"Because of this development, we're moving Winters tonight," Jack explained. "Reinforcements will arrive here by eight, and we'll move from here to the airport."

We spent some time going over the details of the move, including the route and backup plans in case anything went sideways. As the meeting turned to idle chatter, I peered at the clock above the fridge and stretched. Nine hours until Caleb and I were on a plane headed back to D.C.

Jack put his hand on my shoulder. "Something wrong?"

I shook my head. "I can't complain about heading back, but I'm not looking forward to being stuck on a plane with him for seven hours."

"Do you need anyone to escort you two on the flight? He seems to enjoy sniping at you."

"It's nothing that can't be fixed with a couple crushed up sleeping pills in his drink."

A text message from Nicole asking why I wasn't in the office interrupted our conversation. I choked down all emotion as she sent a steady stream of texts reporting that Trevor and Professor Winters were absent as well. Without a word, I raced upstairs and retrieved the disposable phone my friend thought she was calling and texting. I'd forwarded everything on that device to the one issued to me by the Bureau. Another message appeared that I forced myself to ignore. It was time for college student Jessica Ross to disappear. My finger hovered over the button to deactivate the burner phone, a hesitation I'd never made before. After a moment, I pressed the screen. I glanced out the window for a few moments before standing. Fuck, the day couldn't end soon enough.

A check of my secure messages yielded another coded missive from Felton. Reading between the lines, Italy was a bust, and he was headed back home. My fingers flew over the keys as I warned him of the perils of overcooked sardines, my code name for my least favorite family. Even Agent Kenmore would've understood my meaning, but I no longer cared.

The tension in the house increased with each passing hour. After another dinner served in takeout boxes and immersed in silence, everyone settled into the living room to wait for our backup. Caleb seemed resigned to his fate, watching TV on the couch next to me as I played games on my phone. The next time I looked out the windows, night had fallen.

I turned to Jack. "Shouldn't the reinforcements be here by now?"

Cursing, he dialed. Once the call connected, the profanity flowed from his lips as he walked into the kitchen. Kevin moved to stand next to the front window and scanned the street outside while Jason moved to the other window. I felt for my knapsack at my feet, finding the strap as the house went dark. At the sight of the lights still on in the neighboring house, I pulled Caleb to the floor and drew my gun.

"Hold positions!" Jack commanded in a low voice. "Status?"

Tom replied he was near the stairs, and I motioned for Caleb to follow me behind the couch. A gunshot and the sound of broken glass silenced Kevin's voice. Pulling Caleb toward me, I took cover and tried to find the shooters. Another shot followed by a loud thud told me either Jason had fallen or shot someone. Tom crouched down at the foot of the stairs and motioned to Jack.

"Go," Jack whispered, crawling toward the couch. "We'll try to hold them off."

Reluctantly, I nodded. Someone was bound to have heard the gunfire and called the cops, but chances were slim they'd arrive in time. A shot pierced the front door, and he waved his arm toward the back. Caleb grabbed my outstretched hand, and we stayed close to the floor as we made our way to the laundry room near the back door.

The basement was lit by a single emergency light, but it was enough to show me the way to the supply shelf. I raced over and pressed the button on the back wall. As the panel opened and showed a hidden passageway, loud voices and rapid gunfire erupted. I shoved Caleb inside and closed the door behind us. We followed the tunnel down a small incline and climbed a metal ladder, appearing through the plain wood floor of a dark and musty room. Stepping outside, I saw Jack's earlier information paid off, and we were in a shed in the backyard of the house behind the one we'd just escaped.

Angry voices yelled behind us. With my free hand, I gestured to the east and Caleb followed me as we crouched through the backyard. Minutes later I threw my knapsack into the backseat of my car and was behind the wheel, speeding us away from the ambush.

"Where do we go now?" He kept his face on the road ahead of us.

"To the rendezvous point near the airport."

"You think that's a good idea? If they found that place, what makes you think someone isn't waiting for us there?"

I slid my gun under my leg. "Hand me my knapsack."

"So you can call someone and they can fuck us over, too? Absolutely not. Get on the highway and head north."

I turned to ask why when the car lurched sideways. He yelled my name as I gripped the steering wheel and tried to regain control. After several seconds of screeching tires and a few silent prayers, we stopped. However, that didn't stop the black SUV from barreling into us. My head lurched to the side, and the last thing I heard was the crunch of glass as my head hit the window.

• • • • ● • ● • ● • • •

My arms were suspended above my head and felt like they were going to fall out of their sockets. I opened my eyes, only to groan and clamp them shut when the light made my head throb. A low chuckle rose from the faint sound of dripping water. I snapped my head upright and planted my feet when my body swayed. The shackles around my wrists looked old, the long chain twisted around the pipe hanging from the ceiling above me. My heart sank as the sound of footsteps grew louder.

"Wake up!" I couldn't turn to see the man's face, but his voice was harsh. His large hand grabbed my hair and pulled me backward.

My head fell forward as soon as he released his hold, and I tracked his movements until he stopped just to my right. Refusing to look up, I stared at his ugly brown loafers until he let out an impatient huff and pain exploded across the side of my face. His hand gripped my jaw and squeezed as he pulled my head up to meet his hate filled brown eyes.

"Wake. Up," he hissed.

"Fine, I'm awake. Jesus."

He cursed in Italian and stalked away, rolling his sleeves up his meaty arms. Though my view was limited, I looked at my surroundings. The aged red brick walls and cold, damp air gave me the impression we were in a basement, but the smell of motor oil ruled that out. Glancing through the windows near the ceiling above me, I saw a faint blush in the overcast sky. Morning. Not that I expected it to be a good one.

He approached with a grin that made the hair on my neck stand up. Out of pure instinct, I tried to step back which only caused me to slip. His laughter echoed off the walls until his face morphed into one of hatred and his fist flew out and connected with my cheek.

My eye swelled within seconds but held his gaze as I spat a mouthful of blood on the ground. He passed by me and disappeared, only for the back of his hand to connect with the same eye. A blinding pain shot through my right arm just below my elbow. I screamed when he struck the same spot again.

"My goodness, Alfonso. You need to pace yourself or she'll die far too quickly," a calm and heavily accented voice said.

I caught my breath as a tall, athletic older man strolled into the room with an air of nonchalance. Alfonso placed a metal chair about a foot away as the man came closer. He brushed the curly silver hair from his forehead before lowering himself into the seat and crossed his ankle over his knee. We stared each other down before his eyes narrowed.

"Good morning, Signore Sardi. I'd shake your hand, but I'm quite sure your associate has broken my arm."

"And to you, Miss Donovan, I offer my warmest greetings. Please don't trouble yourself for not observing proper greeting etiquette. Alfonso appears to have been rougher than I intended, but that's because he takes my security seriously. You see, word had reached me about this vendetta you have against me. I'm afraid it concerned me a great deal as I don't understand the reason for your hatred."

"It's quite simple. You're the man responsible for the death of my parents, Seamus and Serafina Donovan."

"Oh, I'm afraid I did more than that," he replied. "I shot your whore of a mother in the head."

"Fucking asshole!" I kicked at him until Alfonso yanked me backward and the shackles dug into my wrists.

"Such devotion to family," Gio mused. "I can relate. I feel an intense devotion to my family as well. Take my nephew, for example. He started out from humble beginnings, raised by my mother after his parents died but I knew he was destined for greatness. Once he finished school, he joined the military. He's quite the marksman, so it was no surprise when he became an exceptionally talented sniper for the Army. He soon attracted the attention of the CIA and before we all knew it, he was traveling the world on top secret assignments."

"Fascinating."

His mouth widened to a grin. "It is quite fascinating. He became such an asset to them that when the FBI needed his help with a case, they wanted to recruit him as well."

"Sounds like a popular fellow." Unease settled into my gut.

"He always has been popular. People learn of his talents and will do anything for him. It's well known that nobody can work for both agencies, but they found a way to make it work. Much like I've heard they did for you. Isn't that right?"

My heart hammered in my chest. No. No fucking way. Was that why the first Asset was forced out? Did Felton discover his mob ties? "Oh, but we're not talking about me right now, sir. We're talking about your nephew. He sounds like quite a guy. I can see why you care so much for him."

He smiled and my blood ran cold. "Thank you for the compliments. Would you like to meet him?"

"Might as well. Judging by that look on your face, you can't wait to shock me with his identity."

"That's correct, Larissa. It's someone you know well."

I closed my eyes, deciding to rest while waiting for Gio's big reveal. Raising my head when I heard new footsteps approach, I stared into deep brown eyes I thought I knew. His eyes raked over my body and narrowed at the cuffs holding me in place, but then moved to his uncle. When I remained silent, he shook his head.

"I tried to warn you."

Chapter Twenty-Five

Little Fire

"I DON'T THINK WE'VE been properly introduced, Professor Hypocritical Shitstain," I bit out. "My name is Agent Lying Bitch."

My ears pounded as my hands gripped the chains holding me in place. The bastard stood next to his uncle and lowered his eyes after a few seconds. Heat creeped up my neck at Gio's smug grin. The clank of metal above my head brought my attention back to the present, and I slowed my breathing. Blind rage wouldn't get me anywhere, I reminded myself. Not yet anyway.

Gio gestured next to him and smiled. "I see you've met my nephew, Gianni."

"John."

"Forgive me. He prefers to bastardize his name and go by the primitive 'John' instead. You've met?"

"Unfortunately, yes," I retorted.

"You two have a lot in common. You both have military backgrounds, worked for both the CIA and the FBI. In fact, I believe both of you were in Prague around the same time a few months ago. I'm surprised your paths didn't cross."

I leaned my head back and laughed, earning a glare from Alfonso as he stood in the corner just over my shoulder. Of course John was the asshole who shot at me. Because life had a twisted sense of humor.

"I can't say I recall seeing him," I replied. "But now that I think about it, I recall some pathetic little man trying to disrupt a meeting I had with some of my associates. The culprit got our attention for the briefest of time, but ultimately missed the mark."

John clenched his jaw. "Can we just get this over with?"

I scoffed. "What's your hurry, *John*? It's only natural to want to stick around and watch the fruits of your labor. You did an outstanding job fooling me. Don't be shy now!"

"She really does have your number, doesn't she?" Gio said. "However, I can't let him take all the credit. He was only one of the tools I used for the charade."

"Pretty guilty of my own charade, so I can't be too angry about it. I'll admit I'm curious how you pulled it off." I managed a smile. "Dying girl's last wish? Seeing as how your goons could've killed me when you caught us, I'm sure you're dying to tell me anyway."

He wagged a finger and grinned. "Clever girl. Yes, it was a bit of an undertaking. But it's amazing how agreeable people can be for the right price. All it took was one well-placed leak to the FBI and several checks to get it all in motion. Add a few rogues who owed the family a favor or two to pose as teaching assistants, let the right people spread the word, and it all fell into place."

"Was the FBI in on it? I'm guessing that well-placed leak came from within."

"All the agents at the house," John interjected. "The attack was a clean-up job."

"Hush, Gianni! Don't give away all our secrets!"

His eyes narrowed. "You proved your point. Finish this up and let's get the fuck out of here."

With a small nod, Gio stood and strolled toward me. "I'm afraid he's right. We need to be elsewhere. Alfonso, I trust you'll clean everything up before you leave."

He nodded, appearing from his corner and carrying a small metal baton with a ball on the end. I prayed for a quick death even though I knew it wouldn't happen. Gio bowed his head and headed for the exit while John's face twisted with an emotion I didn't care enough to name before he also disappeared. I focused my attention at the hulking man who stayed behind, studying his face. Our paths had crossed before, I realized. When his mouth curled into a crooked smile, the memory ignited.

"You were at the restaurant at the beach. In the bar." An arched eyebrow was his only response. "Okay, fine. How about a bribe?"

That made him stop. "What could you possibly bribe me with?"

"A quick and painless death."

"And what are you going to give me in return?"

"No, I'll give you a quick and painless death."

He laughed, a full body guffaw, before backhanding me. "Try again."

"My offer still stands."

His hand balled into a fist as he stalked closer, but I was ready. When his body lunged forward, I raised my legs and tucked them against my chest. Once he was close enough, I wrapped them around his neck and hoisted myself onto his shoulders, bringing my elbow down on top of his head. I was not only tall enough to access the pipe above me, but the blow stunned him long enough to give me the precious seconds I needed.

The shackles around my wrists were heavy but, more importantly, so old they weren't adjustable. Once I was high enough to slacken the grip of the cuffs, my left wrist slid free. The asshole regained his wits and sank his teeth into my inner thigh. Screaming, I gripped the pipe as he broke away. His arm came around my middle and yanked me backward. He grabbed my hair and pulled it behind me as my feet returned to the ground.

"Stupid little whore," he snarled in my face. "I was looking forward to having a little fun, but now you're annoying me."

My hand closed around the loose cuff and swung it into his face. He groaned and stumbled backward. I kept a tight grip on the metal and tried to free my right hand. Distracted, I didn't see him approach until the metal baton came down hard on my right forearm. The shackles dropped from my freed hands, but never hit the ground. A few seconds later, he pulled the chain against my throat and stepped closer, trapping me against his body.

"That's right, cunt. Struggle. That just makes the job easier."

I gagged, my arms flailing as they tried to pull at the chain. The evil prick laughed in my ear and tightened his hold. He taunted me by relaxing his grip for a second, only to pull the chain back once again. My hand moved to my chest, feeling the metal of my dad's crucifix. When he loosened his hold a second time, I pressed the red jewel and slid the thin stiletto blade from the cross.

Gripping the knife so tightly it threatened to cut into my own skin, I stabbed his hand until fresh air flooded my lungs. I spun around and sank the blade into the sadistic fucker's right eye. He screamed, and I fell forward, letting out a shriek as my right arm felt like it shattered. I searched the ground until the glint of stainless steel caught my eye a few feet away.

Kicking the shackles out of reach, I dove past Alfonso and grabbed the baton. He pulled the blade from his eye, which bled freely when he turned toward me. At his approach, I smiled and gripped the metal until my knuckles were white. The knife shimmered in the light when he clenched his fist. He lunged forward, and I slammed the metal into his shoulder.

His body spun around and buckled when the baton hit the back of his knee. Cursing in Italian, he tried to stand until I kicked him in the ribs and he fell down. The next round of blows aimed for his kidneys until he rolled out of reach.

"You promised a quick and painless death," he panted.

"No, it was an offer. One you decided not to take."

Securing my injured arm against my stomach, I savored the crack that rang out when the baton hit his forearm. The familiar heat creeped up my neck once again and this time it was a welcome companion. After a few kicks to his arms and ribs, I realized time was running out. Standing behind his curled body, I brought the baton down over and over until the crack of his skull snapped me out of my red cloud of rage. I tossed the weapon behind me and pulled my gun from his waistband. After making sure it was loaded, I stepped over the pool of blood surrounding what was left of the fucker's head and headed for the door.

The narrow corridor was dark and littered with cardboard boxes. I flattened my back against the wall when I heard gunfire in the distance and continued onward, pausing behind boxes to make sure it was safe to continue. My arm burned and throbbed, but all I could do was try to ignore it and be thankful I was left-handed.

After passing several locked doors, I came to the end of the hall and entered another room. Movement out of the corner of my eye brought my attention to a figure running across a metal catwalk suspended from the ceiling. A gunshot broke the silence and the person fell. I hid behind a nearby forklift and scanned the room for Gio's remaining men, as well as the shooter. A man rounded the corner across from me and stopped. He raised his gun, but I fired first and he dropped it in an instant. I moved behind a cluster of metal containers close to the forklift. The stillness of the air had my senses coiled, but unsure when to strike. After listening for any other attackers, I stayed close to the wall and moved to the next hallway, passing more doors and wondering how close I was to the exit.

A small exhale behind me was the only warning I had before two arms banded around my upper torso and pulled me backward. I bucked against the mystery assailant who dragged me into a darkened room. My body was released without warning, only for a light to turn on a few seconds later. I whipped around and pointed my gun.

John put his hands up. "I'm unarmed."

"But my guess is you don't need something trivial like a gun to kill me."

"Liss, I—"

"Pet names aren't a good idea right now. Lucky for you, your beloved uncle is higher on my list of targets than you. So either kill me, say or do whatever you intended when you dragged me in here, and then get the fuck out of my way or you'll move up that list quicker than you'd like."

"I'm not as close to that man as you think." At the incredulous sound I made, he stepped closer. "I realize you have no reason to believe me, but the truth is so much more complicated than you can ever imagine. If you'd just lower your gun, I can explain—"

He wobbled and clutched his cheek as I shook the hand that punched him. Muttering a few choice words, he stared at me wide-eyed.

I shrugged. "You wanted the gun down."

"I deserved that, and you don't know how sorry I am. I need you to understand that I had no choice. If I didn't help him, someone very important to me would've been killed."

"Let me guess. The psycho ex-girlfriend?"

"Please. I can explain, but not here."

I leveled my gun at the center of his chest. "Like I'm going anywhere with you."

He stepped closer. "If you were going to shoot me, I'd already be dead. And vice versa."

"That's close enough, Sardi."

"Not that it matters to you, but that's not my last name. It's bad enough I share a bloodline with the fucker, but please don't lump me in with the whole family."

My curiosity piqued, but only for a moment. The stack of lies from his mouth were enough to make me doubt his honesty if he said the grass was green. I sidestepped and tried to move closer to the door, jerking backward when he held his hand toward me. Swallowing back the scream when I jostled my arm in the movement, I inhaled sharply. His brows creased, but he stayed still.

"Just say what you need to say," I commanded, my voice cracking. "Quickly so I can get out of here before the rest of your goons try to finish me off."

Before I could react, he sprang forward and pulled me to him, careful to avoid my injured arm. My gun fell to the ground, which he kicked out of my reach. When he spun me around and pressed me to his back, I made a frustrated sound and kicked my feet backward until his hand rested at the base of my throat.

"Goddammit, I need you to listen to me if you want me to help you," he growled.

"I don't need your help. In case you didn't notice, I got away from that gorilla you left me alone with just fine."

"Your broken arm says otherwise."

"And I'll take care of it once I get out of here. If you want to help me, just let me go."

"Shh," he whispered. "I'm not here to hurt you."

"I fucking hate you!"

"I know you do, baby. But I don't want you to hurt yourself. Please calm down *mo dhóiteán beag*."

The Irish phrase my father whispered when he tucked me into bed every night as a child made me stop. "How do you know that?"

"I know more than you realize. He called you his little fire. I know how and why you came to be on that assignment in Prague, and I know the middle name on your official birth certificate isn't your real one."

"What is it then? If you think you know me so well?"

"Aednat."

A lump formed in my throat and my eyes burned. It was then that I realized not only had I fallen into the perfect trap, John wasn't the only traitor. Blinking back tears, I struggled to shove my feelings down. I couldn't let him see how much he'd gotten to me.

"I also know you donated your entire paycheck from the Prague assignment to Becek's grandson's treatment, both you and Elle Kingsbury."

"Becek was just another assignment, the same as you," I spat. "I'll need to use my pay from this job to cover a round of STD tests and a long day at the spa to have you completely cleansed from my body."

His arms remained around me, but my body went slack as I stared at nothing and wished I felt the same. The words of comfort he whispered in my ear were just what my heart needed to hear, but I knew anything he offered came with a price I wasn't willing to pay. My emotions were scattered all over, but I clung to one solid desire: freedom.

He pressed his head against the back of mine, loosening his hold on me just enough. My legs buckled, and I slid to the ground. Rolling over, I landed the hardest punch I could muster to his balls. He groaned and doubled over, only to hit the ground a second later when I kicked his legs out from under him. My joints were stiff, but I got to my feet as he coughed and remained curled in the fetal position. Grabbing my gun, I ran to the door.

"Larissa, stop! Please! You don't know the real story!"

The desperation in his voice tugged at my heart. I turned around and he'd rolled to his chest and his eyes were pleading. He tried to stand but froze when I pointed my gun at his head. "Stay where you are."

"Baby, no! You're not safe. I'm begging you to let me help!"

"I'm not your baby. And if you ever have the misfortune to cross paths with me again, I promise I won't hesitate to put a bullet in your fucking head."

His shouts continued as I raced down the hallway and found a door with an exit sign in the next room. Approaching with caution, I crouched underneath a large metal shelf and scanned the surrounding area for any of Gio's men. Finding none, I pushed open the door and squinted at the gray light outside.

The building was in a remote but industrial part of town with hardly a tree or other buildings in sight. Several large trucks drove down the street and turned right at the four-way stop a couple hundred feet away. Keeping my back against the wall, I crept around the perimeter and found a black BMW parked in front. After shooting out all four tires and not seeing any other threats, I did what my mother told me to do that terrible night so long ago. I ran.

• • • ● • ● • ● • • •

Washington, D.C.
One week later

The door from the outer office opened and closed, and I glanced up before turning back to doodling in the notepad on my lap. The clock on the wall above the desk showed it was just before eight in the morning. Right on time as always.

He entered the room and stopped short. My eyes shot to his, savoring the shock and fear. Setting down my poor attempt at artistry, I slid the gun hidden under my leg into his line of sight. His Adam's apple bobbed, a small movement, but one that showed enough. He definitely didn't expect to find a missing agent perched on his desk at such an hour.

"Good morning, Mr. Lynch. Why don't you close the door and join us for a chat?"

His gaze trailed to the man seated in the chair in front of me and widened. He closed the door without a sound and raised his hands when he saw me aim the gun at his chest. "Lissa—"

I motioned toward the empty chair next to Barton. "Jesus, Felton, you raised me with better manners than to ignore other people in the room. Can't you at least greet Special Agent Kane? He hasn't had the best of mornings."

He scooted forward almost as soon as his ass touched the seat. "I know you're upset."

Upset was an understatement. There was no way it described the anger, hurt and betrayal I'd felt over the past seven days. It certainly didn't sum up the confusion that consumed me. How did such a simple job go so wrong on their joint watch? Did the fact I'd survived the past week mean Gio wasn't hunting me?

"Shut up," I said in a lethal voice. "Now that I have you both here, I want someone to explain to me the joint shitshow I was suckered into."

"Lissa, I swear I didn't know," Barton mumbled.

He looked like hell, which was my fault. I'd grabbed him at first light as he left his gym and stuffed him into the back of his car. I didn't mean for him to be shaken up like a warm can of beer during the drive, but the potholes and shitty streets in the area were beyond my control. The bruise on his forehead would take, at most, a week to heal.

"No? So it was just dumb luck I wound up in a safe house full of rogue agents?" I turned to Felton. "And you're telling me you heard absolutely no chatter in Italy?"

"The only oddities reported to me was Gio's increased presence at the port in Bari, and then his sudden interest in buying a nightclub in Rome. I traveled to Italy to investigate it myself and found nothing, which I told you about."

Barton gave Felton a dirty look and turned to me. "The Bureau doesn't know how or why he found you, or how he compromised so many agents. We're taking this very seriously. Both agencies are. We won't rest until we figure out what happened. I promise you that."

"Forgive me if I wouldn't trust either of you to so much as tell me the time," I retorted. "I've run out of fingers to count the number of people who have been lying to my goddamned face for the past few months."

Felton's smug face fell at my narrowed eyes. He cleared his throat and straightened in his seat. "We've launched an internal investigation as well. I swear we'll sort this out."

"Oh, really? Is that investigation going to include how you hired his nephew?"

"I didn't. The original lead of the Asset program, Larry Sullivan, chose the man we hired whose real name we've now confirmed is Gianni Martinetti. I was involved in the program, but not in any leadership capacity and I never met him. Unfortunately, nobody knew the demons haunting that man."

Both men stared at the black cast on my broken right arm. Needing space from their scrutiny, I slid off the desk and stood behind it. At the low hiss I let out when my elbow bumped his chair, they both tried to stand until I shook my head. I ignored their looks of concern as I leaned against the credenza under Felton's certificates and awards that hung on the wall. The silence and accusatory looks circulated between all three of us until both men looked ready to fight each other.

"Where were you, Felton?" He jumped at my faint voice. "I sent you a message that things were getting hot and heard nothing."

He closed his eyes and sighed. "We got a lead on a hidden Sardi warehouse in Molfetta, but it was empty when we got there. By the time my plane landed back in D.C., you'd already disappeared."

"I guess we'll see what the investigation finds, won't we?" I muttered. "What about my father? Don't tell me you've never seen his file."

"As violently as your parents died, I wanted to spare you the knowledge that Seamus wasn't the upstanding citizen you knew him to be. Perhaps he was trying to get out, but that doesn't change the fact he was a cold-blooded killer who would've been sent to prison if he hadn't turned informant. His actions got him and your mother killed. There is no way to sugarcoat that."

"I want his file," I snapped. "From both agencies. I deserve to know what else you two have been hiding about him."

"Lissa, it's not that easy," Barton protested.

"He's right. With the investigation going on right now, it's impossible. I don't know about Agent Kane, but I can try to have it for you by the time you come back from your cooldown."

A humorless laugh slipped past my lips. "Cooldown? Do you think a goddamned vacation is going to make it all better? That I'll magically trust either of you or anyone else in a few weeks?"

"Tell us what you need," Barton said. "What can I do to show you that you can trust me?"

I stared out the window at the rainy street below, wishing for a warm blanket and a football game on TV. Images of laying in the arms of the man whose voice still whispered to me in my dreams invaded and I forced myself to turn toward both men. Their posture relaxed when I holstered my gun.

"Since you're both here, that means I won't have to repeat myself. Leave me alone. All of you. Don't look for me. Don't contact me. Don't send anyone to check on me. If any of your little minions cross my path, they'll come back to you in pieces. Are we clear?"

"As a bell," Barton replied.

I rounded the desk. "And I expect I'm no longer a person of interest in Portland."

It wasn't until Connor met me near the Canadian border I learned I was wanted by the FBI for questioning. Not only was Professor Caleb Winters missing, Karl and Trevor had also vanished. Police pulled Trevor's body from the Willamette River two days after my escape with a wire still wrapped around his neck. It shocked me that I wasn't the prime suspect, but it was a wrinkle that needed immediate attention. Connor all but demanded I find a place to lay low and recover, but it was obvious Gio Sardi wasn't sitting idle, and neither could I.

"DNA evidence we recovered from the wire ruled you out. You're now listed as missing as well as Waters and Fischer."

"Lissa, let me help you," Felton interjected. "Sardi is bound to be looking for you and you won't get far with that broken arm. Let me at least get you out of the country."

I grabbed the phone from his desk and ripped the cord from the wall. Barton flinched but stayed mute while Felton jumped to his feet. I grabbed the knife hidden in my belt and he raised his hands.

"I only need one hand to slice your throat open," I warned. "Back off."

He sank into the chair while Barton shook his head. A check of the clock revealed I'd lingered too long and had a schedule to keep. Grabbing my knapsack next to the desk, I tossed the cord into the trash can.

"Thank you both for your time. I'll be in touch."

Brushing past, I left his office and broke off the doorknob with the ugly rock his secretary kept as a paperweight. Once in the hallway my pace didn't slow until I reached the elevator. A flat voice in my head barked out the instructions needed to keep my body moving. One foot in front of the other. Eyes straight. Breathe in. Out. Repeat.

The metal doors closed, and my shoulders relaxed. I'd done it. Confronted Felton about his lies and broke away, gaining the freedom I needed to take my own path. To figure out what I wanted out of my life. Any decision about my future with either agency would be a rash one at that moment, so I opted to walk away for a time.

A few people in the lobby glanced my way, but my face remained blank and my posture rigid as I continued to the exit. One foot in front of the other. Eyes straight. Breathe in. Out. Repeat.

The ancient looking sedan I "borrowed" from an apartment complex close to Dulles airport sat in the same location I left it. Within moments, I'd hot-wired it and turned onto the highway. The music from the radio was a welcome break from the silence as I glided down the road. Soon I arrived at the regional airport on the outskirts of the metro area. More tension evaporated when I saw the small private jet parked on the tarmac. It was only after we were in the air and I was alone that the first tear fell.

Connor's reminder about keeping my humanity made sense at one time, the need to remain respectful of life even when it was sometimes my job to end it. Even after it was nearly obliterated by IED's and the horror of war, I tried my best to keep it sacred, intact. Now, however, as I struggled to breathe through my sobs, it seemed like another impossible fantasy like my mother's belief in loving someone with every ounce of your soul.

John's deep voice ran unchecked through my head, promising me the world and then scolding me for not heeding his warning. Another sob tore through me and I felt my heart shatter all over again. I'd been a toy, something to entertain him while his uncle plotted to kill me. As if hearing my thoughts, my arm throbbed, and I glared at my cast.

I'd been lucky to escape. Who knew how long that luck would last? Humanity was a luxury I could no longer indulge.

I watched the ocean pass below, lost in the deep blue depths as a plan came together in my mind. Wiping my eyes, I pulled my knapsack into the seat next to me. Glimpsing at the cigarette case, I grabbed a notepad with a map folded inside and arranged them on the table. I studied my notes, circling locations and adding details in the margins.

If the Sardis wanted to play games, I'd happily play one of my own. Mine would be far deadlier, however. I'd come for them all, wiping out every single one of them until only the ringleader and his two-faced nephew were all that remained. For the first time in a week, a slow smile spread across my lips.

Hunting season was open.

Chapter Twenty-Six

Suicide Mission

JOHN

A breeze broke through the curtains, bringing the morning light and the scent of lemons from the orchard. A quick check of the clock on my phone told me it was too damn early; I buried my face in the pillow to see how much more sleep I could coax from my body before getting up to start the day.

A hand brushed mine, followed by a slow inhale. I wrapped my arm around her smaller frame, and she pushed her whole body tighter against me. Her eyes were still closed, but they wouldn't be for long. I swept a loose curl away from her face and her pale blue eyes opened. They met mine and her face lit up with a smile.

"Hey." Her voice had the throaty rasp it always had first thing in the morning.

"Hey. Hungry?"

With a yawn, she nodded. "Starving."

I kissed her forehead and sat up, grabbing my black sweatpants from the foot of the bed. When she moved to sit up, I leaned across the bed on one knee and pulled the covers over her. She opened her mouth to protest until my lips covered hers.

"Stay here. I'll be right back."

She let out a small huff but nodded before I headed downstairs to the kitchen. We'd made breakfast together so many times in Portland, but I wanted her first morning at home, my home, to be special. With any luck

*she'd consider it her home, too. Between gulps of coffee, I cooked every-
thing to perfection and soon was carrying a serving tray upstairs.*

"Breakfast is served," I called, nudging the door open with my foot.

*I stopped as soon as my feet crossed the threshold. The air was too
still. Stomach churning, my eyes went to her still body under the covers.
Had she gone back to sleep? My footsteps were slow and cautious until
I saw the growing red dot on the sheet.*

*Time stopped. Space stopped. Everything. Just. Fucking. Stopped.
Everything except my heart, which beat so loud I barely heard the
crash of the plates when the tray slipped from my hands. This wasn't
happening. It was some terrible dream that I'd wake up from any second.*

*My voice sounded far away as I called her name, waiting, begging for
her to jump up and laugh at the joke she played. After standing in front
of her for what felt like several lifetimes, I pulled the sheet down. Her
eyes, which less than half an hour earlier held joy and warmth, stared
wide and full of terror right through me. Blood oozed from a small bullet
hole in her forehead.*

*I didn't recognize the sounds for several seconds. It was only when
my throat felt like it had been ripped open that I realized the screams
came from me. Sinking onto the bed, I cradled her against my chest and
prayed for the nightmare to end so I'd wake up and hold her for real.
The feel of her blood against my bare skin felt like a final insult when
the barrel of a gun pressed to the back of my head.*

My body jolted upright in the seat, disoriented by the bright
sunlight and the greenery that flew by. It took several breaths to
calm my racing heart, long enough to remind myself I was still in
my SUV and we were headed home from the airport. My hands
shook as I drained the bottled water in the cup holder, which did
nothing to satisfy my thirst.

"Is everything okay?" Benny asked, eyeing me like I'd gone off
the deep end.

"Yeah. Tired as shit. It'll feel good to sleep in my bed for a change." My blood chilled as the words tumbled out. To hell with sleep. I needed a fucking drink. Several of them.

He didn't believe me for a second but acted as if I hadn't been wailing like a crazed banshee. After telling me we'd be home in ten minutes, we both fell silent. Thank god he didn't pry; there was no telling when I'd be okay again.

Larissa's ass kicking gave me a black eye and several bruises. The other black eye, along with the bruised ribs and jaw, were courtesy of her friend Jake when I showed up at his house to tell him he and his fiancée were in grave danger. Luckily, he knew her real identity and took me seriously. By that evening, they were on my private plane headed somewhere I'd never know.

Connor, her former drill sergeant, was a force to be reckoned with. Jake warned me that Larissa headed north after her escape, so she no doubt got help from the old man. Knowing her condition when she left, I expected open hostility upon arrival.

"You must be Professor Hypocritical Shitstain," he greeted.

"Sir, may I come in so we can speak privately?"

The lock had barely engaged when the barrel of his gun pointed at my forehead. "Let's start with you telling me and my buddy Colt what you know about a mutual acquaintance of ours, and why I had to bring a nurse friend of mine to patch them up. I'll warn you now, that Colt is a cranky fucker, so it's not in your best interest to offend him."

I sank onto his couch and laid it all out for him, acknowledging that my forced involvement didn't excuse what I'd done to her. He said nothing, only staring and nodding. When I finished my story, he sat forward in his armchair and stared at the gun in his lap. Shaking his head, he stared at the floor.

"She has a hairline crack in her right arm and a concussion. I tried to get her to find somewhere to hide so she could rest, but she said they'd be after her. And then you show up."

"Sir, I—"

"Relax, junior. It's obvious you aren't looking to kill her. Which makes me wonder why you're here. You hoping to suck up to me so I'll sing your praises to her?"

"My uncle is going to be looking for ways to get to her. If I know she's close to you and Jake, you can bet he does, too."

His eyes narrowed. "What's in it for you?"

"Doing the right thing for once. I've caused her enough pain. The least I can do is make sure the people she cares about make it through this unscathed."

The scrutiny of one old man scared me more than any interrogator I'd ever met. He steepled his fingers in front of his face and watched me squirm on his puke green velvet couch and then simply nodded. After a brief discussion he agreed it was time for him to take a vacation somewhere. The only help he accepted from me was to lug his rifle cases out to the car. After he'd told me the make, model and his accuracy for each one.

He leaned against the trunk of his Buick after it was packed. "You gonna try to find her?"

"I have to. He won't stop until she's dead."

"What she did to your uncle's man scratches the surface of what she's capable of. I've tried to teach the importance of holding on to her humanity. After this shit though, I just don't know."

"I understand, sir."

"No, you only think you do," he barked. "She was barely hanging on by a thread when I saw her. This may have been enough for her to let go of what little she had left. If that happens, she'll burn it all and take herself down with it."

"That's why I have to find her."

He clapped me on the shoulder. "Be careful, son. She won't be happy to see you if you manage to find her."

Gio returned home to Bari and called the family together for a dinner party where everyone could celebrate his "victory." From what one of my grandfather's former men told me the whole thing had been a dog and pony show to stroke my uncle's already out of control ego. He'd described it as a night worthy of all seven deadly sins and, knowing Gio, was all played out to excess. I'd considered myself lucky to have missed it.

The next phase in their plan for Larissa scared me. The hard part was over; she'd been drawn out and was no doubt looking for revenge. Now all they had to do was wait for her to come to them. If she didn't, well, they'd just go find her again. Between my uncle's psychotic enforcer and all the other sick fucks in our world, I had a good idea of the games they'd play. It wouldn't end until they'd ripped her apart and buried her in the cold ground.

She had every reason to fucking hate me when she screamed those words. I was a villain in his scheme. A villain orphaned by the same sick uncle when I was nine years old and raised by my grandmother. In any other mafia family, the current boss's mother and the former boss's wife would've guaranteed her a certain level of respect. Instead, we moved between my parents' house in Verona and my aunt's outside Venice, only traveling to Bari when my uncle ordered her to appear. It was during one of those miserable trips south that he tried to kill her when I was fifteen.

We fled to the U.S. and enjoyed a peaceful life for a while. I enrolled in the Army to pay for college, not realizing that it would lead them straight to us. When I landed in Afghanistan during my first deployment, I learned my grandmother was back in Italy and my servitude to the family began.

In the beginning I simply had to keep my head down, play the good soldier, and not get killed. In exchange, my grandmother, aunt and cousin were left alone. Life as a combat grunt sucked, but it kept everyone at home alive and I made it to a high enough rank to be recommended as a sniper. When I was called to my C.O.'s office toward the end of my tour and introduced to some fed in a suit, I knew the game was about to change.

Larry Sullivan was an abusive drunk who liked to gamble away his per diems and slap around the "dancers" whenever one of his many business trips took him through the south end of Italy. When he roughed up one of my uncle's favorite whores, his rage evaporated once he discovered that Larry's per diems came from the CIA. It was the perfect deal: the CIA gained a former military sniper, and Larry got to live. What did I get? I got to be a pawn and prove our family's worth to the Genovese. The occasional bending of the rule that loaned me out to the FBI was an unexpected bonus for the family.

Infiltrating the agency and passing on false intel was easy. Sabotaging my career was even easier. We Sardi men loved our excesses and Larry wasn't the only one who enjoyed gambling the night away. The movies always made it look like the life of a spy was one of jet-setting to exotic locations and infinite coolness. For a while I bought into it, but it didn't take long for the vices to become more important than doing the job. Being forced to quit should have been a low point, but it freed me from a life I never wanted. The day I walked into my aunt's kitchen and my grandmother's rib-crushing hug was one of the happiest of my life.

The tradeoff was swearing my life and loyalty to the family business in order to keep my loved ones safe. If coming home was the best, then the day I was officially sworn in as a capo was the worst. My men and I were allowed to live in Verona, but as the family's assassin I was at the mercy of the boss's whims no matter how irrational they seemed. Keeping my father's last name annoyed the fuck out of my uncle, but as long as I killed his enemies as commanded, he wrote the check payable to John Martinetti without complaint.

We drove through the black metal gates of my estate and parked near the house. Lucas, my cousin and second in command, rushed forward and my stomach clenched. Time spent in Verona was usually peaceful, but not today. There were too many things that needed to be settled and figured out. The car stopped, and he opened the door.

My hands shook as I stood. "Is she home yet?"

"She got there an hour ago. Mom said she was quiet but seemed okay. She ate dinner and then went to her room."

"Fuck. I tried to keep her out of it this time."

"She knows. She told Mom to tell you she loves you, not to beat yourself up about it, and she'll talk to you in the morning."

We entered my office, and I headed straight to the floor to ceiling windows behind the desk. Lucas locked the door behind him before moving to the bookcase to my left. I peered over my shoulder and watched him pour two double scotches.

He stood beside me and held out a glass as he stared outside. "You look like you need this."

I nodded my thanks and then drained it in one gulp. Stepping away, I refilled it and turned to find him wide-eyed. With a shrug, I strolled back to the window. We sat in silence as I sipped my drink. I wanted to drink the whole damn bottle but needed a clear head to figure out what the hell I was going do to now.

"Do I even want to know what happened?" His voice was calm, but his eyebrows were pinched.

"Which part? The part where Alfonso showed up at the beach, or the part where she treated his skull like a pinata before escaping?"

"Fuck."

My hand tightened around the glass. "The old man helped her get out of the area. After he shoved a gun in my face, he told me we had no idea what we just unleashed."

Connor Minton was wrong; my uncle knew. He was counting on her vengeance. So what if she killed a dozen of his men in her wake? The body count justified any action against her and sweetened the victory when they took her down. The sick bastard would have another banquet just to show off her dead body.

"What are you going to do?"

Steeling myself up for his reaction, I took a deep breath. "I'm going to find her first."

"Have you lost your goddamned mind? That's crazy! That's—"

"A suicide mission. Yes, I'm well aware. But I'm sure the fuck not going to leave her out there unprotected if I can help it. After everything I did to draw her into this shit, I have to try to get her out."

His eyes narrowed as he scanned my face. After a second, he threw his head back and groaned. "You are one stupid bastard. I knew when you came back from Prague your dick would put some stupid ideas in your head."

"That's rich coming from you, asshole."

Fucking Prague. I left that city with more questions than answers. She was far from the usual rats and thieves my uncle commanded me to kill, but also far from the cold-blooded killer the stories made her out to be. I didn't doubt the darkness lingered below the surface, but after hearing Connor speak of humanity, the fact she volunteered for the assignment made sense.

There was no other choice for my job, however. I was to take her out in the line of duty. Her death would've been written off as an unfortunate mishap. For three days I followed her hoping to find an easy way to kill the legend. What I found instead was a woman with a light inside her despite the darkness. When I finally had her in my scope, I couldn't pull the trigger and extinguish that light.

Instead, I bribed my way onto the ambulance and sat in the front like a creep. Just to make sure she made it away from the scene safely, I'd told myself. The compassion in her eyes as she held the professor's hand and updated him on his grandson's recent hospital visit lifted everyone's spirits. Even though my uncle's wrath awaited me back home, I watched her slip into the night knowing I'd made the right choice.

Enraged at what he called my failure, Gio sent me to Portland to finish the job. The original plan was pretty close to what happened: make me appear like a target, stage my abduction, and kill her in the process. It was no coincidence that brought her to the party that fateful night, and I'd hoped the few weeks away from her would be enough to clear my head. The moment I saw her and felt the familiar draw I decided nobody would hurt her. Period.

After a few weeks, I reported there were too many variables and tried to call it off. Gio's new plan was for her to be kidnapped and smuggled back to Italy where she'd be tortured by his sadistic lead enforcer and then killed. The sick look on Trevor's face when I found him over her beaten and unconscious body seared into my mind and stayed there for weeks. Desperate and pissed off for once again being denied his prize, Gio got to one agent on his payroll within the Bureau and soon I was frozen out of whatever new scheme they concocted.

By then I was in too deep, and she was my new addiction. I never expected she'd wind up in my bed, but once it happened there was no going back. It made her safety easier, but I knew the wolves were circling. Taking her to the safe house at the beach had been impulsive and risky, but I was willing to try it if it meant getting her into hiding. When Alfonso showed up out of nowhere, I knew the board was set and we had no escape.

Lucas's voice was sharp. "Are you even listening to me? They found Trevor."

"I didn't have time to hide his body, and the fucker didn't deserve a proper burial anyway. Right now, I just need you to find her. Before they do."

He gulped down the rest of his drink and muttered something under his breath about me being crazy before stalking across the room. "The file is on your desk," he announced before slamming the door behind him.

Grabbing the folder, I sat in the leather chair behind my desk and leaned against the back. I grabbed the two slips of paper on my lap and scanned them before opening the file and gazing at the other two sheets at the top of the stack. Four birth certificates, two from the U.S., and one each from Ireland and Italy, documented her birth, and all four had nearly the same information. It was her reaction to the strange middle name on the certificate proclaiming that Larissa Aednat Donovan was born on Christmas Day almost twenty-seven years ago in New York City that told me it was genuine. The real mystery, however, was why three others existed in the first place.

"Who are you, Liss?"

The phone on my desk rang. Fuck. It was only a matter of time before the asshole reared his ugly head. "Yeah?"

"Gianni, my boy!" His voice was way too cheerful for my comfort.

"What do you want?"

"Care to explain to me what happened with the girl?"

I held one of her pictures and leaned forward in the chair. "What is there to explain? She killed Alfonso and got away."

"Giovino tells me you went back inside."

"And she was long gone when I got there. My part of this shit is done."

"On the contrary. You're going to find her and kill her."

"The fuck I am!" I shouted.

"The fuck you aren't!"

"I did what I was required to do. End of story. You can't force me to do any more."

"You're right, Gianni. I can't. But I can send my people to find her. Should I put Marco on the case? I know how much fun he'll have once he finds her. And of course, once he brings her to me, I'll be so grateful I'll let him play with her a while longer."

Marco was his lead enforcer whose sadism and cruelty knew no bounds. He craved violence and depravity. One of his favorite methods for punishing those who crossed him was to take a female member of the family as a prize to be kept as his slave until he grew bored. All were returned to their families, but most committed suicide within a year. The team I hired to protect my aunt's house had orders to shoot him on sight if he ever showed up, and my crew would do the same if he ever came to Verona. He was an evil that had no business anywhere near us.

"Fine," I bit out. "But you know it won't be easy now that she's in the wind. It's going to take some time."

"Understood, but I will not hesitate to send him the minute I think you're not doing your job."

"Yes, sir," I replied before slamming down the phone.

The picture fell onto the desk as I stared at her face and tried to calm myself. There was no way Marco would ever get his hands on her. If I had to use my last breath to cut his fucking head off, I'd gladly do it. I tried to slow my racing heart, but images of her in pain invaded until I threw my glass against the wall and watched it shatter.

Footsteps pounded down the hall and Lucas tore the door open. "What happened?"

I stood, no longer able to keep still, and ran my hand through my hair. "If I don't finish the job, he'll send Marco."

Sighing, he grabbed the file from my desk and flopped onto the brown leather sofa to the left. "Her FBI and CIA handlers were found locked in an office together at CIA headquarters. She was last spotted at a regional airport outside Manassas, though I haven't been able to confirm it."

I arched a brow. "I thought I was crazy, dumb bastard?"

"Oh, I never said you weren't. But that didn't mean I wasn't going to help you. Now sit your ass down. We've got shit to do."

• • • ● • ◆ • ● • • •

Unknown
Osperale di Roma, Rome
Three Weeks Later

My shoes squeaked on the ugly gray floor as I rounded the corner to the dark metal doors of the ICU. Dr. Rinaldi glanced up at the buzzing sound and gave a small nod. He took a long draft from the paper cup in his hand and made a face.

"That night nurse made the coffee again," his soft voice warned. "Drink at your peril."

"No, thank you. I'm already late."

He made a chuffing sound and looked at the clock. "Two minutes. That's on time for you, Doctor." I lowered my head, and he chuckled. "Joke. It's your third day on this rotation. Come, let us do rounds."

I followed the gnarled hand he held out, and we moved to the end of the hall. Morning rounds on the critical unit were quiet, eerily so. We started with Senora Milanti, who was two days post-op on a double heart valve replacement. I presented the case, going over her vitals and noted the recent drop in levels that were cause for concern. After affirming my suggested course of action, we moved to the next bed.

Seven patients later, we'd crossed the floor and stopped at the last room. Dr. Rinaldi's brow creased at my confusion and then he handed me the folder outside the door. We'd passed over the patient, Maria Rossi, the past two days because tests were being done or a specialist was examining her. He cleared his throat, and I glanced up from the file to see he'd opened the door.

"Since this patient is new to you, I'll present." His voice was low. "Patient is an unidentified female in her mid-twenties. She came in unresponsive four days ago with severe blood loss. Her heart rate stabilized after two transfusions."

"What happened to her?"

"As she's not yet regained consciousness, we've yet to determine that. Upon examination, we found she had a concussion. She also came in with a cast on her right arm that had been partially removed."

"Any other details?"

"Always so eager to solve the mystery," he replied with a small smile.

"I only meant—"

"That wasn't meant to your detriment, Doctor. Your inquisitiveness is a sign that you seek the entire story to better help your patient."

His words were kind. Much nicer than the head nurse in the general medicine ward who answered my questions with rolled eyes and muttered insults. My gaze traveled to the new cast on her arm before moving to the respiratory monitor above the bed.

"What's her prognosis? Or is it too early?"

"It's early yet. Her prior injuries and the item still in her hand when she was brought in—"

A series of loud beeps brought both our heads around to the wall behind her bed. Dr. Rinaldi grabbed his stethoscope and stepped closer. Her face twisted for a moment, followed by a low whimper. He spoke in a soft voice as he turned down the alarm. She moved her injured arm and winced, letting out another distressed sound. I clutched the folder to my chest and stepped closer, stopping when she gasped and opened the palest blue eyes I'd ever seen.

TO BE CONTINUED...

Thank you!

Thank you for reading The Asset. If you enjoyed the story, please consider leaving an honest review.

Review "The Asset" here

Acknowledgements

I would totally suck as a human if I didn't give a proper shoutout to the people who helped me along my journey...

First and foremost, I cannot thank my family enough. To Damien, my amazing husband, thank you for your encouragement and for asking if I was going to go write. Most importantly, thank you for being the best sounding board in the world. From talking through ideas with me to talking me down during the overwhelming times, there's no way I would've gotten through this process with my sanity intact without you. To Zach and Nick, my kiddos, thank you for understanding...or trying to understand...your mom's crazy writing life. To Jackie, thank you for being the world's best mother in law. Your words of encouragement mean the world to me.

A huge thanks to Wattpad. The program was my first step in bringing Larissa to life. Pressing the button to publish my story for the first time was a huge step outside my comfort zone, and while I didn't light up their algorithm with millions of reads at the time they still provided a lot of great resources as I fumbled my way through writing and getting people to read my story.

To Mandy Melanson, thank you for the best conversation in the world where I realized that self-publishing wasn't as scary or as impossible as I originally thought. It's still been a helluva journey, but one I've enjoyed.

To Stephanie and Andrea, my "early crew", thank you for offering up your email addresses so I could test newsletters, messages, and many other crazy things. I told you it would all pay off!

Bonus Chapter

Would you like to read a steamy chapter from John's POV about his worst Monday ever? Click here to join my mailing list. You can unsubscribe at any time.

Mutual Assets: Prequel to The Asset

"Do you know why your employer would pay me half a million dollars to kill you?"

That's the question posed to secret agent Larissa Donovan after a date with her boss's business associate, Victor Acosta. After working undercover for weeks as an au pair, the case certainly gone as she'd hoped and now someone wants her dead. Is it the wife who steals industrial secrets or her art thief husband?

Victor reveals his own issue with the couple and proposes a crazy idea: pretend they're dating and work together to bring the couple down. Larissa is skeptical at first, but reluctantly agrees. Convincing their targets that Victor is using her before carrying through on the hit is easy enough. But is it really pretending when she finds it harder and harder to resist the sexy security consultant?

Mutual Assets is a 28k word short story that takes place a year before The Asset. This story contains adult content and should only be read by those aged 18+.

Available now for free:

Amazon

Other book retailers

Seized Assets

It's been two years since Larissa Donovan walked away from both the CIA and the FBI and vanished without a trace. Hidden away from the world that tried to kill her she struggles to overcome the physical and emotional scars from her disastrous last assignment, only to be abducted by someone from her past.

Is her abductor a friend or foe? As she tries to answer that question she uncovers more explosive family secrets that changes everything she knew about her parents and their murders. Follow Lissa around the world as she deals with these newly discovered secrets and lies and tries to answer one very important question:

Who is Larissa Donovan?

Excerpt

One of my favorite things about my house was the view, and I wanted to catch a glimpse of the sea and the sky before the storm. The moon was hidden by clouds, but with no immediate threat of rain, I grabbed two blankets from the closet and headed to the backyard. I wrapped one blanket around my shoulders before plopping down on the other in the grass. Leaning back, I inhaled the salt air. I shivered when a gust of wind blew past and pulled the blanket tighter around me.

Staring at the sky, I pushed the anger and anguish aside and thought of happier times. Sundays spent on the couch watching football and eating too many snacks. Long talks about anything from the worst album we ever bought to the chemistry of beer. Waking up wrapped around each other and starting the day with a kiss. The lightness in my chest made the decision to give myself a break an easy one. For just that night I decided not to focus on the painful memories. Until I woke up the next morning, it was just a story of a woman who met a man at a party she could've easily fallen for.

Did he miss me? Did our time together matter to him at all? Or was I just a loose end that he now hunted to finish off for his family?

I shivered in the yellow glow cast by the security lights behind me. My thoughts had strayed into dangerous territory. Closing my eyes, I focused on the sound of the water below. I'd always found beauty in the chaos created when the waves crashed against the cliffs. Maybe that was me, enduring despite the endless violence and madness all around.

My body sensed a presence before the shadow approached. I tilted my head to get a better view and the faint sound of his footsteps froze me in time and space. I sat as if made of stone for what felt like an eternity before my mind and body re-fired.

"I knew you'd find me."

Now available!

About the Author

Samara Black was born and raised in Oregon. She started writing short stories and weird poems at age nine. She continued writing as a hobby in college, typing out silly stories with her roommate and came up with the idea for her first book series when she should have been studying for an economics test. After several dysfunctional friendships, toxic relationships, and family entanglements she had enough source material to write stories about characters with messy lives and the even messier problems that come their way.

Samara currently lives in Seattle with her family, including several pets who think they're in charge. In her free time, her hobbies include reading, photography, chasing pests out of her garden, and annoying her teenaged children.

• • • • ● • ● • ● • • •

<u>Social Media:</u>

Instagram: @author.samarablack

www.ingramcontent.com/pod-product-compliance
Lightning Source LLC
Chambersburg PA
CBHW070443300726
48975CB00007B/2017